B. B. GRACE

There's Beauty in my Flaws

A NOVEL

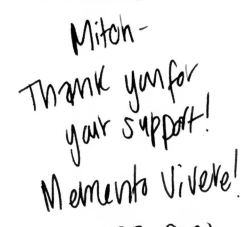

Mitch —

Thank you for
your support!

Memento Vivere!

— B.B. Grace 2020

There's Beauty in my Flaws
Independently Published
ISBN 9781795851671

b.graceful.info@gmail.com

*Written for those
who are still learning
how to pick up their pieces.
You are in good company.*

Death is not the greatest loss in life.
The greatest loss is what dies inside us while we live.

— Norman Cousins

1

"**D**ouble shot of Jack, neat."
I tossed a wad of cash at Ed, seized the rocks glass, and threw it back. As my cheeks warmed, I closed my eyes. It was impossible to stop the next degrading narrative from playing out in my head.

Hey guys, I'm Tally. What beverages are we having today?

They would ignore me. I'd stare, waiting for a break in the conversation they had been carrying on since they arrived – some gibberish about their mergers having an inconsistent philosophy with so and so.

Redressing my irritation, I would try again.
Gentlemen, what can I bring for you to drink?

This time, the one wearing glasses would look up and glare. He would dismiss me with a shoo, his wedding ring almost lost between two swollen skin folds that had risen up on either side to swallow it.

Once I got a few more tables, to the point of busy, the pricks would flag me down and tell me that they are in a hurry; that they have somewhere important to be. *Too bad, assholes,* I would think, while a smile belied my frustration.

I'd had it with being a cog in the machine, shackled to the ever-punishing planet called Earth. My dad was dead; my mother, dead to me. And I was all but dead inside.

I opened my eyes and Ed was still standing in front of me.

"Set me up, again," I told him.

He paused to consider my demand as a frown etched its way across his face. I was losing it, and there was nothing he could do to save me. Ed's only option was to pour another double – to soften my fall. And when he did, I killed it in a single gulp.

"Good luck," I said, saluting him with two fingers while making my exit. I'd never walked out of a job before, but after feeling the power of a reset, I wished I'd done it sooner.

······

The excitement only lasted for as long as it took to pull out onto Daetwyler Drive. There, in the rearview mirror, Fred's Fish Shack stared me down. I wanted liberation, but my brain defied me by scripting the conversation I would have with management the following day when I begged for my job back. I knew I was replaceable, so I needed to come up with an elaborate story – an appeal to whatever iota of sympathy was harbored far beneath their bottomless lust for money.

My vehicle crawled across the southeast side of Orlando in a haze. Pedestrians passed by each other on sidewalks without acknowledgment and commuters filed

2

into sweltering transit buses that would whisk them away to their next destination. An ambulance whooshed by in full emergency mode as I pulled up to my apartment complex, my mind fine tuning the details I would recite to my boss.

The security gate, despite its controlled access, was lousy at keeping unwanted visitors out. One such individual had disregarded the address numbers stamped on the asphalt and stolen my designated parking spot. Scouring the lot, I found what seemed to be the last open space several rows down and next to a vile smelling commercial dumpster whose olfactory assault began before I even cut the engine.

"What the hell was I thinking?" I wailed into the phone.

Sadie corrected me. "You weren't thinking."

Overthrown by rotting trash and the slow creep of anxiety, tears threatened.

"Let me be your voice of reason," she said. "Pull yourself together. Call your manager in the morning and tell him it was a personal matter. You've only got two semesters of college left so just stick it out until then. What's one more year?"

Sadie had no idea I'd quit school a few months before, in the middle of the spring semester. With failing grades, I didn't see any reason to keep going.

It was the fall of my junior year that everyone kept tabs on me, worried that my father's sudden death would derail my ambitions of becoming a journalist. But I stayed the course, kept good grades, and chalked up my determination to accepting the shitty hand that had been dealt to me.

Without realizing it, I'd done myself an injustice. I hadn't slain my emotions; I'd only delayed them. And when they struck, they latched onto me with a vengeance, dragging me down to a low point I had never experienced before. It was then that I needed the check-ins and the words of encouragement. It was then that there were none.

Sadie's prescription of trudging along would require almost no effort. And even though my routine was turning me into a zombie, at least it was predictable.

"I guess you're right," I said.

She laughed. "Aren't I always?"

······

I flung my front door open and went straight to the kitchen. My cat, Eileen, was waiting for me there, sitting at her food bowl with pathetic eyes.

"I'll feed you in a minute," I told her, selecting a random bottle of cheap wine from the cabinet.

Wrenching the corkscrew down, I wondered if the winemaker ever thought about whose hopeless lips would be sucking down his potion. I poured the wine into a coffee cup and inhaled its vapors, smiling at the anticipated contentment it was sure to deliver.

After chugging down half, I tried to pinpoint the exact moment that I stopped giving a fuck. It was probably that night in March when I stayed out late and got drunk even though I was fully aware I had a midterm at seven the next morning. Of course I bombed it.

Or when I snorted my first line of blow in that stranger's car before heading into a concert at the House of Blues. The high was amazing and I didn't want it to end, so I spent an hour trying to find her in the venue to get another bump. And because what goes up must come down, misery followed. The crash kept me in bed for two whole days.

But it could have been that afternoon I went to collect my mail. Expecting a tuition reimbursement check, I tore open the envelope without really looking at it. Instead of a sum of money staring back at me, I found my father's name, beside it, a delinquency total. Enraged by the notion that debt collectors had reduced him to his social security number, I shredded the letter into a thousand pieces and threw them over my balcony where tatters and tears sailed down onto the asphalt below.

The chime of my phone brought me back to the present. I dug the electronic leash out of my purse and squinted at the screen. "Don't forget Uncle Remi's birthday!" the reminder said.

Uncle Remi, my father's older and only brother, was a new addition to my life. I first met him the year before, at the funeral. From then on, we talked every couple months, mostly because he wanted to know how I was and made it a point to keep in touch. Since he lived in Colorado, we only saw each other one other time after that, when he came to Orlando for a Funeral Director's expo the first week of the January.

We had dinner at a fancy steakhouse and he told me stories from his childhood. When he mentioned he couldn't believe he was going to be fifty on the fourteenth of June, I saved the date in my phone. After our meal, he hopped on a plane and headed back home. That was right before all the walls started to crumble around me.

"Happy Birthday!" I shouted when he answered.

"Thank you, young lady." It was good to hear his voice.

"Whatcha up to? Any partying going on there?"

"You know us old people. We go to bed early."

I'd forgotten the time difference. "Oh no! Did I wake you?"

"Yes, but I don't mind the interruption. How have you been?"

Before I could reel it in, the flood gate that was my mouth dropped open. "I'm miserable. I quit my job today and I feel like my life is going to shit."

He laughed – an unexpected response to my misery.

"It's not funny," I told him, partly teasing, but mostly sincere.

"I'm not laughing at you, just your explanation."

"I get it. First world problems."

"Being uncomfortable is a great motivator."

"What about being uncomfortable *and* unmotivated?"

"Well, yes," he said with a chuckle. "That isn't productive."

"Exactly." I swirled my wine along the sides of the cup and took another gulp. "I'm the opposite of productive."

"Tell you what, why don't you come stay with me and your aunt for the summer."

"In Colorado?" I rolled out a mental spreadsheet to list the vast number of obligations that would keep me from going. I had no job. I had no boyfriend. I wasn't taking summer classes. I couldn't think of a single thing holding me back.

"I could use the help," he said. "My secretary is on pregnancy leave."

"You mean, work at the funeral home?"

"That's exactly what I mean. I'll have you back before the fall semester."

There was no point in hiding. I'd already told him everything else. "I dropped out of school."

He hit me with another surprise response. "That's wonderful. So you have no excuse not to come out and see me."

I cradled the phone between my neck and ear while I poured myself some more wine. "I won't be cutting up any bodies?" I asked him.

"Only if your heart desires it."

"Shouldn't you ask Aunt Jeannine first?"

"Ask her what?"

"Well, I don't want to just show up without her approval. We've never even met."

"Natalia, you're family. Jeannie and I would be thrilled to have you."

"Can I think about it and call you tomorrow?"

"Please do."

"I really was calling to wish you a happy birthday," I said. "I don't know how the conversation became about me."

"I'm glad it did. Let me know what you decide to do. Either way, there's no pressure."

"Thanks Uncle Remi."

"I love you, kiddo. Talk to you tomorrow."

And there it was, an opportunity to do something different. A chance at escape. The promise of a reboot.

With an entire bottle of wine coursing through my veins, I imagined myself leaving for Colorado.

2

When I woke up the following morning, I packed my entire closet into duffle bags. I couldn't define the feeling, but it was as if something inside me had shifted.

My unplanned escape placed me behind the wheel of my Chevy, its rubber tires bearing down on the pavement with conviction. Palm trees whizzed by as the sun migrated across the sky in a journey that would end at its new beginning.

An afternoon shower cooled the triple-digit summer heat wave down to a manageable ninety-six. I lowered my window and switched off the A/C to suck in the last bit of sea spray before hitting the state line. Behind me, rain clouds parted to reveal a gigantic double rainbow. In that moment, Florida was conspiring against me. I admired its beauty with an authoritative inner mantra: *Keep on driving.*

"How are you feeling today?" Sadie asked me as soon as she picked up my call.

"So much better," I told her, pulling into Flying J truck stop for gas.

"Great! Did you call your boss yet?"

"No."

"Why are you procrastinating?"

"I'm not."

She snickered. "Did you at least figure out what you're going to tell him?"

"No."

"Look, in order for the plan to work, you have to take the proper steps."

"I've actually taken a great number of steps. I'm all the way in Georgia."

"Seriously?"

"Seriously."

"What the heck are you doing in Georgia?"

"Getting gas."

"Alright smartass. Tell me what's going on."

"I'm heading to Colorado for the summer."

"Colorado?"

"Yep. To spend some time with my relatives."

"Tally, I think a vacation is the last thing you need right now."

"I think it's exactly what I need right now."

"What about your summer classes?" she asked. "Are they online?"

"No."

"So what are you doing about that?"

"Nothing."

"You're doing nothing about it? Did you at least withdraw so your GPA doesn't tank?"

"I never registered for summer classes, Sadie. I quit going in the spring."

"What do you mean you quit going? You just dropped out? You can't drop out. Without a degree

9

there's…" A thought stopped her in her tracks. "Why didn't you tell me?"

I shrugged though she couldn't see it. Why *hadn't* I told her?

"Well?" she asked, her patience wearing.

"I didn't want to disappoint you," I finally said.

"Disappoint me? *You* should be the one that's disappointed."

I thought about Uncle Remi's response. It was so different from Sadie's.

"Honestly, this wasn't the conversation I was expecting," she said. "I trust that you know what you're doing. I just don't want you to fuck something up that you can't go back and fix."

Dejection nipped at the morsels of confidence I had managed to scrape up. What if she was right? What if I was throwing my life away?

"You know, it's pretty brave of you to jump off the cliff."

"I didn't jump, Sadie. I was pushed."

She laughed. "I guess I'm just used to stability and what you're doing – shaking up everything you know – scares the shit out of me."

"That's the thing. I don't know anything anymore. What makes me happy. What I want. Who I am."

"Well, at least you're trying to figure it out."

"Thanks for the encouragement," I said.

"Have a safe drive, Tally. Call me when you get there."

"Will do," I told her, and we hung up.

I pictured the worst case scenario, driving the three hours back to my apartment, climbing into bed, and pretending like it was all a dream. It would be another failure. I couldn't let that happen. I dialed Uncle Remi's number, desperate for him to seal my fate.

· ♦ ♦ ♦ ♦ ·

My drive through the south was uneventful. Every few hours I stopped to fill up on fuel and caffeine, relieve my bladder in grungy bathroom stalls, and dine on packaged food prepared in factories many miles away. As I passed through tornado alley and left Kansas behind, the topography changed.

Just across the border, a wooden sign carved with white painted letters greeted travelers: "Welcome to Colorful Colorado." I gassed up one last time and took a selfie with an enormous green dinosaur.

My four-legged passenger eyed me with sassy feline suspicion as I bit into Sinclair's version of a ham and cheese sandwich. "Don't look at me like that, Eileen. Uncle Remi invited you, too."

I pulled a piece of deli meat off and sat it on the seat in front of her.

"And guess what?" I said when she looked up at me for seconds. "He told me he *loves* cats."

3

The highway's hypnotic spell broke moments before I blew by the I25 junction to Denver. I whipped into the far right lane and veered off onto the North exit which promised to take me to Cheyenne if I let it.

The radio had kept me awake on sleepy parts of the drive, and for that, I was grateful. But if I had to hear another politically motivated advertisement, I was going to rip the damn thing out and smash it. I settled for silence and finished the final leg of my travels thinking about my father.

I'd inherited his hazel eyes and athletic build, physical attributes that served to remind me of the man that contributed to half of my chromosomal identity. He loved to tell jokes.

"Why do elephants paint their toenails red?" he'd ask.

"Dad! You've told me this one a million times!" I would complain, laughing hysterically because it never got old.

He had a knack for storytelling, a voice that dropped you right into the plot.

It wasn't until middle school that I realized my parents were no longer in love. They hid their disputes well because I rarely saw them argue.

Divorce papers were filed on my mother's behalf days after their thirteenth anniversary. She had been fucking another guy for months and finally mustered up the intestinal fortitude to admit her adulterous ways. It was her second failed marriage, but after proclaiming her eternal love for the new beau, she was onto round three.

A product of her troubled upbringing, she sought solace in alcohol. For that, I was able to forgive her. Then she turned her back on her family to elope with a man-child who wanted me out of the picture. Her decision inexcusable, she wasn't Mom anymore. She was Florence. And I no longer vied for her affection.

The exit I needed approached quickly and my Chevy rounded the curve of the off ramp, piloting me into westbound lanes headed for the foothills.

·•◆•·•·

Clouds swelled as shoppers wielding umbrellas bounced from vendor to vendor. Ft. Collins was celebrating its one-hundred and fiftieth year of existence, a proclamation banner stretched between light posts at the edge of its downtown district.

Unleashed canines trotted about the sidewalks and buskers entertained passersby, warming the heart of any soul willing to part with their pocket change. Several barefoot youngsters wearing bathing suits dodged water spouts at the community splash pad. They giggled in anticipation of the spray down.

13

A bluesy voice yodeled from speakers mounted on a transportable stage set up for bands that would be delivering performances over the weekend. Sound technicians adjusted equipment as the fiddle player tuned his instrument by plucking several notes, stopping to tweak pegs at the base of the scroll before continuing his ditty. Groupies stood in front of the stage, swaying their hips to the singer's lyrics while he tested out his mic.

The city's architecture captured me while I was stopped at a traffic light. Many buildings boasted original construction, their stone foundations engraved with the year they were built. Others had been refaced with the same look. Canvas awnings sprawled out from storefronts, and above them, equidistant windows spanned across the second story providing ambient light to urban loft dwellers whose apartments overlooked the grind.

The quaint historical district came to an abrupt end, its few blocks of preservation curtailed by modern fast food chains and convenience stores which returned to dot the road. Brief sprinkles of rain suddenly marshaled into a downpour. I cranked up the manual window in a hurry and engaged my wipers. Heavy rain pounded down as I neared a fork in the main road. Through squinted eyes, I could barely read the names of two canyons with arrows pointing out their direction.

Staying the course, I puttered through a quiet town on the outskirts of the city. Dilapidated farmhouses were tiny against pastoral backdrops, their wooden clapboards peeling paint in surrender. The once active barns had fallen to ruin, no longer the epicenter of agrarianism that had previously dominated the economy.

Houses thinned to uninhabited prairie land and the mouth of Rist Canyon came into view ahead as the unfamiliar landscape drastically shifted again. Mountain cacti and conifers blanketed the terrain, providing refuge for animals skirting the wet weather. Gentle slopes morphed into steep inclines and boulders jutted out on either side of the road. The engine knocked with the climbing elevation, warning it might conk out at any moment.

Rain let up to a drizzle, water particles dancing along my windshield as they celebrated the sun's return. It had poured hard for several long minutes, and my neck was tense from straining at the wheel. I clicked my wipers off and cracked my window to allow fresh mountain air in.

Hal's Happy Hooves passed by on the left, a landmark Uncle Remi told me to look out for when I called him from Georgia.

"When were you thinking about coming?" he had asked, unaware I was en route.

"Soon," I told him.

"Why don't you call me next week and we can pick a date."

"Well," I said, hesitation delaying my message. "I'm actually already on the road."

"We can't wait to see you," Uncle Remi replied without question. He rattled off some directions and bid me a safe drive. "When you get to mile marker sixteen in the canyon, there'll be a sharp bend and a long row of mail boxes. We're just beyond that to the right."

"Almost there," I told Eileen who had finally settled in to life on the road. Our thirty-hour drive was coming to an end.

4

"Turn right onto Sentinel Way," the GPS directed in robo-English. Crabapple trees hugged the road, guiding me to a brick building with a gravel parking lot.

I passed by the mortuary and continued on toward the house which sat slightly elevated in the distance where ominous clouds had transformed into white wisps threatening nothing more than a random touch of shade. Shrubs lined the long driveway and nasturtiums showed off hundreds of blossoms, their vines racing along a two-rail wooden fence that kept vehicles on track.

Weighed down with just about every item of clothing I owned, I rang the doorbell. I couldn't believe I was standing in front of my uncle's home, all the way in Colorado. Making the trip had been a tiny decision in a lifetime of decisions, but it felt huge, as though I were on the brink of a new chapter in life. Hope filled me as the front door swung open, its jamb begging for grease.

"Tally!"

"Uncle Remi!"

He stepped onto the stoop and brushed the sides of my arms. "It's great to see you."

"Likewise," I told him.

"You must be exhausted. Let's go inside."

I followed him into the foyer and closed the door behind me. Richly dyed fabrics in fiery earth tones billowed across the ceiling like a Moroccan tent until they reached the far end of the living room. There, they divided into two masses which dropped down to frame out the fireplace. Several species of happy indoor plants sported rustic pots in their natural terracotta. The furniture, with its mismatched patterns and bohemian designs, brought the décor together in harmonious discord. Unaware that my uncle had been observing me, I met his gaze with a shy grin.

"I wasn't expecting it to be so colorful in here," I told him.

"You can thank your aunt later," he said, moving toward the stairwell. "This way."

I followed him up and consciously tried to stifle my breathing which had become ragged on the climb. At the top, a thick curtain partitioned privacy.

"Jeannie's smudged the room," he said, allowing me entry by pulling the drape off to one side. "She wanted me to let you know you're welcome to perform any ritual you see fit."

"Okay," I said, wondering what sort of *ritual* she thought I'd want to perform as my nose picked up a scent I wasn't sure I cared for.

"Go ahead and get settled in. I'll holler at you when dinner is ready."

Thin air arresting my unseasoned lungs, I inhaled and held it for a moment. When I turned to thank him, he was already heading back down the stairs.

The loft had been modified for my stay, a bed set up in the middle to cut the room in half. On my side, there was a small dresser, a nightstand with a lamp, and an empty clothes hamper. On the other side, floating shelves displayed outdated medical utensils along with several hardcover human anatomy books. I imagined Uncle Remi huddled over his desk, putting the final touches on death certificates that would find their way into the hands of families marked by tragedy.

I made my way over to the large south facing picture window and opened it, the wooden floorboards creaking beneath my weight. In the distance, I could see Forester Funeral Home. An expanse of prairie grass separated the business from the residence, a gravel road picking up where the pavement ended. It felt secluded – worlds away from the quick striding day-jobbers who punched a time clock and then stared at it until it told them to go home.

I was relieved that I wouldn't be taking anybody's order that night. Or the next. And if I finally got my shit together, maybe I wouldn't have to take orders ever again.

·· ♦ ♦ ♦ ♦ ··

Savoring flavors from the first home cooked meal I'd had in weeks, I settled into bed shortly after dinner. Aunt Jeannine's cooking had a soul soothing wholesomeness about it. Her braised heirloom rainbow carrots were a perfect accompaniment to the buffalo pot roast which she boasted was organic and grass-fed. Baked elephant garlic and blue fingerling potatoes were so tasty they could have been a meal all on their own. The apple pie left me in a daze, copious amounts of sugar and cinnamon bourbon the synergistic contributories.

Eileen curled up in the crest of my arm and pawed my skin the way she loved to do each night before nodding off. I was happy to see her adjusting easily, carrying on her normal routine despite our impromptu relocation.

Howling wind bolted me out of bed after what seemed to be mere minutes, but could have easily been several hours. Gusts coming off the mountainside whistled through trees just outside, muffled rain steady on the roof.

"Shit," I grumbled, remembering I had left the window open. I pulled myself from the warm nest I had spun and tiptoed across the room. Cold floorboards let out their wretched moan.

All but a sliver of the moon had been covered by dense storm clouds. I yanked the window shut and secured the latch. Small strands of a spider's web clung to the lower corner of the sill, a cluster of water droplets glistening by lunar glow and a crispy fly carcass stuck in what was left of the silk trap.

Relieved to see that rainwater had not puddled beneath the window, I looked off into the distance. A faint light reached out from the mortuary through the fog. Like a lighthouse beacon, it remained steadfast, guaranteeing the inevitability of death.

Shadows moved back and forth behind the illuminated window. I envisioned Uncle Remi, lost in his work, systematically reconstructing the disfigured face of a woman. Each of his sutures would be meticulously placed, goading her mouth into a natural and relaxed expression, her deserted body presented as if she was living.

A voice called out to me. "Tally, are you awake?"

I raced over to the stairwell and yanked the makeshift curtain aside. "Uncle Remi!"

"By God, what's wrong?"

"The storm woke me, and I remembered that the window was open. I got up to close it and saw you!" I pointed across the room in the direction of the mortuary.

Uncle Remi hurried down the stairs, mumbling to himself inaudibly. I followed close behind.

In one swoop, he put fresh batteries into his camping flashlight, shrugged on his flannel coat, and retrieved his car keys from a hook near the front door. Picking up the weapon from which he was named, he cocked the twelve-gauge Remington and chambered a round of double-aught buck.

"Stay here," he said, and slipped out the door.

I tackled the stairs two at a time, hurling my entire weight ahead of me without any room for error. At the top, I stumbled my way through darkness to the window. I could scarcely make out Uncle Remi's taillights as they faded away.

5

Headlights made their way back toward the house and I rushed downstairs.

"Aunt Jeannine!" I cried, her dark figure swaying in the rocking chair.

"Good morning, dear," she croaked.

"Sorry to have awoken you," I told her, still startled by her presence.

"Nonsense," she said, but it wasn't convincing.

Uncle Remi slammed the door open and shut. "One day I'll catch'em!" Drenched by the rain, water droplets fell to the planks below him.

Eileen, frightened by his return, flew off my aunt's lap. When she found the floor, her fur fluffed and she hissed.

Boots off, and seemingly thrilled by the disturbance, Uncle Remi headed for the master bedroom.

I stood in the middle of the living room, silent and bewildered.

Aunt Jeannine leaned forward and wobbly legs brought her to her feet. "What a riot!"

She fumbled her way to the kitchen with an unsteady gait. "They've been breaking in for years, mostly punky kids from town and weirdos looking to satisfy their morbid curiosities."

Just as she seemed she would topple over, I reached out to help.

"I've got it!" she snapped.

Shocked, I released her immediately.

"I've got it dear," her voice softened. "I'm still getting used to this diseased body. I tell it one thing. It does what it wants."

In the kitchen, she prepared a muslin satchel and steeped it in hot water. "Not matter how bad it gets, I refuse to be nabbed by the pharmaceutical trap."

Aunt Jeannine continued her rant against what she called *Big Pharma*. "The whole medical community is in bed with one another. They don't care if you get better. They just don't want you to die." She hobbled over to the cupboard for a mug.

"If they can keep you on their plan for years, the industry flourishes. Did you know that drug companies are the ones that fund most medical schools? It's ludicrous! I wanted to be a physician, but I just couldn't contribute to the debauchery."

Aunt Jeannine looked strong in spite of her ailing health, a stout Parisian with wide shoulders and medium length curly hair the color of nutmeg, her jaw set sternly in place. "I'm sorry, dear," she said, a tender soul beneath her hard exterior. "I've not been myself, lately."

She averted her gaze to dodge tears, her quivering hands cradling the teacup as if it were a goblet of sanctified elixir. "It's so much more than a physical sickness. They have no idea."

The atmosphere was stuffy.

"Well, that's enough of that!" she decided, shifting her mood like a chameleon. "What would you like to do today?"

I shrugged.

"Your uncle thought you should get started right away."

I looked over at the clock on the stove. It was barely after five but already the dark had begun its retreat.

"I told him to forget it. That you need time to relax."

"Relax sounds nice," I said, grateful she had insisted on my leisure.

"So then, I'll ask once more. What would you like to do today?"

I shrugged again.

Aunt Jeannine shook her head. "You know, you don't get many choices in life. When you do, you should take advantage of them." She offered her hand. "Follow me."

· · ♦ ♦ ♦ · ·

Aunt Jeannine's garden plot was perfectly positioned so that the shadow of the two-story farmhouse would not block the sun as it began to set lower and lower, when the seasons changed, and the earth titled on its axis. In the middle of her photosynthetic masterpiece, rows of heirloom tomatoes bulged with ripe fruits the size of baseballs.

"Zapotec Pleated, Abe Lincoln, Blondkopfchen." She called them by name, pointing with her finger while guiding me through chest high plants. Despite heavy precipitation the

23

previous night, nothing was out of sorts, the land thirsty as a sponge, leaves stretching toward the sky without any regard for gravity.

Feasting on a freshly plucked Black Krim, she continued her identification, every specimen treated pricelessly. The perennials of mint, lavender, lemon balm, and arnica thrived under the watchfulness of their steward, diligently returning each year.

On the far side of the backyard to the east, Aunt Jeannine had created a natural border with flowering plants that swept from the corner of the house to thirty yards out. It stopped at a seasonal brook, one of three that needed to be dredged before the first snowfall which was predicted to arrive in October.

"We get snow early, but our winters are much milder than people think."

As if having divulged a secret, Aunt Jeannine put her hand to her lips, her eyes wide with suspicion that I might tell the whole world about small town Bellvue's favorable weather. I buttoned my mouth and drew an imaginary cross over my heart. A childish grin stretched across her face after deciding I could be trusted.

"It's getting hot out here," she said.

I shook my head and the beads of perspiration that had slithered up through my pores trickled down my back.

"How do you feel about wine?"

6

From the comfort of the deck, we sipped ice cold Chardonnay made with grapes Aunt Jeannine had harvested the year before. Her small-scale vineyard thrived on the edge of their property, juicy clusters ripening perfectly as the temperature swung between night and day.

"Here in this marvelous state, you are allowed to produce up to two hundred gallons without any lip from the IRS."

"It's delicious," I told her, examining the Bordeaux shaped bottle. "I've never been a huge fan of white wine, but I think you've single-handedly changed my opinion of it."

She settled back into her Adirondack chair and closed her eyes to revel in the compliment.

"Have you ever tried Purple Cowboy?" I asked.

"I don't drink anything from California," she presumptively stated.

I applauded her honesty though it was gift wrapped in condescension. She wasn't trying to be a bitch, I decided. She was just astutely aware of her preferences.

"Most wine from California tends to be dilute and unpalatable," I replied, showing off my wine jargon. "But Paso Robles is home to several wineries with superb products."

She opened her eyes and a smirk flattened her mouth into a thin line. "I doubt you could single-handedly change my opinion."

Another zinger.

I was happy for my ballooning bladder which forced a bathroom trip. "Can I bring anything out for you?" I asked, raising sore arms above my head before leaning back to unkink my spine.

Aunt Jeannine didn't answer, her eyes closed again, a contented smile fixed upon her face. When I returned, she was no longer seated. A bag of potting soil beneath her spade clutched hand, her mood had swung.

Sensing my presence, she said, "I suppose we should discuss the details of your new job. The *box* is my endearing term for our beloved mortuary. Refrigeration has to be set at thirty-six degrees or lower to prevent decomposition."

Aunt Jeannine looked up from her transplanting project to see if I would react to her mention of dead bodies. Without the satisfaction of grossing me out, she combed her fingers through the pot plant's roots, its leaves iconic and undeniable.

She went on with her statistics, informing me of how many years Forester had been in operation and how many bodies could be stored in the cold chambers – eighteen and ten, respectively. Uncle Remi depended on the assistance of five employees, two of whom were a married couple on leave to enjoy the birth of their first child.

"You've shown up at a great time," she assured me.

"What exactly will I be doing?" I asked, dreading the answer.

"You are the first point of contact. You'll be scheduling drop-offs from hospitals and healthcare centers, and pick-ups for those who have expired at home."

The sun's descent was underway as Aunt Jeannine watered in her transplant. She brushed her muddy hands together and retrieved her wine glass. "I'm sure you've seen all kinds of whacky stories in the news. Mass graves. People being cremated when they were supposed to be buried. Bodies being sold on the black market for any number of perverse acts. Taxidermy. Necrophilia."

I thought of the intruders from the night before. "Has anything bad happened here?"

She shook her head no. "We have our share of break-ins, but nothing has ever been stolen. Especially not our cadavers. We lock them up at night."

"Why do you think they do it, then?"

Aunt Jeannine brought her index finger to within an inch of her temple and spun it around in a circle.

7

Eggplant from Aunt Jeannine's garden was prepared parmigiano style, lightly breaded and crisped up golden brown. Topped with fresh mozzarella and provolone, she served it alongside homemade pappardelle. Her spicy red pepper tomato sauce laced with dried rosemary, oregano, and thyme was the best I'd ever had.

The wine was not to be outdone, its rich tannins so refined it could have stood alone. By my third glass, I was feeling pretty toasty. Uncle Remi, well on his way to inebriation, rose from the dining table. He waited for his equilibrium to stabilize and then wandered over the entryway table where he selected a ceramic dish nestled among other clay crafts.

Cracking the lid open, he breathed in, his face filling with glee. "Oh, yes," he said to himself. "I've been saving you for a while."

Uncle Remi sauntered back over to the dining room, took his seat at the head of the table, and reached into his treasure chest.

"No seed bank sells this gal," he told me, holding up the two-inch nugget. "Ghost OG is coveted, clones passed from grower to grower in a shroud of secrecy. Kind of like the Holy Grail."

My uncle grinned, his eyes bright. "Ask your Aunt Jeannine. She's had the fortunate luck of handling many prized strains – cannabis cup winners with twenty plus years of genetic manipulation."

I thought about the way she had uprooted her plant earlier in the day as he passed the bud to me so I could share in his appreciation.

"It's been used by humans for millennia," Uncle Remi continued. "The trichomes are where the magic happens. Microscopically, they look like mushrooms."

Battling the wine bath my brain was soaking in, his lesson on botany faded in and out until he asked, "Shall we try her?"

Uncle Remi broke the flower apart and packed the chamber of his long stemmed glass pipe. A conscientious host, he handed it over to me for the first hit. I didn't need to feel any grander but I was ready to move on from the observation stage.

"You just want the heat of the flame," he said, standing up to retrieve a lighter from his pocket. "And always pass to the left."

Although his dictations were meant to be enlightening, he'd made me nervous. I'd smoked weed in high school but had never given proper etiquette any thought. I didn't even know there *was* etiquette.

To Uncle Remi, it meant more than just getting stoned – it was a communion with the cannabis spirit whom he never offended by using the terms marijuana, pot, or weed.

"Cannabis," he said, his voice thick and sensual, "is to be respected."

I kissed the top of the bowl with fire and inhaled with the full strength of my lungs, my eyes closed shut to capture the moment. I breathed out a cloud of smoke and coughed, my throat tickled by sensations it wasn't accustomed to.

Tingly vibrations instantly spread throughout my body, the tenseness in my muscles suddenly obvious. Becoming aware of my own existence, I placed two fingers over my carotid to feel for the pulse.

"Tally?"

My name sounded strange as it traveled along the length of my ear canal. Boundaries were blurring, revealing the interconnectedness of all things. I took notice of my breathing, certain that it could no longer function without my controlled interference.

In. *One, two, three.* Out. *One, two, three.* In. *One, two, three.* Out. *One, two, three.*

Uncle Remi was hovering over me when I realized how baked I was. "You had me spooked, kiddo!"

"Lost in my thoughts," I told him, a goofy grin plastered on my face.

"It'll getcha." He took his first of three consecutive tokes and repacked the pipe before offering it up to me again.

I couldn't fathom going any higher so I politely declined. Uncle Remi took several more drags in solitude, cashing out the bowl before he set the pipe down. I presumed his tolerance kept him in pursuit.

Aunt Jeannine had managed to clear all of our dirty dishes before creeping out of the kitchen and disappearing into the room under the staircase. I wondered what she was up to in her lair.

"We have an early day tomorrow," my uncle said, breaking into my chattery mind.

He slowly came to his feet. Taking his cue, I brought myself to mine.

"We've got three new bodies coming in and an ungodly number of viewings to book." He shuffled several articles on the table and carried his empty wine glass over to the sink where he gave it a quick rinse. "Did Jeannie go over your duties with you?"

I shook my head yes though I couldn't recall the exact terms of my role. A heavy buzz rendered my memory inaccessible.

"Want some water before turning in?" he asked.

"I'm good," I said, heading for the stairs. "See you in the morning, Uncle Remi. Thanks for everything."

I crawled into bed and contemplated my own final departure. Just beyond the last exhale, death loomed, waiting for the right moment to blow out the candle. That night in the loft, I told the reaper to keep his distance.

8

I felt well-rested when I beat Uncle Remi to the coffee maker in the morning. As quietly as I could, I loaded a paper filter with Jamaica Blue Mountain grounds I'd brought from Florida. Steam rose up from the glass basin, the granules percolating in water I filled straight from the tap. I wouldn't dream of using faucet water at home.

I thought about what my day might look like if I wasn't in Colorado. No doubt, I would be in bed. Indolence had become my stall tactic. But as the days kept on without me, I had to face reality: slowly shaving hours off my life wasn't fixing anything.

When the coffee finished its brew cycle, I poured some into my mug, stirred in a little cream, and ducked out the back door. The night was still moist in the air as cool gusts swept across the property. I perched myself on the banister at the east corner of the porch to observe the first light rays that were destined to summit peaks a few miles off in a matter of minutes.

Growing up, summer had always been my favorite season. My father was lax on his curfew when school wasn't in session which gave me several extra hours of outdoor time.

Kickball dominated the street if there were enough participants. If not, roller hockey and four-square made for decent alternatives. When dusk fell over the neighborhood, we would draw up imaginary boundaries for Manhunt, an urban game of tag that even parents enjoyed participating in.

My age and summer ardor shared an inverse proportionality. Instead of logging leisurely evenings as I did in my adolescence, I took advantage of others who were. For weeks, the population swelled with an influx of tourists who would lounge on our beaches and dine in our restaurants.

I had to remind myself that potential profits always outweighed the discomfort of the heat. This, as I bustled around the patio in a long sleeved cotton t-shirt delivering oysters and cocktails, sweat beads rolling down the small of my back to drench the waistband of my jeans.

Sunshine twinkling through leaves in the distance, I sipped my coffee and enjoyed June for the first time in years. I had only just arrived in Colorado, but already I felt a sense of belonging.

"Awesome coffee," my uncle said, having silently joined me on the deck.

I hopped down from the railing and faced him. "Awesome day."

"You're up early," he noted.

I turned to admire the beautiful dawn that was upon us. "It was totally worth it."

Uncle Remi nodded his head toward the sky where two large birds were circling, riding the currents like surfers cutting through crested waves. "Those hawks have been around forever. Got a nest in that cottonwood." He pointed to a patch of trees. "You can borrow my binoculars sometime if you'd like. The night vision ones are pretty spectacular."

Animal watching had never been a sport of mine, but I was willing to give it a try.

"Ever see anything crazy?" I asked him, shuffling across the porch with legs half asleep.

"The Yeti was most interesting," he said, holding the screen door open for me.

I giggled, wondering if the elusive creature really did exist. "Anything's possible."

My uncle smiled. "Ready to get going?"

9

"When a body gets delivered, it's our duty to confirm the identity of the decedent by checking the data on the toe tag." I jotted down notes as Uncle Remi rattled off the basics.

"Initially, the burden of proof is endowed to the family if it was a home death, the hospital if it occurred under their supervision, and the pathologist if an autopsy was performed. It seems rudimentary, but identification is a very important step."

Three knocks on the wall pulled my uncle in another direction.

"Excuse me a moment," he said, ducking into the prep room to assist Darla, Forester's senior mortician.

Left alone, I hunted around the office, snooping through file cabinets to get the gist of what documents I would be dealing with. The paperwork was grouped alphabetically, each surname scrawled in black ink by the same shaky hand.

Uncle Remi returned to the office, just as the phone began to ring. Overwhelmed, he sighed and hit the speaker button to answer. "Forester Funeral Home."

"It's just me." Her voice oozed with sadness.

"I know this has been hard for you Margot," Uncle Remi said, immediately identifying her, "but you have to be strong. Glen wouldn't want you suffering this way." He paused to let her speak. Only muffled sobs were offered in reply.

"Margot," he tried again. The phone line clicked off.

My uncle turned to me, his eyes somber. "Sometimes you have to play therapist around here. People will call, and all they really want is comfort."

I imagined Margot sitting on her couch clutching a picture of her husband, an empty tissue box next to her, wads of soiled Kleenex crumpled up and strewn around.

"Where were we?"

"Identification," I reminded him, my first day of training becoming a lesson in patience.

"Right. Once we establish identity, they get put into the fridge while we investigate their postmortem requests. That's part of your job." He gestured matter-of-factly with his hands.

"If the decedent is to be cremated, you will schedule with Lander's." He pointed up to the corner of the ceiling indicating a location westward, deeper into the canyon. "The other option is embalming."

"How long has Darla worked here?" I asked.

"Since the beginning."

"Like a business partnership or something?"

"No, nothing like that. Her wife, Patty, had HIV. When she died, there was a lot of misinformation out there about the illness. Every funeral home she went to refused to accept the body because of the risk for exposure."

I was surprised by his frank delivery. "But you agreed anyway?"

"Darla said she would to do the embalming herself. She was a flight medic in the Air Force. Blood and body fluids didn't faze her in the least." He shook his head and smiled. "She photocopied reference diagrams in the library and followed along as she went. I marveled at her passion and offered her a job."

"Were you scared?"

"I was heartbroken. People assumed that Patty contracted the virus because she was a lesbian. Of course, that's just ridiculous."

"How did it happen, then?"

"She was born with it. Her mother didn't know she was infected when she got pregnant. Passed right through the placenta."

Darla knocked three more times, signaling she was ready.

I looked over at the door and thought of only one thing. "Does she have it, too?"

"No," he said definitively, disappearing once again.

•••♦••

The office was a chilly ten by ten space, more of a transition between the waiting area and embalming room. One desktop computer sat upon the vintage mocha colored desk, several wire baskets stacked high with papers needing to be filed. Shelves matching the desk were mounted on the lavender painted walls, various medical books and manuals pertaining to funerary practices displayed for quick access. There was an anatomically correct skeleton articulated on a stand, and posters illustrating the entire circulatory system were taped up.

In the corner of the office, a small closet was neatly packed with dated boxes. I peeled back the lid of the previous year and extracted a document from the hundreds that had been stowed in the event of an audit. On the page was an itemized list of various services totaling nine thousand dollars. Stunned by the price, I pulled out another receipt for comparison; its detailed charges were even more expensive.

The phone rang and I froze, unsure if I was ready to deal with whoever waited on the other end. After the fourth ring, I cleared my throat and answered.

"Forester Funeral Home."

"Hey. Is Remi around?"

"He's occupied at the moment." I hoped it was the right thing to say. "Can I take a message?"

"Sure. Let him know Vic is still planning on being there tomorrow. And to call me if that's going to be a problem." His voice was husky and confident, and that was all it took to get me interested.

"You got it," I told him.

"Thanks," he said.

I hung up feeling aroused, a foreign state of being I'd been incapable of since Trevor and I broke up the year before. Not only had he stripped me of my faith in monogamy, he'd also destroyed my sexual appetite. When I uncovered his infidelities, my sex drive was diminished to nonexistent. My pussy had been padlocked for months and even I didn't have the right combo.

The twang of desire brief, I let my thoughts about Vic wash away as I plopped into the office chair and turned on the computer screen. Mousing my cursor across a background of sunflowers, I clicked on the Firefox icon which brought me to the default home page – a religious site with a collection of quotes about death.

I scrolled through a few undecipherable biblical verses before keying in my favorite website for alternative media. It didn't even take ten minutes to realize how little I'd missed since shirking my daily dose of news headlines.

During my internet hiatus, ISIS had continued to behead journalists and climate change was provoking the draft of regulations that would place a tax on carbon use. The mainstream's doom propaganda was slowly infiltrating what had previously been unbiased outlets. All anyone ever talked about was the impending economic crisis or the top five reasons you should vote for a particular political party.

Reports about positive action in the community or people doing well were few and far between. Even then, web trolls would lie in wait, pouncing on any opportunity to post hateful comments because they feel entitled to express their opinions.

Part of my demise the spring semester had to do with my internship, a short-lived probe into the real world of journalism. News agencies, as I discovered, didn't want tenacious writers searching for truth. They wanted sheep that obeyed orders without question – vessels of talent eager to propagate lies for the rich who use their status for manipulation.

When I chose journalism as my major, I saw myself making a difference in the world. I had high hopes of empowering the weary, pushing for restructure of outdated government legislation, and advocating for those abused by both the system and their peers.

Even my greatest of intentions couldn't blind me enough to work alongside self-proclaimed philanthropists masquerading as journalists. All they cared about was getting the most hits on Twitter, more than willing to suck cock for an inside story.

My senior year in sight, I was left in the aftermath of having wasted three years preparing for a progression of successful moments that no longer appealed to me. Humbled by my own ignorance, I quit the internship and slowly withdrew from attending class.

Another call interrupted my thoughts.

"Are you guys planning on spending the night in there?"

I looked out the window and was astonished to see that it was getting dark.

Aunt Jeannine continued on despite my silence. "If you intend to eat this evening, I've fixed a simple meal. But I'm going off kitchen duty. I have matters to attend to."

As if by extra sensory perception, Uncle Remi emerged from the embalming room.

"Tell her we're on our way," he said, the Roman clock above the door beckoning eight-thirty with each passing second.

"We're on our way," I told her, but she was already gone, having said her piece before bustling off to her secret room.

"What does Aunt Jeannine do in her office?" I asked Uncle Remi.

In typical fashion, he answered with a question. "Why don't you ask her?"

We piled into his truck and I buckled up instinctively. The diesel engine cranked over, its sputter almost drowning out a Doors jam emanating from the radio.

He toggled the wheel mounted shifter into reverse. "I admire your safety provisions, but I've got a clean record."

We pulled up to the front of the house, its windows lit by lamps from the inside. I unstrapped my seatbelt and realized how unnecessary it had been to brace for a ride that lasted less than a minute. It was habit though, one that manifested from the *Click It Or Ticket* campaign, and one that had never died.

The sun's rays were preserved in a collection of pink and orange brush strokes painted across the sky. "Know why they fly like that?" Uncle Remi asked, spotting a flock of geese overhead.

I thought for a moment, cycling through archived facts in my head. "No," I finally said.

"The v-shaped configuration allows them to travel further and for longer periods of time. They're defeating wind resistance."

We watched them fade away until they became dots.

"Nature never struggles," he continued. "It evolves."

10

Fogginess was an enemy to be slain when I awoke the following morning. Before even opening my eyes, Vic suddenly came to mind; I'd forgotten to deliver his message. The guilt lasted but a moment, my attention stolen by sexual energy pooling into my pelvis. I reached down under the covers. Even if Vic was a hideous version of the one I'd dreamt up, I craved a man's attention.

I put on jeans I wore the day before and slipped into a sheer camisole. The full length mirror had advice for my chest. Heeding its counsel, I dropped the spaghetti straps down over my shoulders and clipped on a strapless push-up bra which made my breasts appear to be a cup size bigger.

I descended the stairs while wrestling with a blue peasant top that was much more appropriate for dealing with clients than the mini version of a shirt beneath it. Managing to wriggle it on, I sprung off the last step and followed the aroma of coffee into the kitchen. At the table, my uncle was reading his transcripts.

"Vic's coming today," I said straight away, one octave below enthusiastic.

Uncle Remi looked at me over his glasses.

I turned my back and scowled. Hoping he wouldn't spot my interest, I added, "He called yesterday to make sure you guys were still on."

"Oh, good," he said, seemingly unaware as he adjusted his spectacles and returned to his paperwork.

"Morning!" Aunt Jeannine limped into the dining room, her sweet disposition concealing the pain she held in her joints. She kissed her husband on the forehead and staggered over to an herbal entourage which took up the entire corner left of the stove.

I watched her spoon out dried remnants of a plant and weigh them with a small scale no bigger than a deck of cards. Humming cheerfully, she dropped stems, flowers, and leaves into her stainless-steel ball infuser.

"What's your schedule like?" Aunt Jeannine asked my uncle.

He stacked his papers and set his glasses on top of them. "Vic'll be by this afternoon."

"Lovely! Will he be staying for dinner?"

Uncle Remi made his way over to her and wrapped her in his arms. "I don't know, sweetheart. You wanted my schedule, not his."

Aunt Jeannine giggled, their genuine love for one another fresh and untainted by the years.

I excused myself to give them a moment alone but stayed within earshot to wait for any additional details about the guy named Vic.

"Extend the offer if I'm not around," I heard her said. "We have at least five bouquets worth of flowers that need harvesting so I'll be in and out."

"I will, Jeannie," he assured her.

43

Their conversation dwindled to a whisper as I headed off to the truck. Between the two of them, I wondered who would go first. Maybe they'd be on the news, the couple that serendipitously died together, their fingers braided as they shared their final living moments on Earth.

11

The previous day's warm-up had hardly primed me for what was in store on the morning that followed. By the time noon arrived, I had three viewings to schedule for the following weekend and Jefferson, the Lander's delivery guy, had called to say he would be dropping off two cremations.

The mortuary was a square building, its interior walls compartmentalizing the business into smaller squares, each room designed for a specific purpose. I imagined an aerial view of the building, the roof peeled back to reveal a practical layout.

"The box," I said, the edges of my mouth curling up with revelation. Aunt Jeannine's description was quite fitting.

Gravel crunched beneath tires beyond the window and a car door shut. Moments later, there was a gentle knock on the office door which was only partially closed. Chewing the bite of granola I had started on for lunch, I shouted from my seat. "Come in!"

A scruffy middle-aged man with boxes of ashes did not appear. Instead, an Adonic hunk with juicy lips poked his head in, his lovely green eyes instantly paralyzing my heart. I scooped the rest of my granola bar along with the wrapper into the trash and sucked the remaining oats from my teeth with one quick thrash of the tongue.

"Are you Jefferson?" I asked. It was my best attempt to disguise the surprise on my face, but even I wasn't convinced by it.

He smiled and shook his head no.

"How can I help you?"

"I'm here to see Remi," he said, and I immediately recognized his voice.

Vic's thick brown hair was longer on top than at the sides. Instead of gelling it in place, he'd combed it back and allowed the most unruly pieces to fall down over his forehead. He swept his hand across the door to open it wide and pulled himself into my office.

"I'll go get him for you," I told him, coming to my feet. I approached the steel door of the embalming room and pried it open. Formaldehyde saturated air gushed out as I rallied up the courage to enter the place where people were regularly cut open and stitched back up.

Forcing myself into death's domain, the gorgeous man called out to me from behind. "Tell him it's Vic!"

Once inside, I realized I might be walking into an even more uncomfortable situation. I was relieved to see that no one, dead or alive, was around. I knew I would eventually come face to face with a cadaver, but I was happy to be spared another day.

Shuffling feet drew my attention to the opposite side of the room. Darla and Uncle Remi were rolling a squeaky-wheeled gurney to the sink, its tenant draped with a sheet.

"Vic's here to see you," I said, taking in the stench of pungent chemicals used to postpone the decomposition of flesh. Everything was a sterile bright white except for liberally polished stainless steel counters whose surfaces were blemished with dings acquired over the years. Fluorescent ceiling panels provided ambient light, and large operating lamps with posable mechanical arms housed high powered bulbs capable of illuminating the deepest crevices of an exposed chest cavity.

As my breathing hovered above baseline, I scanned wall to wall glass cabinets designed to reveal their contents without having to be opened. Some were stocked with boxes of syringes and tape, others with nitrile gloves and personal protection attire. Several trash bins were lined with red biohazard bags warning of their possible contamination.

From behind a face shield and surgical mask, Uncle Remi spoke. "Perfect timing. Tell him I'll be right there."

When I returned to the office with his message, Vic was still standing, the only available chair perched behind an unwelcoming desk littered with postmortem documents.

"He'll be with you in a moment," I told him, taking my seat as if I had loads of work needing my attention.

"Great, I'll go get my stuff."

I examined Vic as he retreated, and then rushed over to the window to spy.

The sleek black van he drove wasn't the kind soccer moms toted kids to school in. It was rugged and sporty, set above deeply treaded tires ready for the challenge of the toughest terrain. A brush guard and wench were fixed to the front bumper, large waterproof cases strapped to a carbon fiber rack mounted to the roof. There was even a spare on the left back door which swung out independent of the one on the right.

Vic's biceps bulged while he stacked each piece of luggage on an aluminum hand truck painted the same color as his Econoline. As I watched his forearm come up to wipe away sweat from his brow, the embalming room door started to open. I raced across the office to the coffeepot and rummaged around for a filter.

"You read my mind," Uncle Remi said when he entered, pleased that I would think to brew an afternoon cup of java. I smiled at him over my shoulder, glad to have avoided detection.

The van doors slammed in succession and Uncle Remi peeled the blinds down to look out. When he removed the pressure of his fingers, the plastic slats snapped shut.

"Our boy's filming a documentary," he announced.

Stooping low to retrieve coffee cups, I felt the tightness of my jeans up against my inner thigh, a seam in the material gently rubbing against me while I moved about. The resurrection of my libido was welcome, though inopportune. I stood to adjust my pants as I fought for control of my body.

"People need to see a fair account of the funeral business," Uncle Remi went on. "And if showing them what goes on in the parlor is the way to do it, so be it. Not everyone has the stomach for this job, but the least they can do is be respectful. And informed."

Macabre visuals sent my lustful appetite into withdrawal as Vic returned to the office tethered to his gear.

"Man, it got hot out there." He offered Uncle Remi his hand. "Thanks for having me."

"Certainly. We'd like to have you for dinner as well," Uncle Remi told him. "Over for dinner, that is."

Vic laughed, flashing me a sweet smile before venturing into the confines of the torture chamber with his mound of electronic equipment.

As they disappeared, another vehicle pulled up. This time it *was* Jefferson along with what remained of two individuals, their bodies reduced to ash and a few disobedient teeth – the conglomeration of remnants he called *cremains*.

"On average, it takes pret' near two hours at around fourteen-hundred degrees to fully 'sintegrate a body. That's Fahrenheit. Even still," he said, shaking the packages like a kid on Christmas morning, "some are stubbrin'."

Small pebbles jangled around and he grinned, many missing teeth the cause of his impaired speech. His hyperpigmented skin was dark and leathery, his brow hairs wild and wiry.

The longer I appraised him, the less critical I became. Behind glum eyes, Jefferson yearned for attention, his only company those he loaded into the furnace and shoveled out thereafter. He was someone's child, a simpleton in a world of sophistication who didn't deserve cruel judgment. I kept the desk between us anyway.

"Welp, it was nice to meet ya, Tally. I'm the only porter for Mr. Lander's so you'll be seeing me often."

He offered another toothless smile and tipped the brim of his weathered cowboy hat with a stained hand. His ill-fitting boots click-clacked as he retreated to his vehicle which had mostly rusted away save for a few patches of powder blue automotive paint that had been the pickup's original color. I watched him edge away from the mortuary, one taillight refusing to glow as he braked for the stop sign.

12

Prior commitments kept Vic from joining us for dinner. Instead, Aunt Jeannine and I sat side by side on the living room's only couch, both of us engaged in books we were determined to finish. She read from Alejandro Jodorowsky's *Psychomagic* and I picked up where I'd left off in Poe's collection of short stories, not quite halfway through *The Cask of Amontillado*.

"I know we haven't spent much time together," she said out of nowhere, "but I want you to know I've enjoyed you being here."

I started to formulate a response, but Aunt Jeannine continued.

"I don't express myself all too well." She inserted her bookmark and closed the cover. "I'm working on it."

It was my turn to speak so I followed suit by creasing the corner of my page and setting my book down next to hers. We'd each had two glasses of Merlot, the relaxation that comes from sipping wine making itself known.

"I'm happy to be here," I said.

She smiled and waited for me to go on.

"I guess I needed to get away."

"Away from what?"

"The walls were caving in."

"Everyone feels grief differently."

"That's the thing, Aunt Jeannine. It must have been denied or maybe I was just really focused on school. But when he died, I didn't *feel* anything."

"Lack of feeling is indeed a feeling, dear. It's called numb."

Numb. So simple. So uncomplicated.

"I suppose I don't express myself all too well, either," I told her.

"Fair enough." She picked up her book and then set it back down. "How's your mother?"

The question was an ambush. I hadn't spoken to her since my dad's funeral where she sat in the back pew and watched me stumble over the speech I gave to solidify his eternal departure.

"I know you two have had a volatile relationship," Aunt Jeannine offered.

A surge of anger surfaced. Instead of spitting it out with a string of hateful verbs and nouns, I lifted my wineglass and washed it down. Then, without a word, I rose from the couch.

Having known what I was after, my aunt shouted out her request as I made my way into the kitchen. "Grab the *Morris Durif*, dear."

On one side of the pocket panty were hand labeled bottles harvested from her grove, the varietal and vintage marked across a strip of masking tape. The opposite shelves housed store bought bottles, grouped first according to type, then by date from left to right.

52

"It's a Shiraz," she called out, assuming I had lost myself amongst the slew of titles. "Two thousand and twelve."

Having uncorked the bottle in the kitchen, I returned to the living room and poured each of us a healthy glass. "This calls for some chocolate!" Aunt Jeannine picked up a jewel encrusted cigar box from the end table next to her, sat it between us, and threw back the lid. "This here is from a cult Tuscan chocolatier." She held the prized possession up and then set it aside for some special not-yet-planned event in the future. "These are Belgian," she pointed, "and this is from Switzerland."

"Chocolate isn't my forte," I told her. She nodded, made a selection, and then stowed the rest for impending cravings of a later date.

"Where were we?" she asked, unwrapping the 70% cacao Leonidas she'd chosen and handing me two squares from the bar. "Oh, yes. Your mother."

By the time our intermission ended, I'd lost interest in talking about the past.

"Why couldn't Vic come for dinner?" I asked as innocently as possible.

"Who knows. He's tough to nail down."

"Oh," I replied, biting off a piece of chocolate.

"He and Darla will be over on Sunday, instead."

Aunt Jeannine didn't miss the slight smile that touched my mouth. She winked and then returned to her book.

53

13

When I finally roused late Saturday morning, my head ached with dehydration. I wrestled my feet free from the tight bunch of sheets I had tangled around my ankles and Eileen leapt from the bed.

"I'm sorry princess," I told her. "I didn't know you were there!"

More forgiving than most felines, she hopped back up and nudged me with her white-whiskered snout. I had adopted her from the kennel my freshman year of college but what seemed like a plan of mutual benefit turned out to be an emotional and financial struggle. Less than a week after being rescued from impending euthanasia, she was sneezing blood and refused to eat. I took her to an emergency clinic where the vet diagnosed her with a severe upper respiratory infection and acute anorexia – a twelve minute trip to the tune of three hundred bucks.

Eileen was prescribed high calorie canned food the price of steak. When she decided she didn't want to eat it, I had to squirt it down her throat with a syringe.

Weeks of antibiotics and forced feedings made her distrustful, but as her malnourished body responded to the treatment, she regained her energy. Slowly, her kitten instincts kicked back in and she was zipping around the apartment. Our start, though shaky, had bonded us in a special way.

I scratched the underside of Eileen's chin, her purr letting me know she enjoyed my company as much as I enjoyed hers. "Mom's got to get up. Aunt Jeannine is taking me to town." I promised to bring back her favorite treats as I moved pillows under the covers to create a tunnel. She nestled in for a nap while I dressed.

My aunt was waiting for me in the kitchen, reusable canvas bags stacked on the table in front of her. "Have some water," she instructed.

"I'm fine," I yawned, unwilling to acknowledge my hangover.

"Suit yourself," she said.

"Did you eat already?" I asked her.

"I figured we would get something in town."

I looked over at the clock; it was already eleven-thirty. The ride to Ft. Collins would take a half hour, plus the shopping part. I would be famished by then. "Any chance we can do lunch first?"

She stood and straightened the legs of her capris. "Let's go."

· · ◆ ◆ ◆ ·

I tried to enjoy the ride but my head throbbed with the rise and fall of the elevation. I lowered the window, allowing the rush of cool air to pound my sweaty face.

Creeping bile made it hard for me to engage in the conversation Aunt Jeannine had initiated moments after we left the house. For the most part, *Uh huh* and *Yeah* were good enough responses to her questions. The rare circumstance when I had to form a sentence was painstaking. I took my time to answer, waiting for saliva to moisten my mouth.

After what seemed like hours of torture, we finally made it to the sub shop at the edge of town. I felt a spark of buoyancy as I ordered the *Morning After* which promised piles of rotisserie turkey garnished with Swiss, avocado, and house-made honey Dijon mustard, all atop a freshly baked hoagie.

"What's on the menu for tomorrow night?" I asked Aunt Jeannine, who had resorted to reading a magazine while I stuffed my face.

"I don't know. What can you cook?"

"Me?"

"Yeah, you. It's your turn."

"I didn't know we had turns." I jammed the final nub of sandwich into my mouth to circumvent her question. She kept her eyes on me until I was done chewing.

"I know how to barbecue," I said, shrugging my shoulder.

She cackled, my statement the funniest joke she'd ever heard. Inquisitive patrons paused their munching to gawk at us. Embarrassed, I leaned in and whispered. "I'm serious."

"Alright, Tally." She'd come off it a bit, her cheeks still rosy and flushed. I bunched my trash up dolefully.

56

"We haven't grilled out since last season," she said, oblivious to my self-denigration. "If you're up for it, I'd love for you to treat us to some down south cooking."

I hadn't missed home until then. Florida wasn't particularly famed for southern cuisine which contradicted its geographic location. What it did boast proudly were its beaches. I suddenly longed for the smell of the ocean, my landlocked location putting all worthy bodies of salt water more than one thousand miles away in every direction.

I caught sight of her grin and the thought faded. "What's that face for?"

"I'm excited to see you in action."

"You're going to help, aren't you?"

"Maybe. Maybe not."

"Aunt Jeannine! I can't do it all alone."

"Sure you can."

"Well, I don't *want* to do it alone."

"Alright, alright. Keep your shirt on. But trust me when I say, Vic isn't that hard to impress."

"I don't care what he thinks," I lied. "They just don't know my cooking like they know yours."

"True." She folded her sandwich wrapper in quarters and stood. "Let's boogie."

· · ♦ ♦ · ·

Traffic was thick as we made our way through town.

"What in the world?" Aunt Jeannine said to herself.

"There's some sort of festival going on," I told her.

"What for?"

"The city's birthday."

57

"Oh, sure. Yep. They do it every year. I don't remember it being crowded like this though."

She slammed on the breaks to avoid hitting a bicyclist who darted across the street in front of us. His hair was long and he had a guitar case strapped to his back. "Goddamn hippie!"

Caught off guard, I squeaked out a fart. Aunt Jeannine looked over at me with the most curious face and we both burst out laughing.

"Scared the shit out of you, did I?" she squawked.

"It was a close one," I told her, still giggling.

Our minor stall gave the guy ahead of us a few extra seconds to back his BMW out of a premium parking spot.

"Goddamn hippie!" Aunt Jeannine shouted, pleased that our tie dyed friend had altered fate in our favor. "Everything happens for a reason."

She pulled into the vacancy, turned the ignition off, and gathered her environmentally conscious shopping bags. "Alright, Tally. What's on the menu?"

· · ◆ ◆ · ·

The ride back up the canyon was much more enjoyable with a full stomach. Taking advantage of being the passenger, I watched out the window as rocky terrain softened to open meadows which were once again swallowed by dry upheavals of the Earth's crust. It was pure insanity that people had chiseled roads into the mountainside.

"Can you imagine being an explorer back in the day?" Aunt Jeannine broke in as if reading my thoughts. "Summiting one peak to see several more in the distance.

There's an elementary school at the end of this road called Stove Prairie – the poor fools brought their cook stoves with them for miles until they no longer could. Left all of'em behind."

I was silent while she continued her history lesson. "Had they known that was the least of their worries, they would have probably stayed in the plains and built their communities there. It must have been sheer panic when the fires swept through one year, floods the next."

"Didn't that happen recently?" I asked, recalling news reports about broad sweeping forest fires which destroyed a hundred thousand acres.

"Yep, right here in our back yard." She pointed out a few spots where trees were scorched, others directly beside them untouched. "And of course, the flooding followed. We've had a stellar year compared to the previous two."

We passed a white cargo van at the mortuary. I assumed it belonged to Randall, Uncle Remi's transport employee. He and his son, Burke, delivered the bodies.

According to Uncle Remi, Burke was looking to complete his senior year of high school on the second attempt and not at all what you would consider to be *college material*. Instead of pursuing a degree, he planned on learning from his dad until he could eventually replace him. Together, the father-son team delivered decedents to the storage fridge until Darla could get to them on Monday.

Aunt Jeannine parked and shut the engine off. "Thankfully, the universe spared us this time. We were ordered to evacuate and didn't know what we'd be coming home to."

"You got lucky," I said, collecting our bags and bumping the car door shut with my hip. "Did they figure out how it started?"

"Lightning," Aunt Jeannine said shuffling off to the front door without offering to help carry a single thing. "We're prone to lightning strikes around here."

······

I spent the afternoon listening to birds from the basket of a hammock strung between two maples Aunt Jeannine said turned the most outrageous colors in late September. Beneath the shade of the trees, I hardly missed Florida. I watched the woods around me buzz with life before surrendering to a sleepy spell that put me under.

Hours later, light rain started to dampen my clothes. I enjoyed the scent of the wet soil until a tickle on my arm caused me to swat at whatever creature thought it clever to crawl across my skin. No longer a welcome guest in the underbrush, I headed for cover.

The house was quiet compared to the stirring sounds of the outdoors. I was still full from lunch, but I was craving something sweet. I went into the kitchen and dug around until I found the winner. A fistful of chocolate covered pomegranates in hand, I climbed the stairs to the loft.

"How's Florida?" Sadie asked after picking up the line right before it went to voicemail.

"Ha-ha-ha. I wouldn't know."

"I have to say, I'm fairly impressed. Lost that bet."

"What bet?"

"With myself. I figured you would have turned back. No offense."

"Seriously?"

"Hey, I'm just being honest." The words crackled in my ear as I paced, cell service shoddy in all but one area – my bed. I sat before falling backwards onto the mattress.

My narrative dominated while Sadie listened, papers shuffling in the background the only way I knew she was there. I told her I was enjoying my trip and that working in the mortuary wasn't as bad as I thought it was going to be. I had planned on mentioning Vic but decided against it.

"Alright, Sadie. I'll call you in a few days."

"Sounds good," she said, her voice distant and distracted. "Stay out of trouble."

14

By five o'clock the next day, Aunt Jeannine was chopping away at the hydroponically cultivated onions we purchased from a local grower who had propped a tent open on the side of the road. While she prepped, I mixed up some mojitos.

"This is delicious," she told me, taking large sips between loading hunks of veggies and bite-sized beef filets onto skewers.

"Not as delicious as those are going to be. I won't feel right taking all the credit."

"I'm just the help in this one."

She had drained her libation down to ice and soggy leaves. "Let me get you another drink."

I discarded the contents of her glass, added a handful of fresh mint along with the other ingredients, and muddled it all with the back of a wooden spatula.

"Neat," she said, admiring my technique.

The doorbell rang and Aunt Jeannine shimmied off to answer it. After squeezing a lime slice to top off our cocktails, I headed for the living room.

"Perfect timing," I said to Darla, offering her a drink.

"Oh, you're a doll. I hope you won't be offended if I decline." She pulled an expertly rolled joint from her pocket and ran it across the freckled strip of skin under her nostrils. "I quit the bottle years ago."

Darla wedged the doobie between her pursed lips and retrieved matches from the right breast pocket of her plaid blouse. "I'd ask permission, but I know you don't mind," she said to no one in particular before striking a match, the scent of sulfur burning off before being replaced by the earthy waft of marijuana. "Where's your husband?"

Uncle Remi appeared from the bowels of the house. "I knew I smelled you!"

Darla handed her cannabis treat off to him. "It's Grapefruit," she said, tilting her head toward the ceiling to expel a plume of smoke.

"Sure is," Uncle Remi agreed, sucking in his second drag. He looked at me with eyes that advised caution. "Want some?"

"I love grapefruit," I said, stripping the joint off him and taking a baby hit. I passed it over to Aunt Jeannine expecting her refusal. To my surprise, she accepted it.

After several tokes, she passed it back to Darla. "I'm not a prude, you know. I just prefer sativas."

On the brink of a collective high, the doorbell rang again. Darla's dog, Josie, let out a bellow. She'd been laying perfectly still, her snow white paws tucked beneath her body, a lump of brown and black patched fur camouflaged against the wood planks.

Uncle Remi was closest and granted access to our latest arrival. "C'mon in!"

15

The party moved from the living room to the back porch where Aunt Jeannine had arranged chairs in a semicircle facing out to the west. Darla sat on one end, her loyal pooch sprawled out a yard in front of her. The two middle spots were taken by my relatives, and Vic sat next to my aunt, leaving the empty chair next to him for me. I chose to stand, facing them while leaning back against the railing.

Everyone was enjoying their refreshments including Darla, for whom I had prepared a virgin beverage of mint, lime, and club soda.

"What's for dinner?" Vic asked, posing his question to Aunt Jeannine.

"Don't look at me." She motioned in my direction with her head.

"I'll get the grill going soon," I said. Anxiety rising, I lowered my eyes to my feet. The chipped polish on my toenails should have been removed the week before, but instead, stared up to scold me.

Wanting to escape, I headed off to the concrete landing where the grill sat. I put my drink down on the ground and loaded briquettes into the charcoal chimney.

"Still got those matches?" I yelled to Darla. A moment later, Vic's arm was dangling over the banister, the book tiny between his fingers.

"Want company?" he asked, his skin brushing against mine as I took the Diamond Strikes from him. Before I could respond, he was on the porch steps.

I bunched up kindling material and set the charcoal aflame. They would need about twenty minutes to turn their proper ashy grey color. Taking my persisted silence as his cue, Vic initiated conversation.

"Thanks for the invite," he said, as if it were my idea.

"Aunt Jeannine – she seems to like your company."

"They have a beautiful place here." He trawled his head from one side of the property to the other. "Have you done much exploring?"

"Not yet." I poked around at the charcoal with a branch. Darla was mad about something, her voice randomly flaring up with passion.

"First time in Colorado?" Vic asked.

"Mmhmm. I grew up in Florida."

"What brought you here?"

"Change," I told him. He waited for an explanation.

Without providing one, I stoked the charcoal one last time. They were ready. I hoisted the fiery embers into the gut of the grill and closed the vent. Stepping back to retrieve the mesh brush, I kicked my drink over. "Argh!"

Vic chuckled. "We can share this one."

He handed me his half-full mojito, bent down to pick up what remained of mine, and stood back up just in time to watch me suck down the rest of his.

"Sorry," I told him. "I tried to stop, but I couldn't."

"No problem. They taste great." He stared at me until I looked away.

"I'll get us another round," I said, excusing myself from his gripping energy. I was barely noticed as I slipped into the kitchen, the elders debating recent gun-grab referendums aimed at stripping Americans of their second amendment right.

"It's bullshit," Darla snarled, acknowledging my presence with a nod as I stepped back out onto the porch. With the sheet pan balanced in my left hand, and two stiff beverages clutched in the palm of my right, I made my way down the stairs.

Vic was scrubbing the grill grate when I came into view. He dropped the brush and ran to my aid. "Let me help you."

"I'm good." I handed him the cocktails. "I've been playing waitress for a while."

"Those look awesome," he said of the kabobs.

"Why thank you," I replied, adjusting my top and sticking out my chest, rum the conspirator behind my withering inhibitions.

Vic grinned and turned away. "Those, too."

"Will you grab'em for me?" I asked, another innuendo imploring his response. He jerked his head around and raised his eyebrows.

I hoisted the pan to eye level. "Pretty please?"

"Only because you asked nicely," he said, taking the tray from me.

I doused the kabobs with Aunt Jeannine's GMO free, non-aerosol, cooking spray and began loading them onto the grill. By the time I got the last ones down, the first ones to hit the heat were starting to look cooked on one side. I used tongs to give them a quarter turn and continued down the line. The procession lasted until all four sides were browned without overcooking the insides.

"Ready to eat?" I asked Vic when I figured they were done.

"Definitely," he said, peering into my eyes, his stare revealing just how hungry he was.

When all of the kabobs had been removed, I took the tray from Vic and headed off to the house with him following behind. I hoped he was staring at my ass and I swayed it more than usual to tempt him.

•••♦♦••

Each of us took a seat at the dinner table which was draped in a tablecloth, the utensils formally placed on either side of the china. I tonged kabobs onto our plates while Aunt Jeannine filled large globed wine glasses with Malbec.

"Thanks for having us," Vic said, speaking for both him and Darla. "I'm glad I got a rain check."

"Of course, dear," Aunt Jeannine told him.

The rest of us were busy pulling grilled meat and vegetables from wooden sticks, eager to scrutinize the bounty with our taste buds. We ate for several minutes and it was Uncle Remi who spoke first. "I think you might have some competition, Jeannie."

Everyone laughed.

"It's very good, Tally," Aunt Jeannine said.

Darla and Vic mumbled in agreement, their mouths full.

"How much more filming do you have left, son?" Uncle Remi asked.

"We're almost done, Rowan and I. You've met him once before. We've been getting together on Friday's to go over the footage. Do some editing." I supposed that was why Vic couldn't make it to dinner the other night.

"I'd like to get a few more shots of Darla sometime next week if your schedule permits."

"Fine by me," Darla gargled through a mouthful of beef.

All were in various stages of completion when I stood to clear dishes. The dark of night had arrived, swallowing what remained of the fading sunlight. Aunt Jeannine suggested that we enjoy the rest of our summer evening alongside a campfire.

Once Uncle Remi and Vic had the logs going, we ladies joined them with a bag of chocolate covered pretzels for dessert. Captivated by the flames, I faded in and out of Darla's military stories while thinking about Lander's crematorium and the famous Tibetan monk who had martyred himself in an act of self-immolation. From my chair, the fire was hot. I couldn't fathom the pain of being burned alive, especially not deliberately, by my own volition.

"Look!" It was Uncle Remi who stole my focus. He pointed to a swarm of lightning bugs in the distance, their abdomens flickering against a black background.

"How special," Aunt Jeannine cooed.

"I'm sure they're not that special to you, Tally," Uncle Remi said. "Fireflies are native to swampy lands, east of Kansas, where their prey thrives. We don't usually see them here."

"Must be all this rain we're getting," Vic said, linking the chance event with the uncharacteristically wet weather northern Colorado was having.

Uncle Remi shook his head. "Absolutely. Our seasonal stream has been flowing for days. I've never seen it with water this early on. Must be an ideal breeding ground for them."

"Hope it don't make for good mosquito breeding ground," Darla countered. "The city would rather let its people get infected with West Nile than to spray a little damned insecticide."

"You know I'd fight you on that one," Aunt Jeannine said to her, "but I'm starting to freeze."

Underdressed for the rapid temperature decline, we hustled over to the parking area. Uncle Remi and I sent Vic and Darla off while Aunt Jeannine sought shelter inside.

"You guys okay to drive?" Uncle Remi asked as a gust of wind ripped through the valley.

Assuring him they were fine, they loaded themselves into their vehicles and drove off.

16

In my first week, I'd only sampled the funeral business. Jefferson stopped by at ten to pick up a few bodies for cremation and dropped off two that had been reduced to ashes. One of them, Mr. Charles Harvey III, had specified in his will that his cremains be added to the urn which held his father and grandfather – three generations of Harvey's that found peace in knowing they'd be joined after death.

The other a hiker whose mangled body was found at the base of a local bouldering area a couple of miles south near the Devil's Backbone formation. I'd heard Uncle Remi advise the family against an open casket ceremony, given the condition of Waylon's fractured skull and contorted limbs. Reluctant, they agreed to send him up the hill to Lander's where he would eventually travel back down to me, discreetly packed into a cardboard box.

Just before noon, Wilf and Sam stopped in to show off their newborn son, Lawrence. Their young faces were etched with the tired lines of sleep deprivation. I couldn't imagine myself in their shoes, caring for a child – a living, breathing entity that depended on me for its survival.

"He's cute," I said, looking from a distance with no desire to hold him. Babies weren't the adorable creatures people made them out to be. They would constantly cry and throw up, shit their pants, and couldn't be left alone for even one minute without the possibility of getting hurt or worse. Their huge heads bobbled on underdeveloped necks, their skin saggy and loose about cartilage yet to ossify.

"I'll be coming back to work next week," Wilf told Uncle Remi who had joined the show along with Darla in what was becoming the crowded space of the office. "And Sammy is planning to return August first. If you have things covered until then." He glanced at me optimistically and Uncle Remi followed his gaze.

"I'll be here," I promised.

They had the characteristic glow of new parents, completely smitten by the bundle of flesh they had birthed. Soon enough it would be talking back, yelling *Mine!*, and throwing tantrums in public that would make onlookers cringe.

Lawrence wouldn't be any different than the other kids his age. He would skip class, figure out how to masturbate, move on to fucking girls, sneak out at night, and try drinking and driving after a few licensed months behind the wheel. He'd beg for money and then estrange himself in the name of independence, hide his emotions, and keep a secret diary about all the twisted things he'd ever thought.

And if they were lucky, he would go on to graduate high school, possibly go to college, get a crappy job doing something he hated, marry a woman he didn't love, spit out a couple of kids, and realize that his life sucked.

Observing the time, they bustled out with high hopes and big dreams to a lunch date with the grandparents who were equally excited about welcoming a stranger into the family.

Mid-afternoon approached quickly, and I still had tons of documents to file. Phone calls were recurrent, a few of which were the wrong number. Hearing the words *Forester Funeral Home* come across the line unexpectedly would unnerve me. Coincidence? Or synchronicity?

I believed in a creator, but the conundrum of how that creator was created perplexed me. The ages old impasse only became more confusing when physicists came out with statements claiming that ninety percent of matter is of the dark variety which we can't see and that quantum mechanics operate within a framework we don't quite understand and maybe never will.

Puzzling over alternate planes of reality was enough to make my brain throb. Thankfully, the official work day was coming to an end. Dipping out before five wasn't going to offend my uncle who never paid much attention to time anyway.

I held my breath and poked my head into the embalming parlor. Having smelled the stench of death on a few occasions didn't make me any more used to it. I doubted I ever would be.

"I'm heading out," I said, straining to relay my message over the cascade of running water. The faucet shut off.

Uncle Remi worked his way over to the door in medical garb, blue booties covering his shoes, his face masked by nonwoven three-ply paper to defend against communicable pathogens. Splotches of blood painted his apron, the Windsor knot of his tie peeking out the top. He always dressed professionally while on duty, slacks and suit jacket impeccably pressed, heavy starch keeping them shaped even after strenuous physical labor. "That time already?"

"Not quite, but I have a massive migraine coming on."

The crinkle of his brow indicated a frown hidden beneath his protective layers. "Sorry to hear that."

"I'll be alright. Need anything before I go?"

He shook his head no. "Tell Jeannie I'll be home in a bit." That meant a few hours, at best.

"I will," I agreed, shutting myself out.

·‧◆‧‧·

Classical music playing softly in the distance grew louder as I approached Aunt Jeannine's private room. I put my ear to her door and contemplated disturbing her. Over the delicate strum of a violin, I heard methodical shuffling. Deciding not to interrupt, I retreated, staying light on my feet.

"You're no bother."

I stopped in my tracks and spun around. I hadn't heard the door open and wondered how much of my tiptoeing she had witnessed.

"I'm sorry. Uncle Remi wanted me to tell you –"

She cut me off. "Would you like to come in?"

"Sure," I said, the hesitation in my response offending her.

"Unless you have other things to do. I understand."

"No, I don't. I just – I didn't mean to interrupt."

"See this?" She pointed up at the center of the door frame to something. "When this is displayed," she continued, "it means you are welcome to knock. If not, then I'm busy."

She moved aside and allowed me passage. The pineapple charm was tiny and even if I had known the significance, I doubted I would have noticed it. The wood trinket practically blended in with the door. I decided it was meant to be subtle.

A square pub table sat in the middle of Aunt Jeannine's room, its top covered in lively fabric. Iconic statues of Mother Mary, Buddha, and Ganesh graced the altar she had erected, the length of it reaching from corner to corner. Bones, crystals, and other artifacts were displayed with pride, and incense cones let off the warm notes of sandalwood and patchouli.

The large picture window to the east was the same design as the one in the loft. Potted plants were arranged beneath and on shelves surrounding it, the vibrant green of the leaves showing their appreciation.

"The pineapple is universally recognized as the symbol of welcome," she said, my eyes taking in peculiar ornaments and talismans that filled the room.

She had a few wands, and various calendars were mounted to the wall opposite the altar. One had lunar diagrams and another was printed with zodiac symbols. The other two were meaningless to me.

"Here." She pulled a stool out from under the table. A deck of cards sprawled face down, their backs decorated with the Pagan sun symbol I recognized from the cover of my World Religions textbook.

"Cartomancy was practiced by my ancestors. Both France and Italy take credit for its origin." She laughed as she smoothed her hand across the deck. "Ever had a tarot reading?"

I shook my head to let her know I hadn't.

"Would you like one?"

I adjusted myself, lifting my feet from the floor to the rungs beneath the seat.

"There's a full moon this week," she said, "which makes the energy stronger. It can enhance your sensitivity – allow for expansion and understanding." She paused, thumbing the edge of her cards. "It can also wreak havoc, ruffling up your preconceived notions and casting them aside."

My journey to Colorado came about because I needed some ruffling. I couldn't go on with my dull routine any longer.

"I'm ready," I told her, curious what the reading would show.

Aunt Jeannine stared hard at me – through me. A flush of warmth rose up and settled into my cheeks.

"I don't believe you are," she said.

I blinked nervously, feeling like a baited fish that chases the promise of a succulent meal only to find that, after biting down, the worm was actually a rubber imposter used to disguise the barbed hook.

"I think I should go," I told her

"You don't need to leave, dear."

The walls were closing in to suffocate me as I headed for the door. I exited, closed it gently, and all but ran up the stairs to the loft. When I made it to the bed, tears stung my eyes and I quashed my face into the pillow.

17

Friday was half-gone when I looked up at the clock. I penned one last viewing into Chanelle's swelling logbook and closed it.

Because we ran opposite schedules, Chanelle and I hadn't yet met. But one thing I did know about her was she was extremely busy. As the funeral celebrant, she was in charge of memorials. Most of her ceremonies were held over the weekends when family and friends could rally, mourn, and dry their eyes before heading back to work on Monday.

"Forester Funeral Home," I said into the phone after the second ring.

"It's Vic."

"Hey! How are ya?"

"Good. Long week."

"I feel you." Aunt Jeannine had apologized the morning after our strained encounter; she hadn't meant to upset me, she said, but couldn't go against her intuition. I forgave her right away, though the rejection weighed heavy on my heart for days.

"Want to join me at the drive-in tonight?" he asked.

"Those places still exist?"

Vic laughed. "Ever been?"

"I have not."

He laughed, again. "Well, you're missing out."

"Well, I don't want to *miss out*," I teased. "When does it start?"

"Not until after the sun sets. We need to get there earlier than that though."

"I'm all yours," I told him.

"Sweet."

"We can take my truck," I offered.

"Perfect." He told me to be ready around seven. "And bring a coat. It gets nippley."

• • • ◆ • • •

I was waiting out front for Vic when he showed up at seven o'clock sharp. He unloaded himself from his van and gathered an armful of sheets, four pillows, and a thick blanket. I opened the back passenger side of my truck and he set the bedding down on the seat.

"Staying the night?" I asked.

He grinned. "Cinema sofa. If I stay the night, I'll be sleeping in your bed."

My cheeks tingled. I walked around the front of the Chevy and placed myself behind the wheel, hoping the blush didn't look as bright as it felt. I was attractive by most standards, but still, something about him made me feel inadequate.

I started the engine and winced at the roar of the radio. "I don't really know my way around town," I told him, smashing the knob down to kill it.

"No problem. I'll tell you where to turn," he said. "Have you eaten yet?"

I kicked the truck into reverse. "Not enough."

"Do you like pizza?"

I cocked my eyebrow. "Who doesn't?"

•••♦•••

We stopped by Mile High Pies and picked up two large deep dishes, one topped with Canadian bacon and pineapple, the other strewn with every conceivable vegetable.

"We could have gotten a salad, instead," I razzed.

"A salad?"

"Yeah. I mean, if you're watching your diet and all."

"Pizza isn't much of a diet food."

"I know. That's why it's silly that you had them throw an entire salad on top."

Vic smiled. "Nina's a vegetarian."

"Who's Nina?"

"Rowan's wife." He waited for my mental catch-up. "They're meeting us there."

I was disappointed that we weren't going to be alone but I didn't let on. "I was a vegetarian once."

"Really?"

"Yeah. It only lasted a few hours."

We both laughed as I whipped into the left turn lane unexpectedly and steered into the liquor store's parking lot by the grace of a green arrow. "What's pizza without beer?"

"It's nothing!" he shouted. "Do you like micros?"

I shrugged.

"Get the Mojo IPA," he told me when we arrived at the drive-up window.

I ordered and handed the cashier a few bills. He counted back the change he owed me, offered no smile, and closed the service window.

"Must be jealous," Vic decided before we pulled away.

"A good beer would make anyone jealous," I said. "He probably has a few more hours of incarceration before he can get his drink on."

"Nah. I worked at a liquor store for a few months. They all drink on the job. Besides, I meant he was probably jealous of me."

"Because you have a chauffeur?"

"No, because I have a dazzling chauffeur that I get to spend all night with."

He'd managed to do it again, the heat rising to settle on the apples of my cheeks.

"Don't blush. It reveals everything."

"Oh, but it doesn't. You know nothing."

"Well, now I think the blush is on me." Vic's head pitched right. "Shit, we just passed the road we needed."

I smiled. "Are you complaining about the distraction?"

He reached over for my hand. "Not at all."

········

The ticket booth at the Twin, named for its dueling screens, wasn't yet open. Vic spotted Rowan's ride and told me to pull in behind him. His truck was the same model as mine, several years newer and in hunter green.

I parked and cut the engine. When we got out to make introductions, Rowan followed our lead. Nina stayed in the cab, her animated hands slicing through the air, her cell phone glued to her ear.

Rowan's not quite shoulder length hair was tied back in a short ponytail, his features dark and handsome.

"Nice to meet you," I said.

"Likewise." He looked over at Vic, his smile the confirmation of something they had previously discussed in private. They were entwined in a brotherly hug when Nina ended her call and met us on the shoulder.

"It's my only day off," she harped. "Never fails."

Nina was much taller than me, her blond dreadlocks mature and long. She wore large black framed glasses that were more chic than geeky, her left nostril double pierced with small silver hoops.

"Sorry about that. I'm Nina." She put one hand on her hip, the other raised to shield the glare of the sun.

"Natalia." It sounded blunt though I hadn't meant it to. I didn't even go by my full name but it always managed to come out of my mouth when I met someone new. "This is my first time at the drive-in," I added, trying to soften the unintended bitch tone.

"Oh, lucky you!" She winked. "I remember my first time."

"What was that about?" Rowan asked Nina as he and Vic joined us in a loose huddle.

"They got a fresh body delivered and wanted to know if I could come in to help process it."

"You're not," he commanded.

"No way. I told them to fuck off!" She roped herself into Rowan's arms and slipped him the tongue.

81

"Nina works at the morgue," Vic whispered as he pulled me in for a hug.

The ticket booth opened at quarter to nine and vehicles filed into one of two lines depending on the movie they were there to see. The sign on the gate read: "Don't put us out of business. No outside food or drink."

The price of admission was only seven bucks, but Vic handed me a twenty to give the teller. "Keep the change!" he shouted through my window, his charity downgrading our clandestine pizza party to a non-issue.

I accelerated past the posted five miles per hour speed limit to catch up with Rowan, swerving to avoid potholes and darting dogs whose owners were setting up lounge chairs near their rides. His tires kicked up dust as he swung wide and pulled into a spot, his tailgate facing the hundred-foot screen that would be projecting Sloth's gigantic head for the throwback night of *The Goonies*.

Eighties movies were known for their charm: the graininess, their mind-numbing practical effects, the cheesy acting. Vic didn't know it yet, but my father was a huge film buff. I had a whole arsenal of obscure movies to recommend.

After tucking my truck in next to Rowan's, we sipped on a few beers while I received my lesson in cinema sofa design. The sun had completely disappeared behind the foothills to the west and I shrugged into the sweater I'd brought as the breeze Vic promised chilled my skin.

Nina teased a pipe from her pocket, flicked her Bic, and leaned in for a toke. Her features were carved by light into an overtly feminine caricature. She brought her mouth to Rowan's and gave him a shotgun kiss.

Once sufficiently stoned, Vic distributed slices of pizza. We took our seats when the previews started to roll, a booming radio voice informing the crowd of titles and dates for future events. Nina and Rowan were already getting frisky with one another; Vic chucked an empty beer bottle into their bed to let them know we were onto them.

"They're crazy," he said, arranging his pillow. "Are you comfy?"

"I'm great," I told him, snuggling up to his warmth. He returned my gesture and wrapped himself around me as Jake Fratelli faked his death and escaped from prison.

Even though we had each seen Richard Donner's cult classic more than a half dozen times, the opening scene hooked us right in. When Mikey and the gang shot out from the waterfalls, Vic finally broke our silence.

"Man, that would be so fun!"

"They should make a ride at Disney or something," I said, my voice cracking from disuse. No longer comfortable, I sat up to finish the movie. Vic followed suit.

The adjustment put our line of sight just over Horsetooth Reservoir. Beyond the hills, fireworks were lighting up the sky.

"Wow! What's that for?"

Vic situated himself behind me and swept my hair aside. "It's for you," he whispered, his breath hot in my ear.

I didn't resist when he slid his hand down the front of my pants.

18

Eileen nuzzled me awake before I was ready to welcome the day. The weekend had bowed out the way it always did and an early morning rainstorm had dulled the sky a depressing grey. I was achy from the truck bed, my shoulder stiff with a knot I'd gotten from craning my neck to see the movie.

PMS was coming on strong. First, there were chocolate cravings; then, the horniness of a teenager. After that, it was sore tits and tears, and a face full of zits appearing overnight.

Vic's touch was still palpable as I replayed our sexual encounter in my mind. Fantasizing about his genitals, I used the extendable shower head to massage my own while I readied for another day of dead people. With chemical messengers cramping up my back, I packed my bloated behind into a pair of yoga pants and headed out the door.

· · · ◆ · · ·

Uncle Remi left a note on my desk telling me he would be in later than normal. No attempt was made to disclose why. It would be my first day alone. And it was the busiest one I'd had to date.

When the stream of calls waned at lunchtime, I didn't take a break. Instead, I munched on an apple while I looked over the planner. Three decedents were slated for arrival, prescription pill addicts from the upper-class Mountain Ave. neighborhood who accidentally overdosed on a batch of OxyContin they bought off the street and injected. Two were siblings.

Their disheveled mother would be in the following day to select caskets. Tragically, and only months before, she had lost her husband – the result of a rare reaction to post-operative antibiotics given to him after a routine tooth extraction. Now, she was plagued with the inconceivable task of burying her kids.

"This isn't how it's supposed to be." Belinda's voice, slurred from drinking, fractured over the line before she hung up. "I'm so alone."

A woman's scream jolted me from the office chair. I edged into the waiting area and found that the viewing room door – a door that stayed closed unless a viewing was in progress – was cracked open.

Needing a weapon, I unplugged the lamp in the corner and clutched it tight. If my intruder ended up being an invincible Amazonian hopped up on PCP, I would lock her in there and call the cops. That was my backup plan.

Through the bristled fronds of a dwarf palm, I measured her up.

"Idiot." She stomped her pantyhosed foot, the floor beneath her awash with peace lilies. I was at least forty

85

pounds heavier and no longer worried; I could easily subdue her.

"Can I help you with something?" I asked.

My voice startled her and she stumbled back. When we locked eyes, she seemed irritated. "You sure can."

I pushed the door open and gasped. The funerary box was flipped over, next to it, a pin-striped heap.

"He didn't feel a thing," she said, stooping down to grab hold of his legs. I rushed over to help but hesitated. I'd never touched a corpse.

She looked up at me. "What are you waiting for?"

Stuffing my fear, I dug my hands into his armpits and twisted to the left.

"Let's get Mr. Gable on his back," she said, struggling to defeat the weight of his body. When we had him turned, she pumped her fist in the air.

"I thought you were a burglar," I told her.

She snorted. "I was wondering what the lamp was for."

Her features were sharp, offset by her slight frame. I'd seen her face before, printed on a newspaper clipping in the office. It had done nothing to highlight her natural beauty. She was much prettier in person.

"Are you Chanelle?" I asked, turning several plants right-side up. There was water everywhere.

"All my life." She straightened Mr. Gable's clothes, making slight adjustments to his tie and handkerchief. After tightening his shoelaces, she stepped back to assess. "This is the final memory the family has. It must be perfect."

Once the last patch of wrinkles in Mr. Gable's suit coat was smoothed out, Chanelle went to the far wall to look him over from a distance. Then, she checked her watch.

"His wife called yesterday to say the kids missed their flight. That they would need a delay. As you've seen from my roster, it was a real hoot to pull off."

"What time are they coming?" I asked.

"Two."

"Need any help?"

"I think we're all set."

With things back in order, my eyes began to wander. The viewing room was modern, and inviting, and not at all what I'd imagined. Uncle Remi had quarantined off a section of the refrigeration unit and encased it in glass; behind it, Aunt Jeannine displayed her floral arrangements.

Closure was important at Forester's, a concept ignored by other funeral homes operating purely for greenbacks. On occasion, Aunt Jeannine would have the especially heartbroken client over for hot tea which gave her an opportunity to share her ideas about our finite existence – a physical dimension with inescapable rules and a guarantee that no one gets out alive. She'd never finished her PhD in psychology, but that didn't stop her from teaching people how to heal.

Two identical multi-paned windows provided a sweeping panoramic view of the landscape. Genial yellow light fanned the wall above sconces that brought warmth to the cold space which had the A/C cranked down to keep the cadaver cool while being viewed.

"You haven't been in here yet, have you?" Chanelle asked, spotting my curiosity.

I shook my head no.

"Well, let me tell you. I've worked for my share of funeral homes, and this is the only one worth a damn. The others are absolutely wretched, with their dark wood and velour curtains."

The place my father was brought to after he died looked exactly as Chanelle described: drab; a little creepy, even. I'd decided not to see his body because I wanted to remember him as he was – not some shell of his former self, void of the spirit that once animated him. Instead, I waited in the lobby, counting curds on the popcorn ceiling while he was loaded into the incinerator.

The phone beckoned from the office and Chanelle dismissed me. "Go on."

"Forester Funeral Home," I said into the receiver, picking it up just shy of the fifth ring which would deliver the call to voicemail.

"Busy day?" It was Vic.

"You know it!"

"I hope you don't mind me calling there. I never got your number."

After the drive-in, Vic navigated us through the canyon's twisting two-lane highway while I dozed off in the passenger seat of my truck. When we arrived at Uncle Remi's house, he walked me to the front door and placed an innocent kiss on my forehead before venturing back down the mountainside in his souped-up van.

"I thought you moved on," I kidded.

"Actually, I'd like to stop by and see you. Can you can get away for a bit?"

I looked up at the clock. Mr. Gable's family was scheduled to arrive in less than half an hour. "When can you be here?"

"I'm leaving my house now. See you soon."

19

Crows cawed from tree tops, their slick blue-black feathers glinting as they swooped down from branches to peck at bugs only they could see. The sky had cleared leaving behind puffy white clouds, wet grass in shadows the singular indication it had been raining. I stretched my arms above my head and yawned.

Vic's man-van cruised toward me as I continued my calisthenics. I knelt and shifted my weight, trying to loosen the hormonal aches that had begun to bully me.

Through the windshield, I could see his smile. He parked, his distressed leather boot stepping out ahead of him, jeans cuffed once at the ankle.

"Nice moves," Vic said, pulling sunglasses from his face. I greeted him with a kiss on the cheek.

He had a brown bag in one hand, a bouquet of flowers in the other. "What's all that?"

"Lunch. Grab one of my blankets out of your truck."

"Oh, how romantic. A picnic in the park."

"I figured we could walk the property since you haven't had much of a chance to look around."

Mr. Gable's family started to arrive as we headed toward a path broad enough for a tractor to pass through. Foliage was dense on both sides of the trail and spackled sun dotted the ground in patches, most rays blocked out by the canopy overhead.

"Chanelle's got a viewing in a few minutes," I told Vic. "I'm glad I'll be missing it."

He snickered. "She's something else."

"You seem to know everyone around here."

"Pretty much."

"Who'd you meet first?"

"Remi."

"Where?"

"Downtown. When I was at my lowest."

"Is that a store or something?" I asked him.

"What?"

"Milowest."

Vic laughed. "No. My lowest. As in, my depths of despair."

"What do you mean by that?"

"My mom died when I was young," he offered casually. "I had a hard time dealing with it."

"I can imagine," I said. "It hurts to lose someone you love."

"She figured she would go out with a bang. And shot herself. In our basement. On Valentine's Day."

The details hit me straight in the chest and I was shocked silent. Vic's mother had committed suicide on the quintessential day of love, when children were giddy with laughter and getting high on sugar as they collected cardboard greetings from classmates.

"Nothing was the same after that," he added.

"I'm so sorry, Vic," was all I could muster.

"I am, too. I wish she would have seen that there were other options. There always are. It took me a long time to get that. To understand that her decision had nothing to do with me."

The wind kicked up and I took his hand in mine. "Of course it's not your fault."

"I know that, now. But it wasn't easy to accept. Remi and Jeannine have been my rock. They were parents to me. Treated me like a son."

"That explains a lot," I said. Their love for Vic was always apparent.

"The loft was my bedroom at one time. Well, for three years worth of time."

"Why? Did something happen to your dad?"

"It was my birthday – the day I left. My pops said he was heading to the store for a gift and came home two hours later, hammered. He smashed every picture of her. Told me he couldn't stand looking at me and seeing her eyes. Her nose."

"Jesus," I whispered.

"The verbal abuse I could handle. But the beatings were getting old. Used his belt like a whip when he got drunk."

He paused. I chose not to fill the silence. There was nothing I could say. I linked my arm through his and held onto his inner bicep.

"With nothing but the clothes I had on, I walked out the front door and never went back." Vic cleared his throat, his tone falling a notch as he retraced his traumas. "I had nowhere to go. No one to turn to. So I spent the night with homeless people, some addicts, some just down on their luck."

I tried to imagine how Vic must have felt. Desperate. Alone.

"That week on the streets was –" Searching for words, his voice trailed off. "And then Remi stopped to chat with me. Asked if I needed a job."

The footpath widened to a clearing, tire tracks impressed upon mud where the tread had sunk in. It converged on the far side, narrower, and no longer apt for a vehicle.

"Once I opened up about my past, Remi insisted I stay with him and converted the loft into a room. Jeannine even home schooled me. She was strict, but I owe it to her that I got my G.E.D. Have you met Randall yet?"

I nodded.

"When I turned sixteen, Remi let me help him with transport. I did that for a few years and then moved out on my own when I could afford it. Close your eyes."

"What?"

"Close your eyes," he repeated.

"I heard you," I told him, unable to suppress a laugh though the mood was heavy.

"I'll guide you," he said. "Trust me."

"You're not going to chop me up into little pieces, are you?"

A high-pitched sinister laugh was his response. Without my sight, the rest of my senses heightened. The sounds of nature filled my ears as we trudged deeper into the woods.

"We're almost there," he promised. "Annnnddd, stop. Stand there a second." He shuffled around for a moment and then he was at my side again.

"I'm going to sit you down."

It was awkward, but we managed.

"The blind have it tough," I said, louder than intended.

"You can open your eyes, now."

I blinked a few times, letting my irises respond to the daylight. Out in front, grave markers rose from the ground, a few sporadic wooden crosses posted between burial sites.

"Where are we?" I pondered aloud.

Vic was busy unwrapping our sandwiches when he answered. "A cemetery."

"No shit!" I giggled, catching his gaze shift from our lunch to a particular headstone in the distance. He broke his stare and handed me a couple inches of the Cuban.

"Here's a bunch of different mustards. It all looked good." Packets were strewn on the sheet below, next to them, one glass bottle of specialty root beer and a handful of paper napkins.

"I wasn't sure how you were going to take this," he said, watching me nibble.

"How dare you deny me Mr. Gable's crying family members."

Vic laughed. "I know it's not the most romantic spot for a lunch date."

"I've always enjoyed a good graveyard," I told him.

"Graveyard," he repeated. "That sounds so morbid." His eyes shot back out, lingering again upon the same location.

"What's on your mind?"

"You mean *who*."

"Ok, who?"

"I knew I recognized Remi when I saw him in town, but I couldn't place him." Vic brushed crumbs from the creases of his pants and stood. I took his hand and followed him to my feet.

"After the police did their investigation and checked out my dad's alibi, they called in a funeral home to pick up my mom's body. And that's where she stayed."

"What do you mean?"

"My dad never went and got her."

Vic led me over to a grave and propped the bouquet of flowers I thought were for me up against it.

"I helped Randall dig a lot of these holes. One day, I saw my mom's name." He ran his fingers over the letters. *Vivian Aster Kipling.* "Remi tried for weeks to return her. My father wouldn't take his calls."

"Why not?"

"Shame, I guess." Vic cleared his throat. "I was so thankful Remi buried her here, in Liberation Garden. He's done a lot for those that will never thank him."

"Audentis Fortuna Iuvat," I said, reading her epitaph.

"Not bad," he chuckled.

"Latin definitely isn't my first language."

"So you're familiar with it?"

"No."

"How'd you know it was Latin?"

I shrugged. "Lucky guess."

"It's from Virgil's *The Aeneid*. Translations vary but it roughly means '*Fortune Favors the Brave*'."

"I like it," I said, looking him in the face.

94

Vic hid his pain well, behind soft eyes that concealed hard truths. I pressed my lips against his and thrust my tongue into his mouth. He cradled my head as my fingers traced the contours of his torso.

After minutes of impassioned kissing, I stepped back to look him over before dropping to my knees. One tooth at a time, I lowered his zipper. His dick was pressed hard against his jeans. Slowly, I took him into my mouth.

Vic moaned, his powerful legs losing their strength below him. He had his head tilted back, his lower jaw slacked open. Less than a minute went by and he was done.

When I stood back up, Vic embraced me. "You're incredible." He combed at my pants, eager to return the favor.

"Not today," I told him, moving his hands to my hips.

"I want to taste you," he begged.

"I have to get back to work."

"I'll only need a few minutes."

"Not today," I repeated.

"Fine," he said. "When can I make it up to you?"

· · · ◆ · · ·

Our walk back to the mortuary was without conversation until Vic decided to ask me where my life was heading.

"Currently? I'm stumped. What about you?"

"The only thing I ever wanted to do was make a movie. So when I had enough money saved, I said *fuck it*, and moved to Hollywood."

"What brought you back to Colorado?"

"Trouble," he said without elaboration. "But I'm thankful for it. You can make a movie anywhere these days."

Vic kissed the back of my hand. "What are Tally's dreams and desires?"

"Oh, those are long gone."

"Well, what *were* they? Fame? Fortune? A trip to the moon?"

"I wanted to be a journalist."

"That doesn't seem impossible. I mean, isn't it just a matter of knocking on the right door?"

"Sure. There are jobs all over the place. But I wasn't interested in covering sports or fashion. I wanted to expose people. Stir the pot."

"You seem like the type."

I punched him in the shoulder and he threw his arms up in surrender.

"Publications don't risk their image for justice," I told him. "And if you aren't part of the solution, then you are part of the problem. I couldn't convince myself to follow their script."

"Maybe you'd like to follow mine," he teased.

"An *actress*? Not a chance, Mr. Hollywood."

He laughed. "It's a documentary. So no, no acting."

Forester came into view as the trees relinquished our cover. The only remaining vehicles belonged to us.

"Can you fill me in later? I have gobs of paperwork."

"Sure. Do you know when Sam'll be back?" Of course Vic knew her, too.

"Wilf said August when they came by with the baby last week."

"They're a nice couple."

"Different," I said.

"But nice."

We worked our way over to Vic's van, taking our time.

"Let me give you the rest of your bedding before we forget again." I opened the door of my truck and handed items to him one by one. "Sleeping on a bare mattress must be getting old."

Vic laughed and stared at me until his smile faded. "Are you going to stay awhile?"

"I'm here for the whole summer," I told him, smooching his cheek. "Don't forget your zipper."

20

My ringing phone woke me before the alarm could. "Good morning sleeping beauty," Vic said when I answered.

"What time is it?" I asked, the words hoarse.

"Almost seven."

"What are you doing up?"

"I get four hours in a night."

"That's it? I need the full eight."

"I figure if we sleep a third of our lives away and I cut that in half, then I can reclaim about fourteen thousand hours in ten years."

"Whatever you say, Vic. Math was my worst subject."

He laughed. "I wasn't calling to quiz you."

"So, what are you calling for?"

"I have a few more scenes to shoot but I wanted to make sure it would be okay with you if I stopped by today."

"What's it to me?"

"I just – after yesterday. I wanted to make sure we are on the same page."

"As far as?" Of course he was talking about the B.J. Vic cleared his throat and drank from a bottle, the swish of liquid gulping as he swallowed. "I don't want things to be weird, is all."

"Lighten up. I enjoy your company."

"Not as much as I enjoy yours."

I smiled. "Come by whenever. I'll let Uncle Remi know you'll be around."

"Thanks, but he already knows."

"Well then, I'll see you later."

"That you will," he promised.

. . ♦ ♦ ♦ . .

Thick catalogs were mostly to blame for the huge stacks of mail that had been piling up. Their colorful glossy pages paraded coffins and flashy hardware, designer fabric liners, and memory books. Companies offering the upgrade packages were determined to squeeze as much money as they could by guilting families into personalizing their loved one's death. *Why settle for simplicity when you can have decadence?* the limitless options insisted.

There were also a few cards from families thanking Uncle Remi for his services, and various utility receipts marked *Not A Bill* because they were enrolled in auto-pay.

The leaky sensation between my legs captured my attention. Anticipating a disaster, I eased out of my chair and waddled over to the bathroom. Thankfully, it was a false alarm, but I wound toilet paper around the crotch of my panties as an additional precaution.

Vic was waiting for me in the office when I returned, his body dwarfing the chair he pulled in from the lobby, his

99

hands in his lap, his legs spread wide. He dragged his stare from my breasts down to my feet.

I'd worn a semi-professional outfit, opting for a three-quarters length Henley shirt and a high-waisted skirt, pleated, and reaching just above the knee. Not meant to be distracting or sexy, Vic regarded me otherwise. I wondered how long he had been listening to me fumble around in the restroom, yanking length after length from the toilet paper roll.

"Ready for the big screen?"

"Not really. You haven't given me much to go on."

He gave me a sheet of neatly penned topics. The list was short, with few suggestions, and no specific lines for me to say.

"How do you feel, now?" he asked, like he'd squashed my worries.

"Same as before."

Vic laughed and stood. "Don't sweat it. Darla's done this before so she can carry the weight of the interview."

"I thought you were interviewing me."

"No, you are the interview-er. Darla's going to give us a behind the scenes look at what a mortician does."

"Whoa," I said. "I don't know if I'm ready for that."

"You haven't watched the undertaking yet?"

"Why the hell would I?"

"It's so fascinating, Tally." Though the content was dark, I liked the sound of my name leaving his mouth. "She transforms monsters into works of art," he continued, my thoughts distracted and exploring the ridges of his lower lip.

"So this documentary," I started to say, bringing myself back to reality.

"The funerary business is only a portion of it, but the process is important."

"It's about death, then?"

"No," he told me. "It's about transcending death."

"I see." I looked at him blankly, still captivated by his pout.

Vic ran his fingers down the front of my throat, melting me from the inside. He stopped where my lower buttons were fastened and took me into his gaze. "Don't worry about the details."

He retracted his hand, leaving me in silent supplication. "We'll let Darla do her thing and you're going to interject now and then. To keep the dialogue on track."

He picked up his camera bag and slipped on a pair of black framed glasses. "She'll run the show if we let her."

I looked down at my notes to focus, formulating possible questions in my head. Nothing could have prepared me for the next hour of my life.

21

Maroon painted toenails greeted us, the soles free of calluses that would indicate old age. Her lifeless vessel was a slight lump beneath the bleached white dignity sheet, my discomfort growing as I realized she could be quite young, possibly even a child.

"Thanks again, Darla. I know your time is precious." Vic didn't offer his hand, for hers were double gloved and ready for action.

"No. Thank you! I enjoy this kind of stuff, showing people my lovely Frankensteins." I caught Vic's smug glance.

Darla was enthusiastic for her limelight debut. A hint of hairspray crisped her normally unstyled hair, and a touch of rouge kissed her complexion. "Is there anything you want to know in particular as we go along here?" she asked.

"Let me just set up this tripod," Vic said. "And if you don't mind, we'll use your surgical lights. They're brighter than mine." He mounted his DSLR camera and adjusted the elevator column, positioning the lens to capture the entire procedure.

With the tripod secured, Vic dialed in some settings on the LCD screen. "Alright, Tally. I'm going to have you stand with Darla on the far side that way I can get both of you in the shot." He draped a second camera around his neck.

"When I move in to get a close up, let's pause on the conversation. Then I can edit the footage without missing any of the details."

My first embalming session coupled with being in front of the camera made for a cocktail of anxiety. I looked over my cues as the clams of nervousness set in, my muscles aquiver, my heartbeat in my throat.

"You're going to need these if you're standing that close." Darla handed me the same protective garments she was gussied up in. My stomach ached as I contemplated slinking away before the rush of faint overtook me.

"Why don't you sit down for a minute," Darla instructed, recognizing the green symptoms of an amateur. She pulled a stool under me and I slumped down onto it, my limbs slack and heavy at my sides.

Darla looked me over. "This might not be for you, kid."

I refused to be defeated. "Give me a minute."

My thoughts wandered off to the Egyptians, and how they cared for the dead, preserving their bodies for a journey into the afterlife. It was a serious occupation held only by the most qualified individuals deemed capable of assisting the deceased into the next chapter of their existence – the ascension of their souls.

"Well?" Darla asked.

"I'm ready," I said.

Vic studied me from across the gurney. "You don't have to, Tally."

"I want to," I told him, tucking my hair beneath the blue surgical cap and looping the mask around my ears.

"Alrighty then. It's showtime." He turned on his camera, its red recording light reflecting in the glass of his spectacles.

"Let's start with who you are and why you do this, Darla. And then, as you uncover our lead actress, tell us what you know about her."

Darla recounted how she got into the business, her background in military medicine, and the events leading up to her wife's passing. She had never pictured herself working in a mortuary, "But that's just where life took me," she explained.

As her personal profile came to a close, I knew that our guest would soon be revealed; I prayed like hell for it to be an adult. Without warning, Darla slid the sheet down to the cadaver's navel.

"This is Sheila. Even if we knew her real name, we wouldn't use it. Out of respect." Old school tattoos decorated her arms, the work of a novice artist who didn't quite have a handle on his trade. Her platinum hair was wet, two inches of dark roots grown out to disclose her natural color. She couldn't have been much older than me.

"People like Sheila come through our doors all the time. No family. No friends. No one knows she's even missing," Darla continued. I thought of the potter's field at the edge of Uncle Remi's property.

"Our young lady was found by a wealthy businessman out on his morning jog. Obvious track marks on her arms and deterioration of the brain found during autopsy suggested drug use as the cause of death, and that was confirmed with toxicology reports. There's still one mystery no one can answer. Was it an accident? Or suicide?"

I asked my first question. "Darla, thank you for all of the information thus far. What a fascinating case to be part of. I'm curious about something, and our audience may be wondering the same thing. Why is her hair wet?"

"Oh," she replied, realizing she'd left that detail out. "I've just washed her prior to filming. A dead body is far from inactive. Purge fluids expel themselves from openings called orifices. That includes tears and saliva, urine, and even feces."

Darla held up a bottle of soap. "As I disinfect the body topically, I also massage the muscles which have seized up during the onset of rigor mortis. Bodies are refrigerated to delay decomposition, and that makes 'em even stiffer."

She set the bottle back down on the counter and returned to her narrative. "The man that found Sheila felt compelled to finance her burial. She had been lying on her side with a cross necklace clutched in her hand. He believed it to be an omen from God."

Darla adjusted Sheila's head and combed the left eyebrow with her thumb. "Strange things happen to people when they witness death. One time we received thousands of packages of Skittles in the mail sent from all across the country. A young boy had disappeared after school, his candy bag torn open at the bus stop the only clue to his abduction. When his body was found in the ditch near Lory State Park, his anus savagely perforated and his face mutilated, there was a nationwide outcry to register sex offenders."

She paused, pensive. "I hope that's not too graphic for your audience."

Vic shook his head left and right without speaking. Darla continued.

"I'm going to move on to setting the features, which means closing the eyes and jaw for good. What I aim for is the illusion of sleep."

Because everyone onsite was involved in Vic's film session, I had rerouted the business line to my cell phone which started vibrating inside the foam padding of my bra. Approaching the pinnacle of Darla's work, I contemplated letting it go to voicemail. If it was Uncle Remi, I decided, he'd wonder why no one was answering.

I excused myself and ducked into the refrigeration unit which was much closer than the office on the far side of the room. Darla continued her spiel as she retrieved her needle. I was glad to be missing the worst of it.

"Forester Funeral Home, this is Tally."

"Your aunt said I could find you there."

I hadn't heard her voice in almost a year.

"Hello?" she said, when I didn't respond right away.

"Yeah, I'm here," I told my mother, wondering if Aunt Jeannine had contacted her or vice versa.

"You never mentioned you were planning a trip to Colorado."

How could she be so nonchalant? "I haven't heard from you since the funeral. When would I have told you?"

"Well, you have my number."

"The trip wasn't planned. It just sorta happened."

"It doesn't seem like the type of thing that just *happens*."

I rolled my eyes. What the hell did she want?

"But that's beside the point."

"So, if you're not calling to harass me, what *is* the point?"

"Natalia, I'm not harassing you."

An incoming call let me know someone was waiting on the other line. "I'm busy, Florence. Say what you need to say."

"Do you treat everyone like this?"

She knew how to twist me. "Treat you? What about the way you treat me?"

"Natalia. Let's not be like this to one another."

"I have to go." With that, I switched the line over.

"Hello?" I said, forgetting my role as Forester's office assistant.

"Oh, I'm sorry," the caller replied. "I must have the wrong number."

"Forester Funeral Home," I revised, trying to catch her before she hung up. "This is Tally. How may I help you?"

"You sound preoccupied," she said, her English licked by a foreign accent. "Perhaps my business would be better valued elsewhere."

"My apologies," I told her, my mother's voice still digging itself beneath my skin. "It's just that I'm in the middle of something at the moment."

"I see."

"Why don't you give me your number, and I can call you right back." I fumbled for the pen I had tied my hair up with and took off my glove to write on.

"I'll try you again in ten minutes." Before I could thank her, she hung up.

At the back of the refrigeration unit I spotted another door. I slipped my glove on and headed toward it. Unlocked, it opened up into the viewing room. Uncle Remi must have specifically designed it that way to make his job easier. The body could be wheeled out for display, and then wheeled back in until burial.

I'd not paid much attention to my surroundings until then. Fan blades whirred as the chill meant to preserve the dead crept into my bones. I closed the door and headed back the way I'd originally entered. Once in the parlor, I inched my way around the perimeter to stay out of the camera's viewfinder.

"Gotta take this call," I whispered into Vic's ear after approaching him from behind.

He motioned for me to go ahead, his attention focused on Darla who was draining Sheila's blood into a basin near her feet.

"The body takes about three gallons of solution to give it the plump look of a living person," I heard Darla explain as her voice grew more and more distant. "We're in the process of transitioning to a proprietary formaldehyde-free solution. It works just as well, but it's gentler on the environment."

As quietly as possible, I nudged the steel door open and gently closed it behind me. I sank into the office chair, placed my cell on the desk, and switched calls back to the office phone.

I waited. And waited. Rage was rising up inside me.

"Fuck!" I shouted, upset I had represented my uncle's business with an attitude. It was my mother's fault. She had caught me off guard.

Realizing that she wouldn't have known I was in Colorado if my aunt hadn't called her first, I suddenly felt betrayed.

I stewed for ten minutes before giving up on the potential client's callback. If I was her, I wouldn't call again. Not when there were plenty of other funeral homes in town to choose from. Just as I stood to reenter the film set, the phone rang.

"Forester Funeral Home, this is Tally."

"Hello, Tally. We've just spoken."

"Yes, ma'am. I want to apologize for earlier. I didn't mean to be rude."

"No, no. I understand you are very busy."

"Well, that's no reason to treat you without respect."

"It's okay. No problema."

"Let's see what we can do for you. May I have your name?"

"Call me Camila."

"Okay, Camila. How can we help?"

"My husband has passed and I must make arrangements."

"I'm very sorry to hear that."

"He meant everything to me and I want him to be regarded in the best way possible."

"We go through great lengths to provide our clients with the utmost care and respect," I said, recognizing an opportunity to secure her business. "Instead of taking my word for it, why don't you stop by in person? It would be my pleasure to show you around and address any concerns you may have."

She didn't hesitate. "Tomorrow morning, eight sharp."

I would just be arriving for my shift at that hour but I refrained from haggling with her about the time. "Eight is perfect. See you then."

With filming complete, Vic rolled his equipment back into the office.

"Sorry to dip out on you," I told him.

"No worries. I'm sure it was important."

"Just another dead person."

"It never stops," he said.

"Would you want to live forever?" I asked him.

He made a disgusted face and shook his head no. Then, a thought came to his mind, forcing his mouth into a smile. "Not unless I can spend forever with you."

I shoved him and laughed. "Get outta here!"

22

As promised, Camila arrived at eight the next morning, a tight black dress tracing her Latina curves, the length flirting with the middle of her thighs. She removed her shades and strutted through the lobby into the office.

"Camila," she stated, her Hispanic tongue clicking against the front of her obscenely white porcelain veneers. The huge brim of her floppy hat placed much of her face in shadow except for fire-engine red lips that pouted plumply.

I pulled myself from the chair and reciprocated. "Tally."

Standing had barely decreased our height difference. She towered above me in six inch stilettos.

"I haven't much time, so if we could walk and talk that would be appreciated."

A figure entered behind her, his eyes shielded by sunglasses. The blackness of his suit washed out his already ghostly complexion, forcing his carrot orange hair to become the focal point. No man would dye their hair that color; it had to be natural.

Camila looked over her shoulder and then motioned for me to show her around.

"Come with me," I said, working my way around the desk to the door of the embalming area. The watcher remained in the lobby, his presence eerie while he lingered in silent observation. Cold air rushed out as we entered.

"This is the procedural area. It's where we prepare the bodies. Our staff undertaker, Darla, has worked at Forester since it opened," I recited. Flooding light overhead only hinted at Camila's true age, cosmetic surgery, designed to gracefully deliver her into her forties, the secret behind her exquisite skin ironed free of all wrinkles.

"I'm getting ahead of myself," I told her. "Were you interested in cremation? Because we can certainly –"

"No, no," she cut in. "He must be buried in accordance with scripture."

Reasons unknown, she was growing antsier by the second. Sparing further details, I led her into the refrigeration unit which had four new bodies, three in zipped bags and one covered by a sheet that was next in line. Darla had taken Josie to an appointment across town and wouldn't be in until after lunch. The deceased patiently awaited her return.

"I don't care about the cost of your services. I've researched you and know my husband will be in good hands," Camila said. "Because I am still in the process of executing his financial wishes, I will pay for this procedure in cash."

"Cash?

"This will be a problem?"

"Well, no. I mean, I'll have to talk to my uncle about it first."

"I understand. Be sure to let him know I will make his acceptance in this matter worth any extra effort on his part." She paused, apathetic to the corpses surrounding us. "Should I speak with him directly?"

"That won't be necessary," I told her, moving us along.

At the back of the refrigeration unit, I opened the door to let us out into the viewing room. I stepped down and turned just in time to see Camila lose her balance.

"Dios mio!" she cried out. Her feet buckled beneath her as she groped for something sturdy, her ankle twisting out at an awkward angle.

I grabbed hold of her arms to stabilize her. "Are you alright?"

Camila's escort appeared in the doorway, his hand reaching for something in his waistband.

"We're fine," she said, raising her hand to placate his worry. "I've slipped is all."

"I'm so sorry," I told her.

We followed mystery man out into the office, my adrenaline keyed up as the butt of a gun protruded from under his suit jacket. He still hadn't said a word as he exited the building.

Camila's heels chattered along the hardwood floor as she chased after him. "Thank you for your time. I'm sure we will have no issue."

Before I could respond, she was gone.

I watched from the window as she took the passenger seat of a black Cadillac. The heavily tinted glass and several hood-mounted antennas screamed government issued.

Maybe Camila was a politician. Or her husband was a famous movie star. Carrot top looked like he could be

113

someone's bodyguard. The possibility of a high profile death was intriguing. I let my mind wander as I considered their relations.

23

"Namaste, sorry you missed me," Sadie's recorded voice notified. I hung up without leaving a message and dialed Vic.

"Well, hello," he answered.

"Whatcha up to?"

"Cutting some footage from yesterday. In fact, I was just admiring your cinematic beauty."

"Please," I snorted. "I can only imagine how many of my flaws are exposed beneath those unforgiving lights." I had seen myself on film once before, the way the camera adds ten pounds.

"What are you up to?" he asked.

"In bed with Eileen."

"Oh, you've got a pussy palace going on over there."

I imagined Vic laid out on that very mattress, looking up at the same cracks in the ceiling years before. I could hear keys rapping as he worked editing commands.

"I'll let you go. Just wanted to apologize again for not being able to finish up with you guys."

"Don't be sorry. Darla wasn't."

"I'm sure she stepped right up to the plate."

"When can I see you again?" he wanted to know.

"Didn't you say you were looking at me right now?"

"Not the parts I'm interested in."

Sex was inevitable, but I hadn't given it up right away. I wanted to cultivate our friendship, too. Besides, my period was in full swing and I doubted he would be okay with frolicking around in endometrial sloughings.

"I'll call you soon," I said. "Goodnight."

His lips smacked together as he sent a kiss over the air. "Sweet dreams."

I smiled and yawned. It was time for bed.

I scooted Eileen off my chest and stood to remove my clothes. I lifted my shirt over my head and undid my bra, my nipples hardening against the coolness of freedom. Then, I took off my pants.

With the lamp still on, I was pulled into a hellish nightmare. My body was on a steel gurney in the funeral parlor. Darla was there, her eyes crazed, a sharp scalpel gleaming in her hand. Uncle Remi flew about the room, his top hat and clothing that of another century. Aunt Jeannine was crying in the corner, her joints swollen and contorted. Suddenly, I was in a cemetery, Camila punctuating the last rites in Spanish. Vic, shovel in hand, tossed me into a grave and lingered near the edge.

24

Cramps poked at my uterus like Eskimo's with ice picks, womanhood's monthly vampiristic ritual draining me of energy, drop by bloody drop. I popped a handful of ibuprofen from a bottle on the bedside table and forced them down without water.

Sunlight had yet to descend on earth, so I fumbled my way to the kitchen in darkness. When I made it to the oven, I flicked on the lamp above it. There, Uncle Remi had left another note; he'd be away from the office again.

Instead of brewing coffee, I decided to pack up a bit of grounds and head to work an hour early. Before locking myself out, I spotted the skinny strip of light lining the bottom of Aunt Jeannine's door. I smiled at the thought of her solitude as I ducked into my truck and rolled the engine over. It sputtered and coughed, refusing to start.

I pointed at the dashboard and yelled. "Fuck you!"

After lifting the hood, I inserted the safety rod to keep it ajar. Without adequate light, and with only rudimentary mechanic skills, I moved my hand around inside to feel if anything seemed out of place. The battery was completely disconnected.

My eyes shot to the tree line. The darkness of the canopy easily concealed the culprit of such shenanigans, most likely high-schoolers just out of sight, basking in satisfaction as they puffed on stolen cigarettes and smooched their sweeties against the abstinent wishes of their parents. My theory suffered from a lack of neighbors.

Frustrated, I cranked the key and my Chevy roared to life. When I got to the mortuary, the office phone was already ringing.

"Forester Funeral Home," I huffed, my breath labored from sprinting to answer.

"Hey, it's just me."

"Oh. Hey."

"Everything okay?"

"Yeah. I'm not feeling great and my truck wouldn't start this morning."

"Need a hand?" Vic offered.

"No, I'm fine."

"I tried reaching you on your cell."

I patted my empty pocket. "I guess I forgot it."

"Are you sure you don't need anything?"

"I'm just grumpy," I told him.

"Want some company?"

"Nah. My mood will bring you down."

"My mood will bring you up. I'm on my way."

· · · ◆ · · ·

Headlights swept across the office like an outer space beam as a vehicle approached, cold air hanging low in a vast fog that had yet to dissipate. I greeted Vic in the lobby.

"Are you okay?" he asked straight off.

I was helpless as tears poured out for no good reason.

"Hey. Come here." He pulled me into his arms and held me until I pushed away.

"Remember when I took that call during filming?"

"Yeah?"

"It was my mother."

"Okay."

"We haven't spoken since my dad died."

"How long ago was that?"

It seemed strange that I could simultaneously feel his death to be recent yet her absence to be prolonged.

"It'll be a year in August," I mumbled through congested air passages. "I'm sorry to be so emotional."

"Tally, you just lost your dad less than a year ago. You're supposed to be emotional."

"Yeah, but I'm not emotional about him."

"What did your mom say?" he asked.

"She didn't say anything."

"So she called for the two of you to share a moment of silence?"

I cracked a smile.

"Ahh, there's the Tally I know." He reached up to wipe away my tears.

"There was another call coming in so I hung up on her."

"And you didn't call back?"

"No."

"Are you going to?"

"I don't know. Probably not."

"What if she wanted to apologize?"

I laughed. "She could have done that ten years ago, when she ripped our family apart."

"Well, I'm glad you're laughing now." He looked over my shoulder. "Is your around uncle?"

"No. He's in Denver. At the Funeral Director's convention."

"I don't know where that man finds the time."

"Time is not a concept he understands."

The sound of a car alarm being armed stole our attention. We hadn't even heard the vehicle's approach.

As Vic made his way to the door to open it, Camila let herself in.

"Oh, hello," I said, curious why she had shown up unannounced.

Even though it was early morning, she was already wearing her designer sunglasses. She tilted them down to assess Vic.

"Good morning, ma'am," he said to her as she looked him up and down.

Camila slid her sunglasses back on and turned to me with a smile I wasn't sure I cared for. "Handsome *and* polite."

"Glad to see you again," I told her, though I didn't appreciate her checking Vic out the way she had blatantly done. "You left in a bit of a hurry yesterday. Was there anything else you'd like to go over?"

"Do you work here, young man?" she asked Vic, not bothering to turn around and look at him.

"I did at one time," he replied.

"So then, do you mind excusing us for a moment?"

"Yes ma'am. Of course." Vic exited and closed the door behind him.

"Did he break your heart?" Camila asked me.

"No. Why?"

"You've been crying. Your face is a mess."

I swatted at my eyes.

"That's not going to do it," she said.

"I had a rough morning."

She laughed as to say mine was trivial compared to hers.

"What can I do for you?" I asked her, growing upset.

"Do for me? Nothing. I'm here to dispel any myths you may have heard."

I shrugged and shook my head no.

"This town has a vendetta against me. I may not be an angel but I'm certainly no monster."

"Your personal life is none of my business."

"It's not, but you will be brought into it."

"I'm sorry. I'm not really following you."

"Things will work themselves out. I just wanted to bring it to light before they set their plan in motion." Camila lowered her sunglasses so I could look into her eyes. "Always challenge the truth."

With that, she slid them back up the bridge of her nose and left.

"What was that all about?" Vic asked, entering moments later.

"I have no idea."

"Do you know her?"

"No. I mean, yeah. Well, sort of."

"Is this a riddle?"

121

"She called the day you were filming," I told him. "And it was right after my mother called so I was pretty rude when I answered."

"Gotcha. What did she want?"

"Her husband died."

"Just now, I'm saying. Were you expecting her?"

"No. She just showed up."

"And she had nothing to say while I was waiting outside?"

"She commented on my emotional state which is apparently written across my face."

"That's pretty bold."

"Tell me about it."

"What else?"

"Nothing really. She said that I might hear some things about her and not to believe them. Or, what did she say? *'Challenge the truth'*."

"She drove all the way out here to tell you that?"

I shrugged.

"Who is she?"

"I have no idea."

"She looked familiar," Vic said. "I think I've seen her before."

"I doubt you would mistake her for anyone else."

"Wait a minute, wait a minute." Vic sat at the computer and turned it on. "Is her name something like Cameron? Or Carmen?"

"Camila."

"Camila! That's it." He typed out a string of letters on the keyboard. "Bingo!"

"Tell me what it says."

"Camila Dabbencove, former wife of Flynn Dabbencove, taken in for questioning following his death."

"Sounds like a Law & Order episode. All drama."

"You don't think it's more than that? You met her. What's she like?"

"She didn't say much, really. I gave her a tour. And then she left."

"A tour? Cheese and rice."

"What was I supposed to do? I was trying to get her business."

"I'm not sure she has the kind of business you want."

"Why?" I asked him. "Do you think she killed her husband?"

"The police think so."

"That's not what it says."

"I'm reading between the lines."

I shook my head and sighed. "And that's the problem with reporters these days. They plant ideas in the public's mind without offering any facts."

"According to this article, Dabbencove's body was brought to the District Eight morgue," Vic continued. "I wonder if Nina has heard anything about it."

"Oh, good question. You should ask her." The thought of having an in started to excite me. "Maybe she could access the records for us."

Vic took his eyes off the screen and bought them to me.

"Just for kicks," I said.

"I understand this is exciting and all, especially for an aspiring journalist. But let's not forget. Camila might be a suspected murderer."

"She's innocent until proven guilty."

"Isn't that for the court to decide?"

"Duh. It would be fun see what we can find out for ourselves though."

"I don't know, Tally. It sounds... dangerous. Never mind illegal."

"Oh, come on. It's probably just sensationalism. I already told you. The media doesn't care about the truth. They write what sells."

Darla had let herself in which brought our discussion to an abrupt end.

"Good morning," she said, her stare falling on Vic first, then me, then back to Vic.

Vic quickly redirected to insinuate we'd been discussing the film. "Thanks again for the footage, Darla. You were great!"

"Oh, it was my pleasure." She carried herself over to the coffee maker.

With her back to us, Vic mouthed *I'll call you* and then announced his departure. "Ladies, have a wonderful day."

"I can't wait to see his film," Darla commented while I admired Vic's exit. I couldn't help imagining my thighs on either side of his face.

25

Uncle Remi decided to stay the night in Denver. Instead of making a big production out of dinner, Aunt Jeannine and I ate leftover soup and a salad we whipped up from the garden. We were watching the season two finale of *House of Cards* when my phone rang. Entranced by the TV, my aunt didn't even notice me slip away.

"I talked to Nina," Vic said when I answered.

"Woohoo! What did she say?"

"They have Dabbencove's body."

"And?"

"And she knows who Camila is because she visits the morgue quite often."

"Visits? That's a strange way to say it."

"I know, right?"

"How often does Nina see her?"

"She made it seem like it was a daily occurrence."

I felt myself slip into the shoes of Zoe Barnes, the Netflix series' fictional journalist who finds herself mixed up with dueling political interests that ultimately lead to her own undoing.

Vic went on. "According to Nina, Camila shows up unannounced, demanding to speak with Dr. Jahnke. He's the medical examiner."

"I wonder what they're talking about."

"No idea. But apparently after their meetings, Dr. Jahnke's mood turns to shit. At least that's how Nina put it."

"Did you ask her for the records?" I said, hustling up the stairs to the loft.

"Not for them, but about them. She said for whatever reason, the file isn't where it's supposed to be."

"I bet he's hiding it in his office."

"Jumping to conclusions already, huh?"

I laughed.

"He was probably looking it over with Camila and forgot to put it back."

"You're right," I told him. "I don't know why I suddenly want her to be guilty."

"Well, if she did it, then she should be held accountable."

"Yeah, but this is a woman's life we're talking about," I argued. "Forester's job is to take care of her husband, regardless of the circumstances. I mean, imagine being innocent but treated like a criminal."

"True."

"Speculation or not, what do you think? Got any hunches?"

"I'm not sure, either way. Nina said she's interested in Dabbencove's records, too. Let's see what she finds and then I say we drop it."

"Agreed. Call me tomorrow with any updates."

"Talk to you then. Goodnight."

126

We hung up and another call from an unknown number came in almost immediately.

"Hello?" I said to the unidentified caller.

"Tally, it's Camila."

"Camila?"

"I hope you don't mind me calling you on your personal line. I'm feeling really alone."

I was curious how she'd gotten my number but an inquiry wasn't the right move at that moment. "It's normal to feel this way after a loved one dies," I told her.

"It's not that. Flynn had been sick for awhile. It was only a matter of time."

"Okay," I replied, unsure where the conversation was going.

"You think I did it, don't you?"

"Did what?"

"You think I killed him."

I pretended ignorance. "Killed who?"

"My husband!" she shouted.

"Why would I think that?"

"They've launched an attack. I'm on everyone's television!"

"Camila, calm down."

"Please, Tally. Please don't let them do this to me."

"Everything's going to be fine. You said so yourself. They're just after the truth."

Her tone changed. "They have no interest in the truth." And then she was gone.

I heisted what was left of a joint from the kitchen counter and stepped outside before sparking it up. The night sky was clear – a first since I'd arrived. Admiring the stars from the bed of my truck, I listened to the swish of native grasses.

Slowly, the sweet intoxicant began to work its magic, precipitating a philosophical examination of the heavens. *If everything came from one atomic particle that exploded,* I thought, *then why do planetary bodies have different geological compositions?* There was also the question of being alone in the universe.

••••••

A wailing alarm shook me awake. Having fallen asleep in the truck bed, I jolted up, unsure of where I was. Just beyond the mortuary, a car sped off toward the main road, its red break lamps searing their eyes into the night.

Anxiety shriveled my lungs into raisins. I raced inside, grabbed Uncle Remi's shotgun, and returned to my vehicle. Speeding off down the driveway, my hands were like stones around the steering wheel. I slowed as I approached the funeral home. *Why hadn't I called the police instead?*

Fire power in hand, I exited the truck. The front door was closed but the alarm was blaring. With a huge inhale, I flung open the door, simultaneously lifting my weapon and screaming a savage war cry.

BANG!

The shotgun discharged unexpectedly, slamming me against the doorframe where my legs buckled below me. I stood too quickly, my knees shaking as I tried to regain balance. With the blast echoing in my ears, I searched the room.

Not a single document was askew, but on the wall behind the desk, I found an entirely different problem. To hide the group of small pellet-shaped holes, I pulled the nearest poster down, moved it over a few inches, and taped it back up to cover the damage.

When my hearing returned, and the alarm's call became unbearable, I stormed over to the panel and typed in the password to silence it. There, I found that one of the wires had been snipped.

From the security of my truck, I surveyed the landscape. Only darkness stared back. The getaway car long gone, I returned to the house, bolted the front door, and passed out on the couch. When I finally came to, the whole night's affairs seemed hazy and imagined, except I was still cradling the twelve-gauge shotgun.

26

"Is everything alright?" Uncle Remi shouted upon entering. He'd returned from Denver just as a cop arrived to document the break-in.

"Yes, Uncle Remi," I said, not revealing my qualms. "Everything's fine."

"Well, then." He allowed his shoulders to relax. "Tell me what's going on."

The uniformed officer took over. "Forced entry. Motive not identified. No suspect at the moment."

"Not again," Uncle Remi groaned.

"This isn't the first time?" the policeman asked.

My uncle shook his head. "That's why we had the alarm installed. Kids will be kids."

"I'd have a hard time believing it was a kid this go-around." He walked over to the panel. "The perp knew what he was doing. This wire here," he said, facing the tattered end toward my uncle, "it's the one that's tied in with the police."

"A lucky guess," my uncle concluded.

Officer Gilden narrowed his stare. "If that's what you believe, then so be it. I'm going to start writing up my report. After you look over your belongings, let me know if anything is missing. If you want it documented, that is. Otherwise, I'll be on my way."

"All the bodies are locked up and they are my only concern. Besides, it looks like the office is untouched." Uncle Remi looked at me for my opinion. I agreed. Then, to the police officer, he said, "Thank you for your time. Feel free to head out when your paperwork is finished."

As Officer Gilden plodded off to his patrol car, Uncle Remi pulled me in for a hug. "Seeing those lights flashing when I came around the bend had me concerned."

"I'm sorry. I should have called you."

"No, no. It's fine. I'm glad you're alright."

Physically, I was. But crazy thoughts were stirring around inside my skull. Maybe the cut alarm and my disconnected battery were related.

"Are you alright?" Uncle Remi asked, analyzing me.

"I'm fine. Just need to get out of my head."

"I know the feeling. Why don't you beat feet and grab some food? Give Vic a call. Tell him to take you to Big Al's."

"You just got back."

"And I sure am glad to be. Go on, now. The lunch rush isn't something you want to be a part of."

· · ◆ ◆ ◆ · ·

"You're taking me to lunch," I told Vic when he answered. "That's what Uncle Remi said."

"Oh he did, did he?"

"Yep."

"Well that's perfect, then, because I have something to give you."

"Okay. Meet me at Big Al's."

Vic snickered. "Did Remi tell you about the 60/40?"

"No. But he *did* say we need to get there soon or the place will be mobbed."

"Psh. That place is always mobbed."

"I guess I'll need to wear my riot gear."

"And I'll bring the tear gas."

"Great. Where should I park the tank?"

·· ◆ ◆ ◆ ◆ ··

"It's not too bad in there," Vic said when I found him waiting at a picnic table outside the burger joint.

"Should I hide the batons?" I joked, kissing him on the forehead.

Vic stood. "Let's keep them in hand. People will know we mean business."

"Good idea."

He opened the door and held it for me. "Go ahead and find us a table."

"I can wait in line with you," I told him.

In my ear, he whispered, "Do as you're told or I'll have to spank you later."

I smiled and went off to find a spot for two.

When he arrived with our lunch, I was staring out the window. A dorky looking guy in an official looking uniform was walking the street, logging license plates into his hand held unit.

132

"I can't believe they pay someone to do that job," I said.

"Don't worry about him. We're in two hour parking. Besides, it will only take two point five seconds to devour this."

"And what exactly is *this*?" I asked, turning to face him.

"*This* is Big Al's signature patty," he said. "Sixty percent beef, forty percent bacon."

"Damn. That sounds... "

"Amazing?"

"Intense."

"Intensely amazing," Vic concluded.

I lifted my burger from the tray and undid one corner of the wrapper. "Got any ketchup?"

"Right here," he said, pushing a waxed paper cup full of creamy white dressing my way.

"Ketchup," I repeated.

"It is."

I tore a piece of the burger patty from the edge and a pickle slipped out. Leaving it, I dipped the bite sized meat morsel into the sauce.

"That's ranch," I corrected him.

Vic was more than half finished with his burger. He swallowed a huge, barely chewed mouthful. "Colorado ketchup."

I tucked the pickle back under the bun and picked up a French fry. It was covered in parmesan. "Is this another Colorado thing?" I asked, waving it in front of him.

He shrugged, keeping his pace steady.

I nibbled off the end and set the rest back down on the tray.

"Not a fan?"

"Everything's great," I told him. It really was very tasty, but my nerves had hijacked my appetite.

"You can be honest. It won't hurt my feelings."

"That's not it. There was a break-in at the mortuary last night."

"Teenagers?"

I rolled my eyes. "Why does everyone keep saying that?"

"I don't know. That's what Remi thinks."

"Well, why would teenagers break in, steal nothing, and cut the wires on the alarm? Just for fun?"

Vic had finished his entire meal. He wiped his mouth and fingers with napkins, balled them up, and cast them aside.

"I think there's something going on," I said.

"How so?"

"Remember my disconnected battery?"

He looked me over while formulating his response. "You think it's somehow related to the break-in?"

I shook my head yes. "And Camila."

"No way."

"It could be."

"It could be. But chances are slim. Occam's razor."

"I have this gut feeling that there's more to it than coincidence," I told him, my stomach in knots.

Vic mounded up our trash and hauled it away on the service tray. By design, most everything was recyclable or compostable, their corresponding disposal requirements detailed in brightly colored signage above the garbage station. When he returned, he unzipped his backpack and handed me an envelope.

"What's this?" I asked, standing to face him.

He leaned in and kissed me, his sculpted chest muscles prominent under a hunter green V-neck. "I was debating whether or not I was going to give it to you. But I think you could use the peace of mind."

"Tally!" the counter guy called out.

"There's a Shake of the Day waiting for you up there," he said. "I'll call you later."

······

The moment I reached my truck, I tore open the envelope. In it, I found two photocopied documents. One was the coroner's findings and the other was a police report from the initial site visit. Both pages had the decedent's name: Flynn Dabbencove.

As the attending medical examiner, Dr. Gerald Jahnke had scribbled the word *None* under visual findings. According to his notes, he'd collected several samples from Dabbencove's body: hair, nail scrapings, gastric contents, urine, cross sections of the heart, liver, lung, kidneys, and brain, and vitreous fluid. All were sent to the toxicology lab for analysis.

The police incident report was filed the day Dabbencove died, the coroner's a day later. Based on witness testimony by one Camila Rosario Dabbencove, her husband hadn't felt well and was resting. She'd checked in on him at noon and then again just before two. It was then that she realized he wasn't breathing.

Several things had been recorded by Deputy White on his initial inspection of Flynn's bedroom. Among those findings was a list of medications that were noted to have been "lined up on the nightstand." I read through them.

Lipotor, Coumadin, and Lasix were three of the prescription drugs I recognized, a few others being common over-the-counter titles including Bayer, Prilosec, Imodium, and Gas-X.

My phone rang and I looked down with the intention to silence it. Uncle Remi's name appeared on the screen.

"Hello," I said into the receiver.

"Hello young lady. How was your lunch?"

"It was fantastic. Thanks for the suggestion."

"You betcha! They are one of my favorite places to stop at when I'm in town."

"I haven't left yet. Want me to bring you something back?"

"No, no. I've already eaten. I was calling to let you know that the commotion from last night has been solved."

My stomach sank.

"Darla called me just after you left," he continued.

"What's Darla got to do with it?"

"She is the very person who cut the alarm feed."

I was baffled. "Why?"

"She left late last night, drove all the way home, and realized she'd forgotten her insulin." He cleared his throat. "By the time she made it back here, the alarm had armed itself. It does that automatically at eleven every night in case I forget to set it."

"She doesn't have the code?" I asked him.

"I gave it to her but she's never had to use it so it didn't stick."

"What about the wires?"

"Yeah, about that. Instead of getting the police involved, she cut the wire to kill the alert. And she knew the alarm would eventually stop. It resets itself after five minutes."

Darla's shenanigans disclosed, I still didn't believe that my disconnected battery could be explained away.

"I never said she was the most conventional person," Uncle Remi continued. "She was probably stoney baloney if I know Darla like I do. Cops would have made it all the more messy."

"Thanks for clearing the air," I told him. "I'm heading back now."

I stowed Dabbencove's documents in my purse and took a sip of the milkshake Vic had purchased as a parting gift. Maybe there was no interconnectedness. Maybe I was trying to make something out of nothing. It was too soon to tell.

···◆◆◆···

At quarter of three I sat at the computer desk and turned the monitor on. I retrieved the photo copies from my purse, typed the remaining unfamiliar consonant and vowel jumbles into the web query, and waited for the result. Prinival turned out to be a treatment for high blood pressure, and Zolpidem was a drug used for insomnia, more commonly known as Ambien.

Flynn was certainly ill, his medical profile supporting Camila's claim that he had been battling cardiovascular disease prior to his death. He was a victim of the pill train Aunt Jeannine detested, taking one antidote to abate the adverse side effects of another.

137

There, amongst the plethora of inventoried pharmaceuticals, I found a concrete reason to be worried; something that would validate the unsettled feeling within. Corazole, the internet told me, was a drug used to induce seizures in lab rats. Once the animals began convulsing, the newly developed compounds were administered. This type of experimentation allowed researchers to test the efficacy and dosage of anticonvulsants in preliminary trials before sending them to market.

Illegal in the U.S. and difficult to obtain even as a scientist, there was no reason for Corazole to be on the nightstand. But to the deputy, a non-physician whose duty was to simply record items found at the scene, Corazole was just another mandated prescription, not a murder weapon hidden in plain sight.

Dr. Jahnke, the practicing medical examiner and sole authority on every death that occurred in his county, should have been more astute. He either didn't know what Corazole was, and was negligent in his research. Or, he knew very well what it was, and omitted its potential role in Dabbencove's death.

I typed a question into Google: *Can a seizure stop the heart?* Hundreds of thousands of pages were populated by my inquiry.

Referred to by the medical community as SUDEP, sudden unexpected death in epilepsy was well studied. There in the definition was the bit that would allow someone to get away with murder: "SUDEP points no fingers."

There was only one harbinger – the presence of the Corazole bottle. Mechanism established, the motive persisted to evade.

My phone notified me of a new text. The message was one sentence long: "We are on the same team."

A second text followed. It had the name of a place followed by a time. I only had an hour to get there.

27

A Broncos hat pulled low and my hair tied back, I entered Front Range Gun Club. It felt ridiculous to be concealing pepper spray in my purse, but I brought it into the shooting gallery anyhow.

Unsure why I had been summoned, I meandered through aisles, scanning the shelves and pretending to search for something in particular. Bullets concussed at the back of the showroom, behind a wall of double paned glass.

"Can't wait for the new season!" A bearded man appeared from around the corner, his belly robust, one tooth missing from his buttery smile.

"Huh?" I grunted, figuring his comment had to do with some sort of game animal. He tapped the side of his head several times, reminding me of the football paraphernalia atop my own.

"Oh! Me too," I told him, playing the role of a sports fan.

"Donnie, move it along," the voice behind me instructed. I turned to greet an eccentric face rocking mutton chop sideburns. "He means no harm."

I smiled. "It's fine."

"I'm Brad." He took several steps toward me. The bullseye insignia stitched into the upper left corner of his short sleeved black polo matched his hat.

"Jackie," I said, offering a fake name.

"I know why you're here."

I eyed him suspiciously, remembering the text message. "Why?"

"You're looking for a revolver."

"Am I going to need one?" I asked.

"Hopefully not." He worked his way behind a case filled with every handgun model imaginable. "Ever since the paper ran that article about the city's climbing sexual assault rate, women have been flocking in by the droves."

I recalled the two busty females who looked out of place at the register when I first entered, their nails freshly manicured and hair streaked blonde. The clerk was practically drooling over them.

"I haven't read it," he went on, "but I hear the author is a huge gun advocate. He's telling every woman to go out and buy a six-shooter. Reliable. Easy to operate."

"I didn't read it, either," I told him.

"So then, what brings you in, Jackie?"

I stared at him, gauging his authenticity. When I was resolute in his innocence, I realized he was waiting for my answer.

"I had a break in," I said. "Thought I might need some insurance."

Brad's sexy smile dimpled his cheeks, his lips parting slightly to glimpse perfectly straight teeth. "Let me show you a few options. It's best to hold it in your hand."

Under ordinary circumstances, I would have hit on Brad. He wasn't exactly my type, but there was something intriguing about his passion for firearms. I was losing my focus.

"I'm more interested in what you guys have to offer for a membership," I said, steering our conversation away from the front of the store. I still wasn't sure who I was there to meet.

"Of course." Brad locked the case and escorted me to the rental area of the showroom. "You can pay monthly or annually. If you do it up front, you'll save a boatload of money."

I repressed a laugh. He wasn't doing me any favors by swapping out *shit* for *boat*.

"Ammo you pay for, but you can sign out any of these handguns with a membership. We also do a two-hour hold, so if there's something particular you want to test out, give me a call ahead of time and I can reserve it for you."

Brad handed me eye protection and ear plugs. "We usually make you buy these. I'll throw them in for free." It was a nice gesture, but I wouldn't be returning.

He led me along the paneled back wall which abruptly ended where the glass began. "There's fifteen lanes in total."

Men dressed in camouflaged tactical pants and black t-shirts sequestered on the far right side of the gallery.

"Brad, man!" a voice thundered. I looked to my left and my jaw dropped open. It was *him*. Carrot top.

"Don't worry little lady," he said to me, raking his hand through his hair. "I was born like this."

142

Brad chuckled and reached out for the exchange of their handshake, a smack-punch-explode riff they had clearly practiced before. "How have you been, brother?"

"Good man. Real good. You shooting with us tonight?

"Nah, not tonight, Max," Brad told him. "I'm actually heading out in a bit."

Carrot top now had a name: Max. He looked at me and I drew my jaw closed. "I see, I see," he said, turning back to Brad. It seemed he didn't recognize me.

"You're welcome to join us anytime. I know you're here most of the day but we can't get here until six. Later if the SAC keeps us after hours."

"I hear she rules with an iron fist," Brad replied, privy to the abbreviated jargon his comrade was spewing.

"Be glad you got out when you did." Max offered a repeat of the crazy handshake, this time reaching out for a sideways man hug.

"Take good care of my friend," he said, winking at me before heading off to the firing range entrance.

"Sorry about that. He's an old buddy of mine."

I shrugged. "It's no problem."

"I was part of the crew for years," Brad said, the memory of his past a slight twinkle in his eye.

"What kind of crew?" I prodded in mock innocence. "Like a men's league or something?"

He laughed genuinely. "Not exactly."

"Oh."

"Let's just say there are some really bad people in the world. And I'd had enough of chasing them."

143

I continued to gnaw away at his protective wall, determined to find out more. "Ahh, okay. You guys are cops, then."

"No way," he scoffed. "Drug Enforcement."

The details were adding up. Max's demeanor. His conservative attire. The Cadillac.

"I thought Ft. Collins was supposed to be a safe community," I said, keeping up my act.

"The green rush in Colorado has made a lot of people… stone happy." Brad looked at me and smiled before his eyes darkened.

"But it has also made people seriously rich. These aren't poor street kids looking to make a buck. They're businessmen wearing Gucci suits." He shook his head. "I needed to move on."

"Is that why you opened the range?" I asked.

"The range has been around for years. Nel was under contract with the DoD. Our squad came here for shooting practice. They still do."

Brad suddenly looked older, the grating years of law enforcement worn into his face. "I was on my way out of the agency and heard he was selling the place. Hell, I would have taken any business at that time."

"What do you mean, *at that time?*" The question sounded interrogative as it left my mouth.

Brad didn't take offense and offered a simple answer that, to him, explained everything. "Living a double life is a real mind fuck."

The alarm on my phone went off. I fished it out of my purse and looked at the screen. *Birth control, Tally!*

"I need to take this call," I told him, using the opportunity to flee.

"Want to use my office?" he asked, unaware of the ruse.

I silenced the alarm and brought the cell up to my ear. "I'll be right back."

Once outside, I jogged over to Aunt Jeannine's Subaru and started the engine. The tires skidded on the unpaved parking lot as I sped away from the strip mall and pulled out onto Eisenhower Blvd.

Max was definitely the same guy that accompanied Camila when she came for her tour at Forester. But if he had sent the text message that brought me to the gun range, why had he pretended like he didn't know who I was? I didn't see the point. The same went for my disconnected battery. Was he toying with me?

Though Max's ties to the DEA had been illuminated, Camila's connection remained a mystery. I dialed Vic's number and waited for him to answer.

The thrum of red and blue lights in the rearview startled me. I hung up before leaving a message on Vic's voicemail and came to a stop on the shoulder. After removing my hat, I placed my hands on the wheel to let the officer know I was unarmed and not looking for a fight. As the figure approached from behind, I caught a peek of my reflection. Despite puffy eyes and a cluster of pimples raging on my forehead, I would try to talk my way out of any trouble. It had worked in the past.

"Don't move," a woman's voice commanded through the open window, her weapon drawn and aimed at my head.

Out of instinct, I raised my arms into the air.

"I said don't fucking move!" she shouted. I kept them up while she sent a numerical command over the radio attached to her lapel.

"I'm going to need you to step out of the car," she said, pulling the door handle from the outside, her Colt .45's bore hole staring down at me.

"I'm buckled in!" I wailed.

"Go ahead and unlatch your seatbelt. Slowly, with your right hand. Keep the other one up." I obeyed her instructions precisely. Once on my feet, she cuffed me and began her pat down.

"Do you have any weapons in your vehicle?"

"It's my aunt's car."

"Yes or no. There was an armed robbery a few blocks east and you fit the BOLO."

"Armed robbery?" I said, taken aback. "I didn't commit any robberies."

She placed me in her squad car but not before I caught her name. Moments later, a second cop pulled up from behind. He exited, stared me down as he walked past, and joined Officer Blakeson near the Subaru's passenger door. He watched while she searched the front interior.

After a few minutes, Blakeson emerged and reentered, this time through the rear passenger door. She backed out feet first and said something to her partner. He pulled a set of gloves from a pouch, handed them to her, and she went back to work. When the assault on my fourth amendment rights was over, the middle-aged, overweight officer attended to me.

"Miss Forester," he said, having found out my name after looking through my purse. "I'm Sergeant Donahue. Do you have a license for the handgun?"

"I didn't even know there *was* a handgun."

"So, should I interpret your answer as a no?"

"I told her already, the vehicle belongs to my aunt. I didn't rob anyone."

"Well, that's your story. For now, I'm placing you under arrest for possession and concealment of the firearm without a license. You have the right to remain silent. Anything you say can and… "

"You've got to be kidding me!" I shouted at him as he read me my Miranda rights. I had always been on the other side of the law, having seen the inside of a jail cell with a visitor pass clipped to my shirt and the promise that I could leave.

"If your alibi checks out, we will only hold you for the night."

"For the night? I don't fucking believe this!"

"You're cuffed and in the back of a police car. What's not to believe?"

"I want my phone call."

"We'll discuss what your privileges are once we print you." He shut the door hard to let me know who was in charge.

28

"Tell me where your keys are so I can come get you." Aunt Jeannine was distraught I had spent the night surrounded by delinquents with nothing to lose. "Why didn't you call sooner?"

"I've been calling the office since noon!"

"The office? You're lucky I picked up. Chanelle lost her logbook. I was in here searching for it."

"Oh, thank God. I don't think I could have done another tuna sandwich."

"Don't you have your uncle's cell number?"

"Yeah, it's saved in my phone. Which is in your car." I hoped it hadn't been confiscated. Who knows what kind of twisted story the cops could concoct to suit their needs.

Aunt Jeannine hissed into the receiver. "No one commits a single thing to memory anymore. Hell, even I don't know his number by heart. And he's my husband!"

She was right. Long division and correct grammar were also being killed by technology, artificial intelligence capable of accuracy unrivaled by even the most studious of pupils.

I tossed the complimentary sandwich into the garbage and headed outside to wait.

·· ◆ ◆ ◆ ◆ ··

"Cash or credit?" the impound attendant asked.

"I'll pay you back," I told my aunt as she handed over three crisp hundred dollar bills. The chain-link security gate swung wide and she drove into the lot.

"I didn't know you carried a gun," I said as she turned right and counted the rows aloud.

"Me? I couldn't hurt a fly."

"So, whose is it?" I asked, dumbfounded.

"I'm not sure what you mean."

"The gun under your seat."

She laughed. "I doubt it."

"There was a gun in your car. That's why they hauled me in. For unlawful concealment."

"Are you sure you didn't get distracted at the range and walk out with it? It happens. One time I was trying on accessories at the Super Target in town and accidentally left with a necklace, a hat, and a pair of sunglasses I'd forgotten to pay for. Can you imagine that?"

"I didn't leave with a gun, Aunt Jeannine."

"Well, I wouldn't get too worked up. There's got to be an explanation. I'll ask your uncle what he knows about it."

We weaved back and forth through rows of vehicles until we found aisle *G9*. The Suby, as she called it, was a few spots down, jammed between two pickups. My aunt got out and plotted a path to her vehicle while I replaced her in the front seat of my truck.

From the trunk, she weighed her options. Seeing that the passenger door would have more room to open, she hit the unlock button on her keyless entry, sucked in her gut, and pretzeled her way in. Through the back windshield, I saw her scale the center console and plop down into the driver seat. She turned the engine over and backed out, lining her vehicle up with mine so that our windows were parallel.

"See you in a few." She handed me my phone and adjusted her rearview mirror before navigating her way to the exit.

I trailed behind, taking her cue when to break and turn as my mind postulated. Camila's ties with Max, no matter the intricacies, meant that she had nothing positive to offer my uncle's business. And then there was Dr. Jahnke who had failed to investigate why Flynn had in his possession a toxic substance capable of causing the cardiac arrest that claimed his life. There was something going on within their triad that I couldn't quite grasp.

I stopped at the office and watched Aunt Jeannine continue on to the house. She waved goodbye and honked. Darla and Uncle Remi were locked away in the funerary parlor, their vehicles the only indication they were present. I swiveled the chair around and dropped into it.

Several minutes passed while I sat motionless, contemplating my next step. When indecision finally resolved to action, I reached for my cell phone.

"What's new?" Vic said when he answered.

"I think Dabbencove was poisoned."

"Poisoned? No way!"

"There was a suspicious drug inventoried at the scene. It was in the documents you got from Nina."

"Wouldn't the doctor have found it during the autopsy?"

"It's possible he might be involved somehow. I was thinking, maybe Nina could get the toxicology report. To see if anything showed up on the samples. Then –"

"Tally, this is getting out of hand. All of these people can't be involved in a single death."

"Why not? The doctor could have been paid off."

"Highly unlikely. I've already explained Occam's razor to you. Just because it's possible doesn't mean it's realistic."

"Vic, this is murder! Not philosophy. If you're going to kill someone, wouldn't you use as many twists and turns as you could? That's the point of being a criminal. To stay ahead of the law so you don't get caught."

Vic took a moment to formulate his response. "Okay. Let's pretend everything you just said is true." He let the hypothesis rumble. "You need to get the hell out of the way, Tally."

"I've tried."

"Try harder! Or you could be next in the casket."

"It's not that easy, Vic."

"Tell Camila you are too busy to take on another client. Or that there's been a death in your family and the business is taking a sabbatical. Hell, tell her you're shutting down for a month because the mortuary needs a remodel. Get creative!"

Two uniformed officers entered through the front door and I hung up on Vic without saying goodbye.

"Haven't you terrorized me enough?" I shouted, bringing myself to their level.

Officer Piedra looked over his shoulder at his partner, and then back at me. As the senior, he spoke first. "I'm not sure what kind of trouble you've had, but we're not here for you."

The second officer who appeared to be fresh out of the academy figured he would elaborate. "We've been sent to transport one of your clients back to the medical examiner. That's all."

"Normally we do the chaufering," I told them. As far I knew, armed police didn't shuttle dead bodies around.

"There have been some recent developments that require Mr. Dabbencove be returned to the state's custody," Piedra explained. "When this sort of thing happens, which it occasionally does, the M.E. has to go back over the physical findings. Per SOP."

"Standard operating procedures," the rookie cop, Rankin, clarified.

"I know what it means," I snapped. "Dabbencove isn't here."

Officer Piedra held up a yellow legal form and walked it over to me. Forester was listed as the recipient of a sixty-three year old decedent named Flynn Dabbencove.

I was out with it. "What kind of bullshit are you guys up to?"

A pink notice caught my peripheral and I traced it down to the desk. I snatched the page up; it was a carbon copy of the document the police had. Darla's signature lay at the bottom above a line that requested authorization for the transfer. Randall had delivered Dabbencove while I was stuck behind steel bars that restricted my freedom.

"Is there a problem?" Rankin asked.

"I don't believe this," I muttered, reading the second signature on the document: *Dr. Gerald Jahnke.*

Hit with the realization that Dabbencove had already been embalmed, my eyes welled up. Any chance of finding Corazole in his system was unlikely, the poison pumped out of his body, the promise of justice sent whirling down the drain.

Piedra's patience were disentigrating. "He asked you a question."

I shook my head. "There's no problem."

After watching the officers wheel Dabbencove out the back door and into their armored tactical van, I returned my attention to the document in my hand. On the line designated for next of kin, I found Camila's name. Beside it, there was a phone number.

If I backed the notion of her innocence, maybe I could get her to talk. And if she talked, maybe she would slip up. It was a long shot, but I was determined to find answers.

I punched in the number and waited. And waited. And waited. On the seventh ring, my call was picked up.

"This is Martin."

His voice was disappointing and unexpected. "I'm sorry, Martin. I must have the wrong number."

"If yuh lookin' for Flynn," he said before I hung up, "then you've got the right numba. But you must not have heard the news yet. He's no longa with us."

He'd misinterpreted my call, but I planned to use it to my advantage. "I'm aware of his passing. I was hoping to speak with Camila."

The mention of her set Martin off. "Who is this?"

"My name's Tally. I work for Forester Funeral Home."

"Funeral home!" he shouted. "That bitch!"

"This must be a difficult time for you," I said, trying to tame him.

"I hope yuh prepared for what's coming."

"What do you mean by that?"

"Camila killed my fatha!"

His accusation should have been a bombshell, but I was already a few steps ahead of him. I wondered what else he had to say about her. "The paperwork in front of me states that Flynn Dabbencove's death was due to natural causes."

"He did have heart troubles," Martin confirmed, "but it was being treated by his cardiologist back in Brookville. They were only married three weeks, for Chrissake!"

Camila hadn't mentioned being newly-wed.

"I've been suspicious for awhile," he continued, his New York dialect only detectable on certain syllables. "I knew she was afta my fatha's money. He's a millionaire ten times ova, ya know?"

"We don't have access to financial records," I told him, the possible motive behind Dabbencove's murder sending up a red flag.

"I got a family friend back home. Retired NYPD. Had him look into her. Real name's Juanita. Juanita Marcos."

"Why would she change her name?"

"She worked undercova for the DEA. Outta Denva."

I was jolted back to my conversation with Brad. "Doing what exactly?"

"Narcotics agent. She infiltrated gangs. Turned them ova to law enforcement. It brought in thousands of dollas for the city."

Uncle Remi emerged from the embalming room.

"You're here!" he said, gleeful. When he realized I was on the phone, he covered his hand with his mouth.

"She was a nurse in Bolivia," Martin went on. "And now she's a fuckin' murderah!"

I had to keep Uncle Remi in the dark.

"I'll be in touch soon," I told Martin, politely cutting him off before hanging up.

"How've things been?" I asked my uncle, hoping my face was unreadable.

"Great here." A smirk crimped the corners of his mouth. "Tell me, how was your slumber party?"

29

The timing of Flynn Dabbencove's arrival was highly suspect. According to Camila, he was being kept at the morgue until she made her final decision on a funeral home. I called Randall several times, hoping he could provide details about why Dabbencove's pickup and embalming had been rushed.

When Randall still hadn't called back by seven, I decided to leave for the day. The answers to my questions would have to wait. I typed out a message to Vic, asking him to call me when he had a chance.

My phone rang at once. Wasting no time on casual minutiae, I said, "We've got a lot to discuss. Can we meet up?"

"Sure. My sister's out for the night with her friends. Want to come by my place?"

He'd never talked about his sister, nor had he told me that they lived together. I didn't ask him to elaborate before we hung up.

• • • ◆ • • •

Vic's neighborhood was ritzy, the lots sprawling, front yard garden boxes overflowing with produce at the height of their season. Modern ranch houses alternated between brick and stucco, their roofs new, exterior paint fresh. At the end of a cul-de-sac, I parked along the concrete drainage gutter, careful not to damage plentiful green grass that lined the road. I exited and followed the sidewalk up to Vic's entryway. Before I could ring the bell, the front door opened. Vic greeted me, shirtless, his shorts slouching down to reveal v-cut abdominals.

Setting aside my desire to pounce on him, I entered his home and presented the bottle of Colorado produced whiskey I brought with me. "Ever had this before?" I flashed the distiller's modest label.

"Nope. But I've heard of it. Remi loves the stuff."

"It was his recommendation."

Transitioning from a formal dining room into the kitchen was a bar area stocked with wine and liquor, an assortment of glassware offering itself up to any given occasion. He selected two tulip snifters and filled them to half.

"Ice?" he asked, tucking the rim of the glass just under his nose to acclimate his palate.

"No, thanks," I said, taking my portion from him. We sipped in unison, his eyes closed to enhance his tasting pleasure, mine admiring his body.

The house was spotless and I wondered if it was the result of his never-before-mentioned sister's upkeep.

"So, then. Tell me about this sibling of yours."

"Oh. Yeah," Vic casually replied.

I squinted at him. "Is that all you have to say about her?"

"She's my stepsister."

"Does Stepsister have a name?"

"Xandra."

"Is she younger or older?"

"Older. She had a really shitty break up a few months ago. I told her she could stay here until she figured things out."

"Any others?"

He smiled. "Just the one."

The kitchen and common area were huge. All together, the house had to be at least three thousand square feet. Sliding glass doors were flung open, leading to a cozy terrace with luxury patio furniture.

"Do you like it?" Vic asked, catching my eyes as they wandered.

"It's great. Your rent must be astronomical, though."

"I own it," he said, taking another sip of Stranahan's.

"Well, I'm paying on it."

"Impressive."

Vic smiled and made his way over to a plush microfiber loveseat in taupe.

"I spent last night in jail," I said without a lead-in.

He set his glass down on the coffee table and looked at me. "I don't follow."

"I was arrested."

"Arrested for what?"

"Listen. Dabbencove was definitely poisoned." I paused before delivering my assertion. "I'm with the police on this one."

158

I told Vic about the Corazole and how I'd received an odd text with the shooting range address.

"Why the hell didn't you tell me all of this? You could have been kidnapped. Or worse!"

"Google Maps showed it being in the middle of town. I figured since it was somewhere public, there'd be little risk."

"And you're sure Max didn't recognize you?"

"Well, no. How could I be sure?"

"Tally, he's probably the one that sent you that message."

"Yeah, that's exactly what I thought. But now, looking back, I think him being there was a coincidence."

"It can't be a coincidence, Tally."

"That's not what I meant. What I'm saying is that *someone else* sent the text."

"Let me guess," he said, the sarcasm not withheld. "It was Camila."

I shook my head yes.

"Why? Did you see her there?"

"No."

Vic raked his hands through his hair. I didn't dare mention that I'd spoken to Martin.

He finished off what was left in his glass and stood. When he reached the liquor cabinet, he brought the bottle of whiskey to his mouth. They took their time parting ways.

·· ♦ ♦ ♦ ··

We drank more than driving allowed, so I didn't resist Vic's insistence that I stay the night. Our first time having sex wasn't the grandiose event I had anticipated.

159

Instead, it was belligerent lust spawned by too much booze. Deep penetration, without any result, continued for too long. Spent, we both passed out and remained coma-still until morning.

I rubbed my eyes and reached over the side of the bed for my phone. It was already after six and I had to be to work by eight. There was no way I'd make it on time.

Vic's arm pulled me close. "It's Sunday."

A smile stretched its way across my mouth when I realized he was right. I twisted around in his protective clench to face him and easily fell back asleep. Hours later, the room was still a dark cave untouched by the sun.

"Time to wake up," Vic whispered into my ear after planting a soft, wet kiss on my forehead. "It's almost noon."

"Ugh," I groaned, the sickly taste of my whiskey binge lingering.

"Are you hungry?"

"Mmhmm."

"Good. I made us breakfast."

"I thought you said it was noon?"

"It is." He slinked away from the bed, the smell of syrup galloping in on the heel of his breeze. "You should never skip the most important meal of the day."

I met Vic in the kitchen wearing one of his shirts and a pair of lacey spankies that had been discarded from the bed onto the floor at some point during our sexcapades the night before.

"I'm drained," I yawned, taking my seat at the breakfast bar. Cheesy scrambled eggs and two pieces of French toast were waiting for me.

He razzed me over his shoulder. "Wuss." Boxer briefs were the only thing he was wearing, their pliable fabric squeezing the contours of his ass cheeks.

"Try this," he said, turning to deliver a cappuccino he'd whipped up with his espresso machine. The front of his underwear was also tight and left nothing to the imagination. I took a precautionary sip and stuck my tongue out at him in disgust.

Vic returned the gesture.

"Do you always walk around half nude?" I asked, taking another sip.

He tossed me a *pretty much* shrug.

"Really?" I looked off in the distance.

"It's my house. Besides, she doesn't care."

"Don't get me wrong," I told him. "I'm *definitely* not complaining."

"It sure sounds like it." He smiled. "Eat up."

There was only one plate between the two of us. "Aren't you going to help me?"

"No. That's for you. I already had mine."

"Oh. Well I'm glad you didn't wait on my account," I teased, heaping eggs onto the fork. I bucked them off and played around with the toast instead. Dabbencove was on my mind.

"I talked to a buddy of mine this morning," Vic preempted, reading my thoughts. "He's going to trace that text you got."

"Yeah?" I said. "I'll get the number for you."

I laid the fork down and turned to stand.

"He also mentioned that he could get the 911 call Camila made the day Dabbencove died."

I twisted back around. "Go on."

161

"Nash said the medical records are only part of the story. He thinks the dispatch recording might be more telling."

"Do we have access to that?"

"He does."

"And he volunteered to get it for us?"

"I wouldn't use the word *volunteered*. Nash works for Ft. Collins P.D. but does some P.I. stuff on the low."

"Vic, is he going to help us or not?"

"That's the problem. You are looking for different answers than I am."

"Don't we both want the truth?"

"People die all the time. It's not your job to figure out why."

"Can't you see this was thrown into my lap? I didn't ask for it."

"You enjoy it in some strange way."

"Dabbencove deserves justice." I picked my fork back up.

"If you're not going to eat," he said after watching me relocate food from one side of the plate to the other without bringing it to my mouth, "maybe you'd be more interested in a shower?"

He left the question to simmer as he sauntered off to the bathroom.

· · · ◆ · · ·

Worn down, I returned to Uncle Remi's house and conked out. Hours passed, and when my phone rang later that evening, it surprised me.

"Hello?" I said, dazed. The smell of garlic and Italian herbs taunted from the kitchen, their aromas wafting up into the loft to stimulate my appetite.

"You're not going to believe this."

"Hmm?"

"I've got the call to the dispatch center."

"That was quick," I told him, coming to.

"Yeah, well I was expecting to put your worries to rest. Now it has me curious as hell."

I sat straight up, my heart thudding hard against my chest. "What do you mean, Vic?"

"It needs some work, but I think I can hear squabbling in the background."

"Like, an argument?"

"Yeah."

"About what?"

"Can't tell yet. I'm cleaning it up as we speak."

"I'm on my way over."

30

Vic didn't meet me at the door, so I let myself in. "It's just me," I shouted, announcing my arrival in the entryway and adding my shoes to the collection of other pairs that had congregated at the carpet's edge.

A lean figure with a sassy pixie haircut appeared in the hallway.

I gasped. "You scared me!"

She stared in silence, which added to the awkward first meeting.

"Sorry to barge in. I'm Natalia." I didn't offer a handshake, my arms full with food Aunt Jeannine had sent along with me.

The olive-skinned woman said nothing. She was buff, her physique clearly the result of a dedicated exercise routine and healthy eating habits. She and Vic had that much in common.

When she still didn't engage, I tried the only ice-breaking strategy I knew of: ask a question. "Are you hungry?"

"In here!" Vic called out from a room I hadn't noticed on my previous visit.

Without a word, she faded back into the darkness, clicking her music on before continuing to fold items from the dryer.

"What's your sister's problem?" I whispered as I approached Vic from behind. He was seated in front of two flat screen monitors, his ears covered by noise-cancelling headphones that drowned out the world around him. On the screen, squiggly lines in neon green undulated as he keyed in commands.

"Definitely three voices," he said, removing his headset and spinning around to see me.

"First booze, now dinner?" Vic stood and placed a chaste kiss on my cheek. "You really know the way to a man's heart."

"Aunt Jeannine," I told him. I hadn't mentioned where I was going, but somehow she just knew.

"Jeannine makes the best damn sauce."

He took the Tupperware and led us out from his electronic filled grotto into the kitchen.

"Aside from the dispatcher and Camila, I can hear another person in the background," he said, dishing out generous helpings of Bucatini from the plastic containers onto ceramic plates. He spun long pasta noodles into bundles by twirling his fork into the scoop of a spoon. "It's faint, but I think I can enhance it."

"Who do you think it is?" I asked.

Vic waited to answer until after he swallowed. "Tough to say."

We put the vocal dismemberment chat on pause while we finished eating. Vic buttered a few slices of bread and handed me one. I hadn't realized how hungry I was and beat him to cleaning my plate.

"That was *so* good!" he said upon finishing. He washed our dishes, wiped his hands on a small kitchen towel, and organized the counter back to its previously tidy state. "Let's go."

Vic dimmed the recessed kitchen lights and off we went.

Xandra's bedroom was directly next to Vic's office, Puscifer's *The Mission* thumping from behind her closed door. Our shared taste for Maynard somehow made her brashness less offensive. I abandoned my premature assessment of her and reminded myself of my own apprehensions when meeting new people. Reticence was probably just her defense mechanism. That, and I imagined she was going through a lot mentally – breakups weren't easy no matter how long the relationship had lasted.

Vic slid headphones over his ears and turned his attention to the frequency he intended to isolate. While he manipulated digital dials with his cursor, I rooted around his room.

It was modestly decorated save for well-utilized bookcases lined with hundreds of movies, their spines facing out, the titles in no particular order. Floating shelves were installed on the wall that bordered his stepsister's room; their contents ranged from large, irregularly shaped geodes to Streampunk type gadgets. The carpeted floor was home to every color and size extension cord on the market, their rubber protected wires tidily wound and twist tied.

He continued to play the audio clip over and over, dragging the rule back to the segment in question and then toggling the controls as needed. I selected a book from his collection and opened to a random page. There, a poem began with the words *Sinister smile of deceit*. How fitting.

On the inside cover was an illegible message addressed to Vic. Her loopy, artsy signature concluded the paragraph, its characters also impossible to decipher. I wondered if she was an ex-girlfriend or maybe a friend of his sister.

"You've got be kidding me!" Vic shouted.

Startled, I snapped the book shut.

He removed his headphones and spun the high-backed leather chair around. "It's another person, alright."

His bare foot bounced fretfully, his heel nearly hitting the floor before springing back up. When Vic realized that I was waiting for him to elaborate, he swiveled around to face the computer and snatched the headphone cable from the tower.

"This is the unedited clip," he said, cranking the volume to counteract Xandra's encroaching music.

The female dispatcher's voice came over coolly, her neutral response perfected over the years. "Nine, one, one, what's your location?"

"Please send an ambulance, my heart – husband having heart attack." Camila's voice was panicked, her words jumbled together. She sounded genuinely alarmed. "Please, hurry. Please!"

"Calm down, ma'am. What's your address?"

As she recited the numbers, I committed them to memory. The rest of the file played out with Camila stating her husband was not breathing and remained unresponsive. EMTs arrived on the scene within five minutes.

Vic turned to me, his face devoid of emotion. "Now, for the enhanced version."

The female voices went back and forth as dispatch pleaded with Camila to calm down.

"I need to ask you some questions, okay? Is he breathing?"

"I don't know!" Camila screamed into the receiver.

Losing patience, the dispatcher tried again. "I need you to calm down and check him. Is he breathing?"

"No!" she yelled.

A third voice barely registered on the display.

"He's not breathing?" the operator confirmed.

"No," Camila repeated.

"Check his mouth and make sure it's clear. Is he awake?"

"No, he's totally gone."

The phone crackled as if it had been set down. And then, there was a man's voice. "You said you were going to get an ambulance."

My eyes were on the monitor as the voice presented itself in the form of a wave. Vic's blank stare was cast upon the wall, his ear in perfect alignment with the speaker.

"I know that," Camila said to him before returning to the phone and addressing the dispatcher. "Okay, he's on the floor."

"I'm going to tell you how to give mouth to mouth. Take a couple deep breaths."

Camila listened to the directions and then disappeared from the line again.

"Get away from me," the male faltered, struggling with Camila. Struggling with the poison.

"Give up!" she ordered in the distance before retrieving the phone.

"What were you doing?" The dispatcher wanted to know.

"We were taking a siesta."

"What?"

"A nap," she translated.

"No, just now. What were you doing? I'm trying to give you CPR instructions."

Medical personnel started to arrive and Camila shouted to them. "Come in!"

The operator's voice came over the line one last time. "Disconnecting. Rescue on scene."

"Martin said she's a certified nurse," I told Vic. "How could she not know CPR?"

"Who's Martin?"

I swallowed hard, realizing my mistake. "He's Dabbencove's son."

Vic narrowed his eyes.

"Flynn told Camila to get away," I continued. "He must have suspected she was trying to harm him."

"More importantly, we've caught her in a lie."

"Exactly! Camila claims her husband is already dead but we just heard him talk to her."

Vic shook his head. "She even responds."

"We need to call the police."

"Not a chance."

"Vic, we have to!"

"We are committing a crime right now. Probably several."

"I'll tell them everything we know. About the Corazole, and the gun club, and –"

"Tally, are you listening to yourself? You know it doesn't work like that. Especially if there really is some sort of collusion happening. They'll throw the book at us."

I paused to collect my thoughts.

"What's up, Tally? I don't like that look you have."

I jotted down Camila's address. "I have a plan."

"I can't believe this," he complained.

"You can stay here if you want."

Vic sighed and came to his feet. "You're not going alone."

31

"I know it's late," I said when Martin answered. "I don't sleep much these days."

"I have the 911 recording that Camila made on the day your father died," I told him. "She tells the dispatcher that Flynn is unconscious but you can hear a man, presumably him, talking in the background."

"I knew she was involved! I need that tape!"

"Martin, listen. It's more complicated than that."

"My fatha is dead and she's the killa! Simple as that!"

"I hear you. But the call won't prove anything on its own. There needs to be physical evidence."

When he said nothing, I continued. "The police found something called Corazole on your father's nightstand. It's a drug that causes seizures."

Martin gasped. "Oh my God!"

"It's possible it could have interfered with his medication or stopped his heart. The problem is, I found out in an unorthodox way. Do you understand what I'm saying?"

"Sounds straight forward to me," he argued.

171

"Yes, but that piece of information wouldn't be admissible in court because of the way I obtained it. Besides, we have another hurdle." I took a deep breath before compounding the bad news. "Your father has already been embalmed."

"No," he whispered. Then, rage. "No. No. No! How the fuck did that happen?"

"It was without my knowledge."

"I want to see him."

"I'm sorry, but he's no longer in our custody. There was a court order issued to bring his body back to the medical examiner. The cops transported him themselves."

"They can't just do that!"

"Listen. Your hatred for Camila may have been valid, even if it was speculative until now. But there's no way she could have done this alone. There must have been some orchestration. Some covering up. I don't know why, yet."

"She wanted my fatha's money. That's why. I'll kill her!"

"Martin, you still have options."

"Options? What options? He's dead. Now she needs to suffa!"

"Request copies of the investigative report. It will show that Corazole was inventoried at the scene."

"If they are all in on it, who do I trust?"

"You can trust the evidence."

"Won't the poison be out of his body now that he's embalmed?"

"There's no way to know for sure. An independent autopsy needs to be performed to test for it. There are a lot of moving parts. You have to take this one step at a time."

"Why are you helping me?" he asked.

I hadn't expected the question. "If I were you, I'd want someone to help me, too."

32

The four-acre lot on the west side of Ft. Collins sat on the corner of a major street, tucked behind protective evergreens. A decoratively lit driveway wrapped around the entrance. It looked warm and inviting, a palatial home that was expansive enough to house a large number of guests who likely attended social events hosted by the wealthy couple who appeared to be happily in love.

Alarmingly close to Vic's own residence, I imagined Camila driving past his neighborhood, showing off her sporty ride while concealing hatred in her eyes with name brand sunglasses that cost more than my entire wardrobe. She could have easily shopped in the same grocery store as Vic, crossed paths with him in the toilet paper aisle, or waited in line behind him at the register.

"I'm surprised she doesn't park that in the garage," Vic said, spotting her jet-black Aston Martin in the driveway as our vehicle slowly passed the Dabbencove spread.

"That's where she keeps the Rolls Royce," I told him.

Vic's glare was incredulous.

"I'm kidding," I laughed. "I don't know what she has in there."

"You better not, Tally. This is the one and only time we're coming here."

"Fine." I craned my neck to look for cameras. Surely, with her background in law enforcement, she used surveillance equipment to keep an eye on her property.

Headlights turned down the road behind us. A dead end with few other homes on the street, Vic pulled to the curb, pretending to have found our destination. Instead of passing us, the car pulled in next to Camila's ride.

"What the fuck?" Vic whispered. He watched in his rearview mirror while I adjusted the one on the passenger side.

"Did you get a good look?" I asked him.

"Not really."

"Well, what color was it? Did you see the driver at all?"

"Honestly, it looks like a cop."

If my calls were being monitored, it was possible we had been followed. "Does it have lights?"

He shook his head no. "It's got antennas all over it."

"No way!" I undid my seatbelt and spun around in the seat. "It can't be."

"Can't be what?"

I looked at Vic, and then back at the road behind us.

He tried again. "Can't be what, Tally?"

"Max," I said.

"Forget this."

I turned Vic's camera on. "We're so close, now."

"Close to what?"

"Pictures."

"Pictures of what?"

"Them. For proof."

"Proof? That won't prove shit!"

"Yes, it will show they are working together."

"No, Tally. It won't. I can't believe I let you talk me into this."

I rolled down the window and peered out as I contemplated his rebuttal. He was right. Pictures alone wouldn't be enough. I needed to get within range of their conversation to record it.

I yanked on the door handle and moved to exit. Vic grabbed at my arm but I wrestled him off.

"Point us toward the main road," I instructed through the window. "And keep the engine running."

Vic met my eyes with disappointment.

"I'll be right back," I told him, pulling the hood of my black sweatshirt over my head and fading into the night.

My confidence had deteriorated by the time the sprawling two-story fortress came into view. Pressing the thought of being caught far in the back of my head, I pushed through the dense plant border lining the property's perimeter. There, I found my first hurdle.

Bright circles of illumination were cast by landscape lights which had security cameras bolted to them. Carefully avoiding the hot spots, I stooped low and waddled over to the side of the garage. As I approached, a rustle in the tall ornamental grass sent me into hiding. Beads of sweat rolled down my chest as I ducked behind two large trash cans.

I weighed my options if I was caught, deciding that I would run away as fast and far as possible instead of implicating Vic by making him my getaway driver. He'd be pissed, but I wasn't going to bring him down, too.

My legs became cement as the sounds drew closer. When the urge to flee peaked, a doe and her fawn emerged from the brush. I sighed and the mother deer looked in my direction, pronounced eyes wide and glistening. A door from around the back of the house screeched open, startling us all. She leapt away instinctively, her baby close behind.

"You can't just show up whenever you feel like it." It was Camila.

"I don't *feel* like it," Max corrected. "I'm over this bullshit."

"Don't be like that, baby. It will all be over soon."

Their lips smacked as they kissed. I hit the record button on Vic's camera, more interested in capturing audio than video. I wasn't sure how far away the sound would be picked up. I had to get closer.

Inching my away along the side of the house, primal grunts and heavy breathing filled the night air. "Right there, baby," Camila panted.

Glass shattered to the ground and Max shouted. "Fuck!"

"It's okay, sweetheart," she giggled, tipsy. "I want you inside me."

I continued to snake around the back corner of the garage, edging closer. My foot crunched down on a twig and it snapped.

"What was that?" Max demanded.

"Deer," Camila moaned. "Don't stop. I'm almost there."

After a number of unsuccessful thrusts, Max quit on her. "I can't."

"You're pathetic," she growled. Just out of view, I watched as she snugged her robe around perky breasts, hopped down from the picnic table, and went inside.

Max brought his arms up and wove his fingers together before placing them behind his head. With his pants unbuckled, and his shirt crumpled on the ground beside him, he stared out into the back yard, the flame of a tiki torch dancing above its citronella scented reservoir.

Camila came back through the sliding glass door to deliver her final message. "It's over."

Max ripped his zipper up and buckled his belt. He stomped on his discarded shirt as he passed it by, taking the foot path at the bottom of the porch steps that would navigate him straight toward me. Without hesitation, I heaved a handful of pebbles in the opposite direction.

Max spun and drew a gun from his ankle. I worked my way back around the side of the garage and slipped through the hedge.

"Are you okay?" Vic asked as I strapped myself into the passenger seat.

"I'm alive," I wheezed, recovering from the sprint.

The Cadillac's tires squealed as Max backed out of the driveway and again when he turned onto the main road.

Vic expected the worst. "Are we going to follow him?"

"Nope. Show's over."

"Did you get what you were hoping for?"

"Just a case of erectile dysfunction."

Vic forced a laugh. "That's embarrassing."

·· ◆ ◆ ◆ ··

The drive back to Vic's neighborhood was short, and I was glad I hadn't been chastised for the covert mission he dubbed Operation E.D. Although there wasn't a stitch of dialogue suggesting Camila's culpability, I wasn't ready to give up.

"I'm going to head out," I told Vic when we parked in front of his house, a frosty snow globe keeping the entryway aglow. All the inside lights were off.

"Are you sure you don't want to stay the night?"

"I've got to work in the morning and can't be late. I owe Aunt Jeannine for bailing me out."

"Don't want to be fired?" he teased.

Our goodnight kiss progressed to making out. Before fondling led me to his bedroom, I broke it off. "Gotta go."

"No, you don't." He swept the back of his hand across my cheek.

I kissed him again and exited the vehicle. It was after midnight, sleepiness and anxiety clinging to my joints as I staggered to my truck.

"Sweet dreams," he whispered across the lawn before disappearing into his house.

I waved goodbye and ducked into the driver's seat. I could see us being lovers, but I was only going to be in Colorado for another month. Even if I wasn't leaving, I wasn't ready to sacrifice my independence. I wasn't sure I knew how to anymore.

"Interpersonal relationships alter your bio-chemistry," Sadie told me after I kicked Trevor's cheating ass out. "When you feel threatened, there's a thickening of the theoretical shell, the protective layer that grows between you and the world."

Through her analyzing microscope of causation, she deemed every situation the result of a previous action. She even blamed inaction. "As you become marked by trauma, the ego shields the inner child from harm. Blocking the hurt is disastrous for emotional development; you're going to hinder appropriate responses to future attacks."

"The system sounds flawed," I challenged.

"Of course it is. By design, egocentric behavior masquerades as selflessness."

"Enough of the verbal diarrhea. How do I stop it?"

Her solution was simple. "You don't."

33

My body roused to the demand of my alarm before the sun showed itself through the drapes. I'd ditched the comforter at some point when the sheets had become so saturated with sweat that they started to stick like a second skin. Dreams had kept me from restful sleep, but when I tried to recall them, I couldn't.

I gulped down a double dose of vitamin C and apologized to my immune system for the inadequate nourishment it had received for several consecutive days. I'd traded my predictive routine for the promise of truth and understanding, replaced scheduled meals for lukewarm afterthoughts, and gained a few sugar pounds from drinking too much liquor.

When I showed up at the office close to eight, a silver Mustang was waiting for me in the parking lot, its windows rolled down, the engine cut. Unfamiliar with the vehicle and its occupant, I stayed in my truck.

A middle-aged man dressed in khaki shorts, a collared shirt, and loafers emerged. He waved and headed in my direction. I cracked my window as he approached the driver side door.

"Mawnin', miss. I'm looking for someone that works here. Name's Tally."

"And you are?" I questioned anonymously, taking note of his accent.

"My apologies. I'm Mah-in Esdan. Not used to making introductions through winduhs."

He shuffled his hands in his pockets. His dark hair and features were stern, but even a practiced smile and smoothly shaven face couldn't neutralize his heavy heart. I pushed the door open and stood.

"Tally," I said, offering my hand. "Nice to properly meet you."

Martin accepted my handshake warily, his eyes scanning me with inquisition. My phone etiquette suggested that of a suit wearing office assistant well versed in dealing with the public. Clad in a lacey tank-top and faded skinny jeans, Martin voiced his surprise.

"You're much younguh than I expected."

I ignored his comment. "What are you doing here?"

"I think you know," he said, stepping closer.

I took a step back and the truck pushed me from behind. Martin closed the distance.

"I need that 911 call."

I wondered how long he had been parked there, waiting for me. Rolling the request around in my head, I could hear Vic's cautionary voice of warning. "For my own protection," I told Martin, "I don't know if I can do that."

"I fig'ed as much." He rifled through his pocket and produced a small thumb drive. "This is our conversation from last night. For *my own* protection."

After searching my face, Martin said, "When I get the 911 call, you get this."

I stared at him without blinking. He was so close I could taste his cologne.

"Why should I believe you?" I asked him, considering whether he might somehow be involved in his father's death. "You could have another copy."

"I could." He dropped the USB back into his pocket and shrugged. "But I don't."

Martin had more reasons to be mistrustful that I did. Besides, Camila needed to pay. The call would give him a shred of hope to keep him going, to keep him digging, to keep him sane. Figuring out all of the answers would take the rest of his life, and even then, he'd always have an empty hole inside him from losing his father.

"I'm sorry for your loss," I said after concluding my analysis. "I'll have a copy of the recording for you tomorrow. Where do you want to meet?"

"I'm headed over to the courthouse afta this to request a copy of the autopsy."

I shook my head to tell him I agreed.

"Why don't I call you lata this evening so we can work something out?"

"That's fine."

He headed for his sports car with steps of deliverance, eager to tackle the next phase of his investigation.

"Good luck, Martin," I called to him before he slipped behind the wheel. It was all I could say. I had underestimated his tenacity. If I could get a copy of the call to dispatch without Vic knowing, then I'd be able to avoid an argument with him.

Once inside the office, I set to cleaning. I washed the windows, steel wooled the sink, and even scrubbed the toilet. The physical labor was exhausting but it felt good not to meddle. Sweaty and sore, Darla was a welcome distraction when she stepped out of the funeral parlor.

"Jeez, woman. I've never seen this place so sparkly."

I wiped hair out of my eyes and adjusted my bandana. "It needed it."

"I'm surprised to see you with so much energy these days." She winked.

"What do you mean?"

"All that time you've been spending with Vic." She thought for a moment. "Then again, you kids can go on, and on, and on."

I her gave a look of pure torment.

"Oh, don't worry. You've managed to settle the score for us. We were beginning to think Vic was asexual. Or closet queer."

"*Queer?* Isn't that like a taboo word or something?"

Darla laughed. "Queer is a socially accepted term in the correct context. Some people are sexually queer. Others are gender queer. Anyway, we were never quite sure about Vic. Now we know."

"I'm glad everyone is talking about my sex life," I groaned.

"At least you have one." She walked over to the window and ran her finger across the ledge to inspect for dust. There wasn't any. "I'm heading to Bar SS with a few of my lady friends if you want to get away for a bit. Us vintage lesbians can be quite entertaining."

"I thought you didn't drink?"

"Yeah, but lucky for me, they don't interrogate my preferences at the door."

"I didn't mean it like that."

"I'm teasing. If you're going to hang with my friends, you'll need thicker skin. Toodles."

Darla left me to ponder. Based on Vic's looks, I assumed he'd racked up a whole list of partners. But if they never saw him with anyone, maybe I was wrong. That, or he hid his flings well.

I found my keys and headed for the exit with a shower on my mind. Then, I'd decide if I had the stamina to meet up with Darla and her crew. The phone began to ring on my way out, my conscience overruling the idea of letting it go to voicemail.

"Tally, its Mah-in." I was not excited to be hearing from him again so soon. "My fatha, he's gone."

"Gone where?"

"Camila signed the release and overnighted his body to New Yawk. Buried him this aftanoon."

"How can she do that?" I asked, but I already knew. She had used her title as wife to legally allocate rights into her own hands. Flynn's property was signed over – all of his belongings; even his money. She was the sole benefactor to his entire estate.

"I'm gunna file an injunction to exhume." Martin was grabbing at straws, the chance to redeem his father's injustice slipping away.

"They'll never go for that," I told him. "You've got to take it one step at a time."

"He's already in the ground!"

185

"Look, if you start demanding crazy ideas, they will think you are crazy."

"Well, maybe I am!"

Regret punched me in the face. Contacting Martin was a huge mistake; of course he would want revenge. I was beginning to see why Vic thought my entanglement could be dangerous.

34

Wilf had been back to work for a week already, but I hardly noticed him as I went about my duties with a fog hanging over me. Randall and Jefferson migrated in and out, the words exchanged between us sparse. Chanelle didn't make an appearance which was completely normal. I had sent Vic a few text messages which were unreturned and left him a voicemail on Friday which was also ignored.

Sadie's phone rang several times before she picked up, chipper voices laughing in the distance.

"Man, I thought you died," she said, unaware the stakes of my sleuthing were escalating.

"Not yet. Got company?"

"Theo threw a surprise party for me."

Guilt simmered in the pleats of my stomach. I'd completely forgotten.

"Happy Birthday, Sadie."

"Thanks, babe. Hold on." Doors slid open and shut, and then it was silent. "You still there?"

"Yeah. I don't mean to keep you," I began.

"It's cool. I need a break." Sadie met Theo in a class she'd taken the semester before – Ethics in Human Experimentation. She the student and he the teacher, they weren't practicing ethics when they decided to explore more than just research together.

"How have you been?" she asked.

I told her about Vic whom I had only briefly mentioned the last time we spoke. Now I'd fucked him and stayed the night at his house.

"Game changer," she said, aware of the consequences sleeping together brings. I didn't tell her much about Dabbencove, except that a series of strange events had resulted in my arrest.

She laughed at my incarceration. "That's just silly."

"Anyway, Vic's been AWOL for a few days now."

"Want my opinion?"

"Of course. Why *else* would I be calling?"

"Being in Colorado was supposed to help you focus, not run away." She took a sip of something. "You're letting yourself be distracted."

I cleared my throat.

"As for Vic, who cares? Maybe he just wanted to get in your pants. But whatever. Win-win. You really needed to get over Trevor. I mean, you hadn't gotten laid in how long?"

"Going on a year."

"Jesus, Tally."

"I know, I know."

"Now that the streak is over, you should feel great about yourself. Energized. Libido is an indication of overall health. To tell you the truth, I was worried about you."

Guitar strumming and loud singing spilled into the quiet space where Sadie had retreated.

"Tell whoever that is that you've got to go," a male voice slurred.

"In a minute," she told him, but he already had his hands on her, pulling the phone away and tickling her vulnerable spots.

"I love you, Tally!" she squeaked between giddy laughter. "Call you soon."

The phone clicked off and I knew I wouldn't hear from her any time soon. We were growing apart.

She was pursuing her dream of being a psychologist, had a live-in boyfriend who worked for a prestigious college, and didn't have to think about money as long as her grades were good.

I was on the total other end of the spectrum. It was much easier to relate to one another when we lived in the same city. Hundreds of roads separated us now.

35

"**B**lack usually has the most caffeine. If you still need some pep, I'd go with this one." Aunt Jeannine pointed to a blend of curly leaves, cardamom pods, star anise, and peppercorns. "A homemade Chai if you will. Great with a dash of cream, just like you would your coffee."

I leaned in for a sniff. "Smells wonderful."

"I love it in the fall."

"The spices would play out well with a bit of cold weather. And some pumpkin pie."

"Pumpkin pie is good year round," she said, sorting through her tea chest. "So, tell me, is your coffee consumption bringing you down?"

"I actually feel great today," I reported, instantly regretful for not having considered the wrath of her M.S.

"I'm feeling good, too," she said. I was glad to hear it. "But back to you. Coffee is known for mycotoxin contamination. It can cause some pretty nasty symptoms."

"I don't know about all of that," I told her.

"It also messes with your hormones." Aunt Jeannine raised her eyebrows.

"I have some things I need to think over," I said, not indulging her in whatever conversation she wanted to have about my hormones.

"So, you're looking for something mellow?"

"Mellow, but not sleepy."

"Stay away from chamomile and valerian, then. Those will put you out." She searched until she found what she was looking for. "Here we go. This is what you want."

She poured warm water from her kettle into two generous mugs and dropped the bags in. "Lightly caffeinated green tea, peppermint, ginkgo biloba, and rosemary," she recited. As the cognition improving remedy steeped, Aunt Jeannine asked me about my plans for the day.

"I thought I would take a notebook and go out on the trail."

"That sounds like a great idea. Have you written much since you got here?"

"No. I kinda stopped in the spring."

"Your uncle mentioned you were having trouble staying interested in school."

"I guess that's a good way of putting it."

She smiled. "I miss reading your stories."

"Oh God. The angsty ones from high school English class?" My father had sent out a collection of them in Christmas cards that year. I was mad at him for weeks.

"Everyone has a story to tell," Aunt Jeannine quoted from the one about why I wanted to be a writer.

I covered my face with my hands. "That seems like a lifetime ago," I told her. "Besides, I don't do fiction anymore."

"How come?"

"I don't know. It seems senseless to create fake scenarios when there are real-life stranger-than-fiction stories to report on."

"Don't you want an exciting career? Something colorful? Journalism can be so bland."

The tea timer sounded and Aunt Jeannine extracted our bags.

"I think today will be a nice reset for you," she added. "Nature can be extremely stimulating. Not in an interference sort of way."

Her lips seasoned, she brought her mug straight to her mouth. "Your surroundings speak to you always, but you've got to pay attention."

My belly interrupted with a growl for breakfast. On cue, Aunt Jeannine sliced home-baked cinnamon raisin bread and smoothed honey butter across its surface.

"Here's something light." She set two pieces on a napkin down in front of me. "When you get back, we can cook up a fresh pot of soup. It's supposed to get chilly tonight, and I've got a bunch of veggies that need to be used up before they spoil."

"Maybe we can try out that Chai, too?"

"Splendid," she said, busying herself in the kitchen. I detected a hint of pain in her right hip and decided she wasn't feeling as well as she led me to believe.

After delivering the last of the crumbs into my mouth, I finished off my tea and stood. "Thanks for everything," I told her, tossing my napkin into the garbage and setting the cup on the counter.

She rinsed a few dishes and dismissed me. "Get out there and enjoy the day!"

．．◆．．．

Sunshine was abundant and warm as I set out on the footpath toward Liberation Garden. I took in fresh woodsy scents: floral blossoms awaiting pollination, sweet saps of juniper and pine, and decaying leaves leaching nutrients into the ages old soil. Two baby woodpeckers chipped at bark in search of a delicious insect meal, the parents unseen but surely watching from a nearby branch. Pairs of squirrels chased one another up and down tree trunks, rustling the underbrush as they played.

Nearing the cemetery, a semi's horn blared, severing my engagement with the spirit of the land. I thought the trail led deeper into the woods but the bustle of traffic meant the main road was close. On the far side of the plot, a family of deer rested peacefully, apparently undisturbed by commuters trekking along the strip of asphalt in rolling metal boxes that carried them down the side of the mountain into town.

I was guided by invisible forces to the middle of the graveyard where Melani "Lani" Marseille had met her final resting place. She was clearly the first to take residence, and all the other headstone markers emanated out from hers in concentric rings.

Small patches of light shining through the trees had dried sections of the grass below. I selected the driest real estate and sat cross legged. Breathing slow and deep, I lowered my pulse, and quieted my mind.

Lines from Thoreau's Walden rose up from somewhere within. *I went to the woods because I wished to live deliberately, to front only the essential facts of life, and see if I could not learn what it had to teach, and not, when I came to die, discover that I had not lived.*

Relaxing my muscles, I closed my eyes. A previously practiced mediation helped guide me to an inner sanctuary where the nagging voice of insufficiency was snuffed. There, I found contentment. Acceptance. Freedom.

Before I was ready to let it go, the moment was lost, the sounds of my environment dragging me back to reality. I flung my eyes open, suddenly uneasy and vulnerable. The sun's orbit had shifted, leaving me in shadow.

I picked up my pencil and started writing. My stream of free word association began with *Warm* and ended three pages later when a cool breeze touched my bare shoulders. With the dampness of evening settling in, it was time to head home.

In the distance, a red fox wriggled out from a tree crevice and crossed my path. It stopped momentarily, stared at me, and moved on.

·· ♦ ♦ ♦ ··

Onions and garlic wafted from the kitchen as I unlaced shoes caked with mud. I found Aunt Jeannine at the counter cutting butternut squash, her fingers stained an orangey-yellow.

"I wasn't sure how long you'd be," she said, moving on to dicing celery, and then carrots.

Hours had slipped away, gone forever, propelling me toward an uncertain future.

"Maybe we can put this in with all the rest of it." I held up the mushroom I'd found.

Aunt Jeannine grinned at my discovery. "Did you find it, or did it find you?"

"I suppose it was mutual."

"Any others around?" she asked.

"Not that I saw."

Aunt Jeannine scratched at its flesh and the surface blued. "You won't want to add this little one to the soup."

I looked at my hands and wondered whether or not I had brought them anywhere near my mouth. "Is it poisonous?"

"Nope, just better to be eaten alone." She washed the stump with water and patted it dry, then placed it on the ledge of the kitchen window. "Ever taken a psychedelic trip?"

"No." Images flashed in my mind: tiny pills shaped like hearts; dehydrated teens passed out on the dance floor; paramedics poking IVs into collapsed veins. "But, I know a few people who have. They said it was scary."

Aunt Jeannine found my response hilarious and let me know with unbridled laughter. "I'm not mocking you, dear." She limped about the kitchen, adding vegetables to a stock pot of water that had been brought to boil.

"Trips can't be good or bad, they just *are*." She stirred salt and pepper into the broth. "Ever heard the story of how we ended up with this place?"

"Vic told me the owner died in a freak accident."

Aunt Jeannine nodded. "Lightning. A priest, mind you. And God stuck him dead." She sampled the soup and dropped in some bay leaves. "Remi was visiting South America when it happened. That was way back, when he was still an apprentice. Father Edward was Remi's first. Embalmed in the very place he once owned."

"What's in South America?" I asked.

"Soul renewal. My sister Lani was there, helping a medicine man with *ayahuasca* ceremonies."

195

"Lani?" I blurted before I could contain it.

"I take it you've met."

"What happened?"

She turned to look out the window while she dipped into her memory.

I shifted in my chair, wondering if I had broken an unspoken rule.

"I didn't think much of it when she disappeared. Lani was good for that. We would go months without talking. Then, she'd turn up out of nowhere, often in a different state, sometimes another country all together. She didn't tell anyone when she took off to Peru."

Not interrupting, I watched as Aunt Jeannine poured effervescent white wine into two glasses, carbonation bubbles rippling the surface before dissolving. I suspected her daily drinks were to combat not just physical pain.

"Pacari, her shaman, disappeared one day. Gone. Vanished out of thin air." She paused. "Lani felt forsaken. She slipped into a deep depression after that. I convinced her to move here, to get a job, to be close in case she needed anything."

Aunt Jeannine turned her back to the window and leaned against the counter for support. "Your uncle was beside himself when she came though our doors in a body bag."

My curiosity boiled over. "How did she die?"

"Her life was taken." She brought the wineglass to her mouth before continuing. "I believe the truth will be revealed some day. Cults aren't easy to penetrate from the outside. But when loyalty breaks down, they will start to turn on one another."

"Who are *they*?" I asked.

Aunt Jeannine shrugged.

"Why Lani?"

"Have you ever met anyone that just had it? Good looks. Great vibes. Excited to be alive."

Sadie came to mind.

"That was my sister. They were all so jealous of her."

"Jealous enough to kill?" I tried to imagine being that envious of someone and thought of Camila. Aunt Jeannine swallowed the rest of her wine; mine was still full.

"Anyway," she said. "Let's change the dial here."

I had more questions but decided not to pry.

"We've got to get ready for the new moon."

36

It was just the two of us, again. Uncle Remi skipped dinner to catch up on work he'd missed while lecturing at the convention. When we were finished, Aunt Jeannine ladled vegetables and broth into a plastic container for him to enjoy later. She always cleaned up right after cooking and I wondered if Vic had learned that habit from her. I hadn't talked to him all week though I'd tried to get in touch. I was upset with him for avoiding me.

I piled pounds of Aunt Jeannine's crystals into a wheelbarrow and shuttled them outside for her. She led the way, holding our Chai lattes, the steam rising up with scents of vanilla and licorice.

"Know much about lunar cycles?" she asked, stopping at the stone altar she used for charging her metaphysical tools.

I shook my head no, watching her unload jagged chunks of earth. Some looked like nothing more than cracked open rocks of what I would consider rather ordinary.

"The new moon is perfect for setting goals. It's a time for fresh beginnings."

From her sack, she pulled out slices of orange and lemon, a vial of sea salt, and a ceramic basin she said was for water.

"These are offerings I set out to give thanks. Less messy than animal sacrifice." She winked and slurped her tea. "What do you think?"

I brought it to my lips to form an opinion. Before I could tell her I liked it, Aunt Jeannine ducked behind a trellis of honeysuckle, her scissors snipping away.

"I saw a red fox in the woods," I said.

"Ah, the great problem solver," she offered, her voice hushed by the thick foliage between us.

"I figured you would know what it meant."

"Only you can know that, dear." She made her way back to the altar, her basket overflowing with beautiful blooms. "But when a vixen appears, she represents the balance between persistence and patience, virtues that, when in unison, work to solve a difficult situation."

She placed her tarot deck among the plethora of other items. The sight of it made me flinch.

"I came here to find clarity," I told her, my eyes lingering on the cards. "Lately, I've been feeling more lost than ever."

"You sound like Lani," Aunt Jeannine said, her sister continuing to occupy her thoughts. "That's why she was purging in Peru."

"What do you mean by purging?"

"A magic root grows in the Amazon. The indigenous people make their sacrament from it. Cleans you from the inside, out." She chuckled, recalling her husband's mystical experience. "Your uncle had the runs for days after. He said his plane trip home was excruciating. Especially for the rest of the passengers."

Aunt Jeannine took a seat on the bench nearby, enjoying Chai between delivering details about the entheogenic plant.

"Basically, the process starts with reducing food intake to a strict vegetarian diet, and then tapering that off to a fast prior to ingesting the potion. As *La Madre* starts to work, it forces you to expel anything harmful from your body; that includes physically, mentally, and emotionally."

"Why was Uncle Remi there? He always seems so balanced. And happy."

"You can thank the ayahuasca for that."

"What about Lani?"

"Many junkies go there to defeat addiction."

"She was a junkie?"

"Aren't we all?" Aunt Jeannine pulled a bar of chocolate from her bag. It was the special Tuscan brand she had hidden away when we last looted her stash. After folding the box open, she removed the foil, broke off a piece, and placed it on the altar.

"Just a small amount for the Gods," she said, popping a square into her mouth.

"I think I need some help from La Madre," I told her.

Aunt Jeannine smiled. "Grandma may not always give you what you want, but she'll certainly give you what you need."

"I just want answers," I said.

"Yes, dear. But are you asking the right questions?"

"How do I know?"

Aunt Jeannine lifted her mug and drained its contents. She retrieved her tarot deck from the altar and

200

began shuffling in her rhythmic, almost intoxicating fashion. After what seemed like an eternity, she addressed me. "Let's consult the cosmos."

Before I had time to protest, she turned the first card over. "The Hanged Man."

"I don't like the sound of it," I said, apprehension like sludge in my throat.

"Relax, Tally. You're ready."

I shook my head ever so slightly. "I trust you."

"I'm but a conduit. Trust the universe, my dear."

She revealed the next card while I fought off my nerves.

"The Emperor," Aunt Jeannine dictated, a quiver in her voice drawing me to look at her. "I usually present all three cards before interacting with my client but I feel inclined to speak now. Is that okay?"

I gave her permission with the nod of my head.

"This is the past position." She pointed to the Hanged Man. "He represents powerlessness. Surrender and acceptance are his motto. When I first drew it, I immediately thought of your journey to Colorado, leaving familiarity behind, and conceding to the universe's wishes."

Aunt Jeannine paused and looked down at the second card, for almost too long.

"Then, we have this," she finally said. "In your present position. The Emperor – embodiment of male energy: dominance, authority, and leadership."

"Who is it?" I asked.

"In this instance, the past card may be more of a recent past. Not what I had originally envisioned." She looked dismayed. "Serves me right. Anyway, before I get ahead of myself –" She turned the third card to progress the reading and her jaw dropped open.

I stared, analyzing her disbelief.

"I'm sorry," she whispered. A frown dimpled her cheeks. "I didn't realize how much you'd been struggling."

"What do you mean?" I shrieked.

"The Fool is in your future position. All three are Major Arcana. In a deck of seventy-eight, there are twenty-two majors and fifty-six minors."

Get to the point! I'd had it with the suspense.

"It's unusual to draw a Major card for every position. When that happens, it often suggests that events taking place in your life will be in the hands of destiny. In other words, there is nothing you can do to alter their course." Rain clouds congregated into a grey blanket above while she let the gravity of her deduction sink in. "Even though we search for meaning and resolution, there are things we simply have to accept."

Thunder clapped in the distance.

"Lack of answers to the questions you ask may mean that you aren't fully prepared for dealing with the inevitable."

"I am prepared!" I argued.

Aunt Jeannine studied the spread as she came to her feet. "*A fool thinks himself to be wise, but a wise man knows himself to be a fool,*" she said, stopping at the altar once more before weaving through the backyard to the house.

As I digested her words, Mother Nature penned a follow-up message. *Don't think too much,* she warned, sending with it a pack of howling coyotes. I obliged Her and took off for the house.

"That thing's been ringing all day," Aunt Jeannine yelled after me as I darted up the stairs. Vic hung up before I could answer; he'd already tried me five times.

Wanting to prove a point to him, I switched the volume to silent and tucked my cell away. He had ignored me all week. It was his turn to do the waiting.

⋅⋅◆◆◆⋅⋅

By Monday morning, Vic had called a total of fifteen times. I listened to his three voicemails on my way to the mortuary – two were hang ups and one was, "Call me back. It's urgent."

When I got around to returning his calls, it was lunch time. He answered on the first ring.

"Where have you been?" he demanded, not waiting for a reply. "I've been trying to get ahold of you."

"The same could be said for you. You just disappeared."

"Have you seen the news?" he asked without justifying his absence.

"No."

"She's dead. Camila's dead!"

"What? How?"

"Her house was set on fire."

"Slow down," I ordered, unable to process Vic's barrage. He didn't.

"F.C.P.D. took Max into custody this morning."

"Max?"

"He was on the security camera."

"We saw him leave," I protested.

"That was almost a week ago. This happened last night."

"Why would he want to kill her?"

"You heard what she said to him!"

"I'm heading over there."

"What? No."

"Yes."

"Why, Tally? There's nothing more to be done. They found the body last night. Nash was there with ATF."

I was already tuning him out as I penned a note to let Uncle Remi know I would be back after lunch.

"Tally, don't do this," Vic pleaded, my truck's engine roaring to life.

"I have to. See you there."

37

Traffic was mild until I neared the property, rubberneckers slowing down to gawk as black smoke billowed from the mansion that had become the scene of Ft. Collins' newest homicide. Satellite-topped news vans crowded nearby streets, journalists delivering their stories as cameramen panned tripod-mounted video equipment from left to right and back again. Vic flagged me down as I made a parking space out of a stretch of overgrown weeds.

"Thanks for meeting me," I said, pulling myself from the truck cab.

"Of course." He shut my door behind me.

First responders had secured canary yellow tape around the perimeter to preserve forensic evidence. Rain slickers the same yellow as the barricade tape protected journalists as they commentated, a light sprinkle doing what it could to help firefighters extinguish the last of the flames that refused to die out.

My shoes squeaked in the wet grass as I approached the police line, camera flashes fluttering like soft lightning.

"It's unclear where the fire originated, although there has been a lot of activity near the garage which is on the lower east side –" her calculated voice trailed off.

Another reporter standing under an umbrella picked up the story from a different perspective. "She just lost her husband last week to heart troubles," he said, "and now the family will be dealing with this unfortunate news."

"Bitch got what she deserved," Vic spat, the hood of his jacket swallowing his head, his eyes smoldering with disdain.

An argument unfolding on the steps leading up to the house stole everyone's attention.

"Sir," an officer barked. "You can't go in there."

Martin stood his ground. "This is my fatha's house. I'll do what I want!"

"I understand you are upset. We are just here to do our job."

He threw his head back and laughed. "You obviously need some help. News flash, pig. Camila was a murderah!"

The crowd gasped.

"I can't imagine the stress you are under right now." This time, it was a female who addressed Martin, her hair pulled back in a tight bun, a business suit proclaiming her rank. "I assure you, we are following every lead we've been given."

"Bullshit!" Martin shouted at her.

She'd had enough. "If you don't leave on your own recognizance, Mr. Esdan, we will be forced to arrest you."

"Oh, yeah? Fuck you, then." He turned and faced the audience of hungry sharks hanging on to every piece of bait he was tossing into frenzied waters.

"You guys want something to report? Go talk to Tally at Forester Funeral Home. That's F-o-r..."

Martin's voice grew faint as Vic scrambled to navigate me through the crowd, his hands gripping the backs of my arms to steer me.

"What an asshole!" Vic bellowed when we reached the road. He drove the side of his fist into my truck's rear quarter panel.

"It's all my fault," I managed to say, the shifting of my equilibrium causing me to lose my footing.

"I've got you," Vic said before I collapsed onto him, the world around me fading to a hole of darkness. "You're going to be alright."

38

I laid low at Vic's house while Uncle Remi dodged inquiries about a woman named Tally who was said to have inside information regarding the death of Flynn Dabbencove.

"I have no idea what the man's son is talking about," he told several correspondents looking for their next story. "Dabbencove was embalmed at my facility before being returned to the medical examiner, per his official request. We only do what is asked of our clients and will remain neutral in your ongoing investigative reporting. If you have additional questions, please direct them elsewhere."

Uncle Remi eloquently delivered his message and then returned to business as usual. Everything he said had been truthful. He didn't know a thing about Dabbencove or Camila. I was thankful I'd kept him in the dark.

When Aunt Jeannine dropped by Vic's with my clothes, she was happy to provide updates. "I think your uncle likes it in the limelight."

"Him and Darla both," I told her. "Maybe we should start a reality show and make a million bucks."

"You can count me out."

"Same here. I've had enough drama for one lifetime."

Vic had set the record straight, smoothing out some details and completely omitting others. He denied that we had any notion Camila could have been involved in her husband's death.

"Basically," he said, "I told Remi that Camila came by Forester and then Martin called looking for his father. He said he was concerned about the way Flynn died so you told him to contact the authorities."

I thought about the USB drive Martin had threatened me with. Vic still didn't know about it. "What if someone saw us at Camila's house?"

"No one saw us. Besides, everyone thinks Martin is crazy. We should leave it at that."

"But he's not, Vic. This is all becoming one gigantic lie."

"What are we supposed to do, Tally? We don't know the whole truth."

He was right. For the sake of Uncle Remi's livelihood, for my safety, and for Vic's sanity, it had to be left alone.

Frustrated, I turned on the TV and flipped through several channels until I found a local news outlet. Max's mug shot filled the screen.

"The FBI has been called on for help with what appears to be a homicide perpetrated by one of most decorated agents in the department of justice, Maxwell Levi Homestead." The bubbly newscaster's head jerked as she enunciated each word, delivering facts about a man she'd only known for as many seconds that it took to read the prompting monitor in front of her.

"You just can't let it go, can you?" Vic jabbed. I ignored him.

"Here with us today is the district attorney who will be presenting evidence on Camila's behalf," she went on, "assuming there will be a trial. Won't this go to a jury, Dr. Alby?"

"Certainly, it will," Dr. Alby confirmed. "When someone viciously beats another person and then sets them on fire, the people want justice. Mr. Homestead is a federal agent and very well respected in the law enforcement community. But that doesn't mean he gets immunity. It's my duty to see that Camila is rightfully represented as she isn't here to defend herself."

"Have you spoken to the police chief yet, Doctor?"

"Yes, Frieda. I have. Charlie will be giving us whatever resources necessary for a thorough investigation, and to retrace any phone records leading up to the event. Of course, we need manpower to obtain statements from witnesses who knew the victim and also those who knew her accuser so we can start to form our defense. Mr. Howes has always been very attentive to my office's needs."

The feed switched back to Frieda who thanked District Attorney Thornton Alby for his time. She continued on to the next story about prairie dogs testing positive for bubonic plague in the Boulder area.

I clicked off the television and stood to peer out the window at another sunny day I chose not to enjoy.

Vic wrapped me up in a hug. "Everything's going to be fine."

Camila had gotten what she deserved, but I couldn't help feeling angry. "I'm glad it's over. It's just that she'll never be held accountable for killing her husband. Even if

Martin can prove his father was poisoned, there's nothing that can be done. She's gone."

"The world is a better place without her," he told me. "It's time to move on."

39

Vic and I worked on his documentary into the early morning hours, running through clips of footage he and Rowan shot before my trip to Colorado had even been an idea.

"What attracted you to film?" I asked him, looking off into the distance to rest my eyes; fuzzy spots danced around on the wall.

"Honestly, I'm not sure. It always called to me."

"Is this your first project?"

"It's the first one I'm proud of."

"I'd like to see some other things you've made."

"No way."

"Why not? I won't judge you."

"Most of it is really dark and depressing."

"I can relate," I told him.

"Doubt it. You would run far, far away. Trust me." He turned in his chair to face me, the stubble of day old facial hair growth shadowing his jaw in the glow of the monitor. "I really like you, Tally."

"I like you, too," I told him, leaning in for a kiss. His tongue gently swirled around mine.

"Let's go to bed," he grinned, nuzzling my neck with beard bristles that tickled my skin into goosebumps.

Vic made sweet romance novel love to me, first by massaging the muscles in my feet and calves with his hands, then by soothing the ache between my thighs with his mouth. Just before I reached orgasm, he mounted me.

Conscious of his sister being down the hallway, Vic stifled my moans with his hand. His mouth opened in elation as he pulled out. We cleaned ourselves up and Vic drifted off to sleep almost instantly.

I was still wide awake an hour later. I'd thought little about Camila while we churned out scenes for Vic's film, but at four in the morning, she had me searching the internet for information.

Max had been officially charged with Camila's death and the city was in the process of setting a date for the trial. Dr. Alby promised to make an example of Max and he was living up to it. The media did its part in running a smear campaign, every local news outlet plastered with the worst picture of Max they could find. Along with his psychotic photo, there was always a caption with the same message: *DEA agent indicted for murder of ex-lover; refuses to issue statement.*

All of the articles were mashed up versions of one another, each with the same data stitched together by different authors. On an obscure website, I found something that no one else had published – a statement from Martin.

When asked about the loss of both parents in such a short period of time, he responded, "I'm not sad. I'm furious. And I will get to the bottom of this."

To the public, it sounded like retribution. But I knew the real meaning. I imagined Martin was grateful for Max, and glad that Camila was dead. What he really wanted was the truth about his father to come out.

Even though Martin had outed me, I understood why. He felt threatened. In a way, it was my fault. I didn't deliver on my promise.

I dressed and tiptoed down the hallway to Vic's office. The 911 recording wouldn't bring Flynn back, but I was determined to reconcile.

I found the file, connected my phone to Vic's computer via the USB cable, and clicked the transfer button. An error message popped up. Of course it wouldn't be that simple. I asked Google why.

Apparently, the WAV format was owned by Mac's biggest rival, Microsoft. I needed to convert the file to one my iPhone would recognize. After reading through a few posts on a forum, I found a protocol written by someone named HackintoshGuru. I was thankful for his instruction and followed his step-by-step guide.

Once the MP3 was created, I crossed my fingers and hit the transfer button again. This time, it worked. Before I could disconnect my phone, I was interrupted.

"Sex turns me into an insomniac, too," the gritty female voice behind me rasped.

I clicked out of the window I was reading and spun around. "I didn't mean –"

Xandra put her hand up to cut me off. "Everyone needs a good hard fuck now and then."

I felt myself blush. Wisps of smoke trailed out from her joint, the cherry beaming a fiery red as she puffed.

"Here." Her hand reached out toward me. "This'll do you right."

I dropped my phone into my pocket, put the computer to sleep, and turned the monitor off before joining her at the doorway. The first toke hit me straight in the chest and I gagged.

Xandra smiled. "First time?"

"No," I said, between a string of coughs.

She took the joint back. "Probably the tobacco. My throat is used to it by now."

"Tobacco?"

"I dilute Vic's herb with it. The shit he grows is just too damn strong."

Nicotine stormed my head. "Vic grows pot?"

"Oops," she replied unapologetically. "What are you up to in here?"

"Trying to find friends in the area," I lied.

"I'll be your friend," Xandra said, winking. "Ask Vic, I get more chicks than he does."

She swept my hair out of my face and brought the joint to my mouth. "Difference is, I don't mind sharing."

Pressured, I took another drag. My unease was palpable. When I could no longer handle her advances, I fled. "Goodnight," I whispered, brushing past her.

As I tucked myself beneath sheets cold from my absence, my thoughts lingered on being intimate with a woman. I could find beauty in the female figure, but that didn't necessarily equate to lesbian sex.

While trying to decide my feelings on the subject, Vic's beefy arm lifted up and curled around me.

40

I woke up alone at an unknown hour and dressed into sweatpants and a tank-top, the same outfit I had worn for several days in a row. The house was quiet, my footfalls the only noise as my strides carried me down the hallway to the main living area. Vic wasn't in the kitchen or his computer room. I walked over to the formal dining area which I'd never once seen used and yanked the blackout curtain aside. The driveway was empty.

Back in Vic's room, I dug through a pile of dirty clothes that had started to collect in the corner. My purse was all the way at the bottom, my cell phone inside it. There was an unread text message: "Went to the gym. Got a few errands to run. Be back later." It had been sent almost three hours beforehand, at nine that morning.

I suddenly realized that I'd forgotten to erase my search history on Vic's computer the night before. He would be livid if he found out I was still prying into Dabbencove's case.

I sprinted across the house to his office. Several minutes passed as the beast chattered away, processing thousands of files and organizing all its programs. The home screen came up just as a vehicle pulled into the driveway.

I clicked open the browser and toggled through the tool bar. The engine rumbled for a half a minute in the drive before it cut. My pulse racing, I shut down Vic's computer and clicked the monitor off before rushing into the kitchen to pull out leftovers from the night before.

The front door opened and closed, keys jangling more loudly as they approached.

"Hey," Vic said, his tone flat.

"Hi!" I replied, almost too chipper. "I was just making some lunch for us."

"Oh, cool. I'm starving." He swigged the last few sips of water from his sports bottle. "I thought you might sleep all day."

I laughed but my hands were shaking and I knocked cauliflower onto the floor below me.

"I didn't know cooking was that much of a work out."

"Huh?"

"How come you're out of breath?"

"Oh. My phone was ringing and I thought it was you." I didn't like the way I was beginning to construct lies so effortlessly.

"Who was it?" he asked.

"Who was what?" I was barely listening, my nerves still short circuiting.

"Who was calling?"

"Oh, right. It wasn't anyone. Just my imagination."

"I hate when that happens."

I was glad he agreed before I slipped further into deceit.

"It's like when you swear someone said something but they weren't even talking. Or when you watch a scary movie by yourself and think someone is breaking in."

"Stress-induced auditory hallucinations," I told him, pleased that the conversation was moving in a new direction.

"How clinical."

"You can thank Sadie, the aspiring psychologist. I've been subjected to many of her post lecture lessons. She's actually dating her professor."

"Nice! Hot for teacher."

No one could accuse her of not getting the most out of her college education.

41

Aunt Jeannine answered the phone swiftly, talking before I was given a chance at hello. "I miss having you around. When are you coming by?"

"I'm on my way up the canyon now, actually. Just giving a courtesy call."

"Nonsense! You're welcome anytime you'd like."

I hadn't worked or even been to Uncle Remi's property since the media manhunt Martin had called for. And the last time I'd spoken to my aunt was when she came by Vic's, her backseat piled high with my belongings.

I stopped into a teahouse and, with the help of the brew master, blended a few concoctions that I thought Aunt Jeannine would enjoy. At the nearby wine shop, I picked up a bottle of Purple Cowboy for her to try. Aside from beverage oriented items, I bought a beautiful succulent that was marked with a label touting its requirement of *minimal watering and care.*

Things mandating energy input, like fish and puppies, never appealed to me as gifts. I found it unfair to bestow ownership on the recipient without their consent. However, the butterflies etched around the pot caught my attention, its raku fired glaze iridescent in the sunlight when I walked past a clearance table set up outside the flower shop I'd parked in front of.

The other purchases I made were ordinary groceries, including whole dairy cream, stone ground bread, free-range eggs, and a few pounds of locally sourced chicken raised and slaughtered only miles from the supermarket. Even if I could save them a trip to town, it wasn't enough to repay them for their hospitality.

I turned onto Sentinel and a large bird greeted me by circling above. White tail feathers contrasted its dark plumage, the wingspan a number of feet across. I swung my truck around and backed into my old parking spot.

"I thought you were an apparition," Aunt Jeannine said from the front stoop, the awning shading her from what was shaping up to be a warm day even for summer. "Are you moving back in?"

"No, these are for you," I told her, gathering bags in my arms and kicking the passenger door shut.

Her eyes were fixed on the sky. "Now, isn't that special?"

I placed the goods on the concrete landing and shielded my eyes as I followed her gaze.

"Kinda early for migration," she continued. "Ever seen a bald eagle before?"

As the bird flew closer to the canopy, I spotted its white head and yellow talons. "Only on dollar bills."

I collected the groceries and jockeyed through the door while she held it open for me. The house was far less tidy than I expected, a reminder that my aunt's medical battle likely rendered her immobile when it was at its worst.

"I picked up some devil's claw in town. The tea shop employee said it would be good for your inflammation." Setting everything on the counter, I rummaged through the canisters of tea until I found the one called *LocoMotion,* its constituents the rheumatoid fighting trifecta of willow bark, eucalyptus, and boswellia.

"Shall we try it out?" she asked.

After stocking her kitchen with the items I'd brought, we sipped tea at the dining table.

"How are you occupying your time?"

"Unwisely," I confessed. An envelope with my name on it was stacked above other mail parcels. "Is this stuff mine?"

"Oh, yes. I've been meaning to bring those by."

I leafed through them.

"One is from me," Aunt Jeannine said. "That one there. Hand it to me."

While she removed the stamp to save for a later date, I slid my finger inside the closure of an envelope marked with the words *Open Immediately.*

The document, printed on police department letterhead, went on to say that the gun I had been charged for possessing was traced back to Front Range Gun Club. Its owner, Brad Dempsey, was glad to have had his property returned and wasn't interested in filing a lawsuit.

I refolded the letter, tucked it back into its envelope, and tossed it onto the pile. Taking another swallow of tea, I constructed a scenario inside my head.

Camila had lured me to the range. She had planted the gun. She had called the police with a description of my vehicle which set the BOLO in motion. And while I was

221

locked up, she had put in the order for Flynn to be embalmed, any evidence of foul play washed away.

Aunt Jeannine cut into my thoughts. "The greeting card might be a bit redundant after what I'm about to say to you." The statement brought my eyes to hers. "Vic and I had a long conversation."

"Okay," I said. She took my hand.

"We both think that you could use some counseling."

I pulled away. "For what?"

"Tally, don't be offended. People get therapy all the time."

I crossed my arms and looked over to my left. On the back of the couch, Eileen was basking in the sun. She was completely oblivious to the turmoil of modern man.

"Your troubles will catch up with you no matter how far you leave them behind."

"I needed to get away," I told her.

"Your environment does have a part to play, I'll admit. I absolutely loathed California. But changing your scenery doesn't get to the root of the problem." From the corner of my eye, I saw her bring her hand to her chest. "It doesn't get to what's inside."

"So, what exactly did Vic say?"

"Let's not get into the details. It won't do you any good."

"I've got to get back to town."

"Are you upset with me?"

"Of course not." I was fuming on the inside when I stood and hugged her.

42

I darted into the first liquor store I saw and chose a cheap bottle of green apple vodka. Without a mixer, I downed warm shots in the nearby parking lot of a bustling steakhouse.

Drunk, I dozed off for a few hours, the sun replaced by the smoky grey of dusk when I woke. I was still mad at Vic who had been calling since I decided to kill my ringer around four; it was almost ten. My phone lit up the cab of my truck as he tried my line again.

"Yeah?" I answered distractedly, turning the key over.

"Hey. Where are you?"

"Out."

"I haven't heard from you all day."

"Oh," was all I said.

"Is everything okay?"

"Tell me about your conversation with my aunt."

"What do you mean?" he asked, nonplussed.

"The one where you told her I should see a shrink!"

"No, I never said that."

"Well what exactly did you say, then? That I'm unstable? Reckless? Crazy?"

"Tally, why don't you come home and –"

"Home, Vic? I live in Florida!" Tears threatened.

"I'm sorry, I just –"

I cut him off again. "You really hurt me."

A couple linked arms and made their way to a vehicle parked a few spaces away in the row ahead of me. He opened the door for his dolled-up date, snaked around the back of the car, and took the driver's side. Through the windshield, I watched them kiss.

"I'm so sorry," he pleaded. "I shouldn't have talked about you behind your back."

"Fuck you, Vic." I ended the call and jacked up the volume on the radio, the music blaring while I screeched my tires in reverse.

·•••••·

My eyes slowly cracked open to surroundings I didn't recognize. Cotton balls lined the inside of my mouth which hadn't seen water in almost twenty-four hours and it felt like I'd been hit in the head with a hammer.

I brought my fingers to just above my left eye. There was a huge knot and dried blood. When my vision focused, I found the culprit of my injury.

The details were patchy, but there was only one possible conclusion: I'd swerved off the road, struck the tree, and passed out. The damage wasn't too bad; just a smashed headlight and a dented bumper.

When I checked my phone, I wasn't expecting to see Sadie's name. According to my call log, we'd chatted for eleven minutes. There wasn't a single second of remembrance that I could stir up.

"What the fuck happened last night?" I said when she answered on the first ring, an atypically quick response that was the result of her worry.

"I've been waiting for you to call me back. You were hysterical and in no shape to drive."

"I guess so," I told her, whiplash settling into my neck.

"Did you make it to the Stupa?"

"The what?"

"That's exactly what I said. I looked it up online. It's some sort of Buddhist shrine."

"I don't see any shrine," I reported, thankful for the location of my accident. A few yards head, the unpaved road ended abruptly before dropping off to a ravine. I cringed at the thought of plummeting to my death.

"I'm glad you had enough sense to pull over before you became a statistic."

The decision to stop hadn't been mine, but I let her believe that it was. She didn't need to know about the collision. No one did.

"I tried to talk you out of driving but you had already made up your mind to go there," she went on. "You said someone had mentioned it while you were waiting in line at the package store."

Scattered fragments came to me. I was eavesdropping on two men that told the liquor store cashier they were going to a meditative retreat in Red Feather and wanted some booze to get them by. Their wives had signed them up for a couple's workshop that was supposed to enrich their relationships. The guys didn't see the point of vegetarianism and chemical abstinence, even if it was only for one weekend while they worked on connecting with their spouses.

"Good luck," the bag-eyed clerk said as they scooped up more than a dozen shooters of tequila and headed off with their ulterior motives.

Agitation set in as I made my way to the counter to transact my purchase. All I wanted to do was tie one on, and those two assholes were standing between me and the register, telling Josh, the cashier, a bunch of shit that didn't pertain to him. I set the bottle down hard, my passive aggressive way of letting him know I was sick of waiting in line while he carried on with customers in meaningless drivel.

"Eight seventy-five," he requested in a throaty cigarette-tainted voice. "Ever been to the Shambhala Mountain Center to see the Great Stupa?" He laughed as he said *Stupa.*

I handed him exact change and exited the shop without a word.

"I'm glad you're okay," Sadie said, interrupting my backtracking thoughts.

"I'm in one piece, if that's what you mean."

"That's a start. Now that you're sober, tell me what's going on."

"I probably just overreacted."

"I'll be the one to decide."

"Well, I told you about Vic."

"I thought we were past him?"

"I've been staying at his house."

"You're not staying with your uncle?"

"I am. I mean, I was. It's complicated."

"You're choosing to make it complicated, Tally."

226

I hadn't told Sadie about the Camila ordeal and decided it wasn't worth rehashing. That chapter was closed. And I knew if I brought up Aunt Jeannine's counseling recommendation, Sadie would certainly agree. I had no interest in her clinical evaluation.

"I feel more in control today," I said. "I'm going to create some space with Vic and stay these last few weeks with my uncle."

"That sounds like a solid idea." She muffled the phone and ordered her coffee black, requesting it to be extra hot and freshly brewed.

I revved up my truck and pulled away from the guardrail. "I just don't want any sympathy."

"Tally, get a grip. They care about you and want to see you well." She thanked the drive-in teller and coins clanked against the hard surface of whatever she dropped them into.

My pocket of good cell service waned and static filled the line. Before I lost the call, Sadie had one more nugget of wisdom to deliver. "Before you leave there, you need get your shit together."

I embraced the peace of the mountains while contemplating her advice. At that elevation, leaves were already beginning to take on the coppery tones of fall. I felt more confused than ever, like I was running in place.

I hadn't yet found my destination when I spotted a sign that told me I was nearing 287, which would lead me away from the canyon and back to town. I had sought the Stupa's positive healing, but it wanted nothing to do with my negativity.

When cell service normalized, I picked up my phone and called Aunt Jeannine. I wanted to thank her for her concern and tell her she was right. I needed to get back into a routine. I needed her guidance. And if I could stay with them for awhile longer, I would be able to get on track before heading home to Florida.

"Hello?" the voice half shouted. I looked down at my screen to see if I had called the wrong number.

"Tally, its Darla. Your name came up on caller ID."

I instantly knew something was wrong.

"How've you been, doll?"

"Fine, I guess. Is Aunt Jeannine around?"

Darla hesitated. "Tally, there's been an accident."

43

The parking garage elevator doors couldn't close fast enough as I rapped on the button for the main floor, the only other rider aboard a hospital employee decked out in seafoam green scrubs. She paid no attention to my lack of patience.

I pushed through the sliding doors before they opened completely and jogged to the concierge desk at the center of the lobby. "Forester," I wheezed. "Jeannine Forester."

"And you are?" the desk clerk asked, her eyes fixed on the computer monitor.

"I'm her daughter," I lied.

"Head down that way," she pointed, uninterested in confirming my identity. "Take the elevator up to the fifth floor. She's in room three."

I didn't thank her and hurried down the hallway she told me to follow. Only hours after I'd left her house, Aunt Jeannine had tripped on her way up the loft stairs. She then tumbled backward, broke her leg, and hit her head against the bottom steps. Uncle Remi found her bleeding and unconscious.

"Is she alright?" I asked Darla over the phone, mashing the gas pedal to the floorboard and weaving in and out of traffic as I raced to the hospital.

"We won't know until she wakes up from surgery. It's kind of a miracle," she said, "if you believe in that sort of thing. They found a brain tumor we had no idea about."

"A brain tumor?"

"Yep. The doc went in and removed it. Said it was a basic procedure. Well, basic as far as brain surgery goes. But here's the kicker. That golf ball sized growth could have been the reason for all these terrible symptoms she's had the past few years."

"The M.S.?"

"That's the one."

I exited the elevator on the intensive care unit and located room three which was the first one past the nurse's desk. An extraordinarily tall, matronly framed woman with bleached blond curly hair and a stethoscope draped around her neck eyed me out over her reading glasses as she scribbled notes on a clipboard. If someone told me she was an ex-wrestler, I wouldn't have questioned it.

Machines inside sterile bedroom chambers tracked pulses, breathing, and brain functions. The squeaky floors reeked of disinfectant, their surfaces scrubbed clean of contagions. Pastel colored art clung to bright white walls, their images subtle and uninteresting, the subjects feigning joy. No music played and, other than the beeping of monitors, an eerie silence fell over the entire unit. When the staff spoke, they whispered, adding to the ominous tone set by dimmed lights.

Uncle Remi stood close to the mechanized bed, the rail on his side dropped down so he could hold Aunt Jeannine's hand. Plastic tubes snaked up from her arms, some delivering powerful pain meds, others for hydration. Bloodstained gauze bandages wrapped her head and a sling supported the weight of her casted left leg. I imagined the pain of snapping a bone completely in half and shivered.

A rosy faced woman stood next to Uncle Remi; she looked a lot like Aunt Jeannine. On his other side was Nina, wistful and teary-eyed.

"I think we're at our limit," the conservatively dressed woman I hadn't met yet said as she moved around the foot of the bed and exited.

I took her place next to my uncle and side hugged him. He continued to hold his wife's hand, placing his free arm around me and pulling me close.

"Jeannie," he whispered, "we're all here for you."

Her eyes remained closed, a greasy strip of Vaseline lining the slit of her lids to keep them moist. The anesthesiologist had placed her in a medically induced coma to immobilize her while the brain recovered.

The hulking ICU nurse stopped in. She squeezed Nina's shoulder with a huge paw as though they knew each other, and then, without speaking, manually checked Aunt Jeannine's blood pressure and heart rate with her stethoscope. She documented her findings on a chart and left us to continue our vigil. Nina followed her out.

"Thanks so much, Ronnie," I overheard Nina say as I excused myself to join them in the hallway. "She couldn't be in better hands."

Ronnie looked at me and then at Nina. "It's my pleasure."

Her voice was less intimidating than her build. "The most important part will be her recovery. It was really nice of Vern to come stay a few weeks."

"She's amazing," Nina sung.

"I sure miss her," Ronnie said, the unremitting high pitched beep of a machine inconveniently summoning her to the aid of a distressed patient. Despite her size, she gingerly trotted off, leaving Nina and I to watch as she ducked into the room a few doors down. Several other nurses followed in behind her.

"Thanks for coming up to visit, Nina."

She hugged me, holding on a little longer than I was comfortable with.

"Jeannie means a lot to me, too," she said pulling away, her bottom lip quivering as she held back tears. Nina's usual confidence was shattered, the lenses of her glasses smudged, her face puffy and seashell pink. She coaxed a used tissue from the front chest pocket of her blue cotton scrubs and swabbed her nostrils. "Got time for a walk?"

44

"Vern used to work with Ronnie in the ICU," Nina said, filling in details as we made our way to the cafeteria. She'd arrived from California by plane just as Aunt Jeannine was being wheeled into the operating room. "You know she's your aunt's sister, right? I mean, they look like twins."

"I didn't know she had more than one."

"She doesn't," Nina said. It wasn't clear whether she was being technical or if she was unaware of Lani all together. I let it go.

We rounded the corner and joined the line leading into the food service area. For standard hospital fare, the salad bar looked fresh, offering compartmentalized toppings including cucumbers, pine nuts, hard-boiled egg crumbles, and one variety of tomato. Nina, avoiding the ham and turkey chopped into bite-sized cubes, tonged mixed greens and a prodigal helping of edamame onto her disposable paper plate. She drizzled a citrus vinaigrette over her veggies and proceeded to the checkout line.

"Not hungry?" she asked, clueless that I'd been following her around instead of making meal selections.

"I think I'll just have a coffee," I said, tossing my empty plate into the trash.

"It's good here." She worked an apple juice from the ice chest, her other hand balancing the flimsy disposable platter that was beginning to saturate with salad dressing.

Nina waited for me as I stirred cream into the larger of two Styrofoam cup sizes and we made our way to the register together. She set her plate on the scale and took my coffee from me. "I'll get that."

"Hey sweetheart," the bright smiled cafeteria employee beamed. Her badge touted twenty years of service, its surface decorated with commemorative pins awarded for various recognitions she'd received over the course of her employment. "How you been?"

Nina's face reddened and her eyes welled up while she quietly waited for the total price of our purchases.

"Tomorrow's another day, baby. Don't you worry." She acknowledged me with a nod, her brown eyes closing and opening rapidly, a cluster of moles speckling her upper cheek. "As for today, lunch is my treat."

"Rita, you don't have to do that," Nina objected, digging around in her purse.

"I know I don't have to, baby. I want to." She broke open a roll of coins and closed the drawer. "The Lord heals all. You ladies enjoy the rest of your afternoon."

Nina showed me to a table at the back of the café where the window overlooked a pond filled with geese. "Vic told me about your fight," she said, opening her juice and taking a sip. "He means the best."

"He doesn't even know me. How could he know what's best?"

"Do you really blame him for being worried? I mean, come on, Tally. You were getting obsessed with the Dabbencove case. His wife could have damaged you."

"She's dead, now."

Nina studied my injury. "What happened to your face?"

I reached up for the bump. "Must have knocked it on the nightstand."

She shook her head and looked out the window; the geese took flight unanimously. "I think you guys should start over. I haven't seen Vic this happy in a really long time. Actually, never."

"How long have you known one another?" I asked.

"Since we were kids."

"Did you grow up together?"

She turned to me. "Sort of. I met him at the Redirection House."

"I don't know what that is."

"Oh," she laughed, taking another sip of her juice. "That was the name of the place your aunt and uncle were running back then. I moved in after my grandma died."

So that's what it was – an orphanage of sorts. I knew why Vic was there, but why was Nina? "What about your parents?"

"My mom was arrested for prostitution when I was nine. When she got out of jail, she took off."

"And your dad?"

"Never met him."

"I'm sorry, Nina. I don't mean to be nosy."

"Eh, no worries."

"How old were you when your grandma passed?"

"Fifteen. I was spiraling out of control. By some stroke of luck, I got linked up with Jeannie and Remi. They loved me unconditionally. Treated me like a daughter."

"So you lived with Vic?"

"Yeah, we were pretty close."

I searched her face for a deeper meaning.

"Not like that!" Nina howled, usurping the attention of several cafeteria diners. "Gross. Vic was like my big brother back then. That is, until he started drugging. God, I hated him after that."

"He never told me."

"Man, he was a fucking animal."

"What do you mean?"

"Just, so damn angry. Aggressive. Self-destructive."

"Did they kick him out?"

"He kicked himself out. And checked into rehab. It was the clearest thought he'd had in almost a year."

"This is news to me."

"I'm sure you were pissed off that he didn't call you last week."

"Wow. So he *was* avoiding me."

"Not exactly. There's a substance abuse camp a few hours west of here – a sister company of the treatment center he went to. They have a no phone policy."

"Did he relapse?"

"No, he's the senior counselor there. They do workshops and team building exercises throughout the summer."

"I wish he would have said something about all of this. About his addiction."

"It's not the type of thing you tell a girl you're into. At least not right away. I'm sure he would have eventually opened up about it."

"Maybe," I said, skeptical.

"He's been clean for a long time."

"Alcohol doesn't count?"

She laughed. "That's like drinking water compared to the things he used to put in his body."

"You can't tell by looking at him. That he was an addict."

"He's a gym rat, now. Still an addict, sans the life-threatening consequences. And mentally, therapy has really helped dig him out of his hole. You can see why he would think it might help you."

Nina had mostly just moved pieces of lettuce around on her plate when she checked her watch. "I've got to get going."

45

Poudre Valley Memorial was a labyrinth Nina knew well. She descended to her dungeon of morbidity as I tracked my way back to the ICU according to her directions. There, I found Vern standing outside of Aunt Jeannine's room.

"I'm Natalia," I said, extending my hand. She hugged me instead.

"I've heard great things about you, Natalia."

We detached and I peered over her shoulder, into the room. Uncle Remi was leaning over Aunt Jeannine's bed and whispering in her ear.

"Tell Uncle Remi I'll be in touch."

"I sure will," she told me. "Nice to finally meet you."

I thought about Vic on the walk back to the parking garage. Nina was right. His conversation with Aunt Jeannine wasn't a covert dissection of my character. He thought of her as a mother – someone caring and insightful with tons of wisdom to offer.

The word *therapy* had sounded so clinical coming from her mouth. Like a diagnosis. I wasn't ready to accept the recommendation even if it was to my benefit.

"Hey," I said into the receiver when Vic answered.

"I'm sorry about everything, Tally." He sounded run down. "It's great to hear from you."

"I just saw Nina."

"Oh, good. I let her know about Jeannine."

"She was in the ICU when I got there."

"Are you okay?" he asked.

Reception crackled in and out as I navigated the packed parking garage, my stomach loopy from the circular exit. The call dropped as I closed in on the teller. While looking down to redial Vic's number, something darted across the front of my truck. I jacked on the brakes just in time to avoid hitting a pedestrian. He threw his hands up and sulked on past.

I inched up to the attendant's window to fork over my fee. Preoccupied by the newspaper in her lap, she hadn't noticed my near hit. She stuck her hand out the window to retrieve my money and pressed the button to lift the gate.

Traffic lanes were congested with swerving food seekers desperate to find something to eat before their hour-long lunch breaks expired. Once I reached the cruising speed of forty, I felt around for my phone to call Vic back. He beat me to it.

"Hey, sorry about that," I said as soon as I answered. "I was in a dead zone."

"I was talking for a few minutes before I realized you weren't there." He paused. "Can you come by so we can talk? This is feeling really impersonal."

"I'll be there in a few," I told him, noting the ringing in my ear as I hung up. I started to sweat. Then my heart rate rose. When the road ahead became fuzzy, I pulled into the

239

closest parking lot, closed my eyes, and pleaded with my body.

The urge to puke passing, I opened my eyes and realized I was in a familiar location. The sub shop Aunt Jeannine and I had eaten at the last time I had an empty, hung-over stomach was staring me in the face.

Few people ventured in as I waited for two sandwiches to be made by the kid behind the counter who was more interested in flirting with his cute coworker. She twirled her hair and giggled while she rang me up.

I paid and made my exit just as a group of rowdy skater boys swarmed the sandwich counter. Through the windshield of my truck, I watched them sprawl out in almost every booth available. I forced down a bite of toasted turkey club, the same sandwich that had previously come to my rescue, and waited for my glucose levels to recalibrate.

With my vitals in check, I returned my thoughts to Vic. If Aunt Jeannine hadn't toppled down the stairs, I'd be staying a few more weeks in the loft. There, I could ponder. I could replay conversations in my head a thousand times. Ultimately, I could let time pass, and with it, wash away my feelings.

"No," I told myself. This was exactly what Aunt Jeannine had pointed out. Avoiding problems doesn't make them go away. It delays the resolution.

But before I headed to Vic's for reconciliation, I needed to cover up the gash in my forehead. If not, he would ask questions. I pulled concealer from my makeup bag and got to work.

46

"Here, eat this." I handed Vic a curried chicken sub. It would stall the conversation for few minutes at best, but at least I'd have a little more time to think about a tactful approach before we got into the thick of things.

"This is killer," he said of the grinder.

"Supermarine's," I told him.

"I've driven by that place a million times, but the name always deterred me. If you have to say your shit is super, then it probably isn't."

"I think it's a play on submarine. Like sub sandwich."

Vic still didn't get it. I continued to spell it out for him.

"Sub means below. Like sub-standard."

"Oh." He laughed at himself. "Hell, when they're putting out food that tastes this good, they can call it whatever they want."

Vic corralled his last bite, and before swallowing, stared down the other half of mine.

"It's turkey. You can have it." Looking to buy more time before addressing our issues, I searched the fridge for something to drink. There was nothing.

"I want you to know I've thought a lot about you for the last two days," he prefaced after I filled a glass from the faucet. Expecting to be the initiator, he caught me off guard. I stared at him.

"Don't worry, she's not home."

I felt nauseous, again. "Can we do this outside? I think I need some fresh air."

I followed him out to the back porch and sat cross-legged on a cushioned wicker loveseat facing another of its kind. Vic chose to stand, positioning himself against a concrete pillar that looked out over his yard. It was a welcomed lack of eye-contact.

"I shouldn't have reacted the way I did," I started.

"It was a little over the top," he said. His wasn't the response I wanted.

"You're going to accept some of the blame," I told him.

"Well, yeah. I was just agreeing with you. That it was dramatic and everything."

Insulted, I rolled my eyes and looked away.

"I apologized," he said. "I don't know what else you want from me."

The conversation had barely begun but I was already getting irritated. "What I *want* from you?"

"I'm sorry, Tally. Jesus."

"Just because you're sorry doesn't make it okay," I sneered, so far removed from my feelings that I wasn't sure if I wanted to laugh, cry, or break his nose.

"It was wrong of me. I shouldn't have gone behind your back," he said, refusing to look in my direction once my eyes clamped onto him.

"You shouldn't have, but you did. And before you started the blame game, I was going to tell you that I understood why you would go to Aunt Jeannine."

Vic finally looked at me. "You were?"

"Yes."

He crept up behind me and massaged the base of my skull. Even though I was upset with him, his touch was soothing. I had missed him, too.

Vic sat, folded his arms around my chest, and trailed reconciliatory kisses along the nape of my neck.

"You're always on the defense," I said. "Why is that?"

"Not always."

I eyed him over my left shoulder without physical engagement. "I want answers."

Frustrated, he backed off and stood. Seduction was his go-to problem-solving solution but I was determined not to be instantly swayed. This time, he would have to talk.

"We've been spending a lot of time together," I told him. "And it's been great. But I feel like I know nothing about you."

"We know each other," was his reply.

"Honestly, Vic? What about Xandra?"

"What about her?"

"You never mentioned you had a sister."

"Yes, I did."

"Not for weeks! I was kind of shocked when you told me. I don't know. I guess I just felt like we *did* know each other, and then boom. You say you have a sister and it makes me think we don't really know much about one another at all. You only share pieces with me."

"Isn't that the point of dating? To get to know the other person?"

"Yes, Vic. But so far we have just been kind of feeling things out. We never committed to a relationship."

"Well, I haven't been seeing anyone else."

"That's not what I'm saying. Why are you being difficult?"

He looked away, reeling himself in for protection.

"Nina told me the reason you moved out of Uncle Remi's," I said, trying to gain some leverage on him. "About your addiction. Why didn't you tell me?"

"I don't like to think about it." He shrugged, reluctant to let me in on his past. "I guess I never got over her suicide."

"We can talk about it. I'm here for you."

"Listen," he said, bringing his eyes to me. "There were a lot of demons inside me back then. Trust me. It won't benefit you to know all of the shit I went through."

I met him on my feet. "If we are going to tear down the walls between us then you have to stop putting them up."

"Masonry runs in the family," he joked. Forcing him to share his past was futile. He'd do it at his own pace.

"Do you believe in God?" he asked after staring into my eyes for what seemed like forever.

"There's got to be something, right?"

"I have an idea," he offered, taking my hands and swinging my arms back and forth. "Why don't we set you up in the basement? That way you can have some personal space."

I thought about my living options. Vern would be staying in the loft while she was in town. Even if I was welcome to the living room, couch surfing wasn't going to be an ideal situation since Aunt Jeannine would be heading home to recover.

"I know you don't have many places to go," he added.

"I don't need your sympathy."

"Stop. I didn't mean it like that. Who's being combative now?"

I grinned. "Do as I say, not as I do."

"Double standards," he said, linking his right arm through my left. "C'mon. I'll show you to your new room."

47

Vic's basement was an aquatic haven. Fish tanks spanned wall to wall, floor to ceiling.

"I didn't know you operated a pet store in your free time," I said, my eyes adjusting.

He took my hand and led me to the first aquarium which housed an innumerable collection of snails, their sizes ranging from the infinitesimal to the gargantuan. "This is my latest addition."

"Why?" I asked, the interest in keeping so many slimy creatures evading me.

"I was finding them in my other tanks. First a couple; then, like fifty at a time. They can be beneficial, but not if they reproduce too rapidly."

He plucked one large specimen off the glass and cupped it in his hand, bringing it close to me for observation.

"Instead of killing them, I drop them in here. They love being pet."

"You pet your snails?" I teased, rubbing its shell with my index finger.

"Careful. They're easy to fall in love with." He returned the docile invertebrate to its home and continued with my guided tour.

"This whole section is fresh water." Vic pointed. "Most are communal, but a few bad boys and girls get their very own. Like this one here."

I indulged him. "What is it?"

"Tiger Oscar."

"Oh, I know Oscars."

"The bigger they get, the more predatory they are. I used to keep Juno with tank mates, but once he outgrew the others, he started picking on them. Now he lives alone."

"They're cute," I commented of the neighboring tank where the school was moving in unison.

Vic laughed and dropped a few live worms inside. The fish destroyed them in seconds. "Piranhas."

"Nah uh?"

"I adopted them from a family that didn't know what they were getting into. It happens a lot. Most fish end up being flushed down the toilet instead of being rehomed."

I thought back to my childhood years of fish keeping. I'd managed to kill them all off.

"Parents buy their kids fish because they're cheap and misrepresented as easy to care for," Vic explained. "Tossing a betta into an unfiltered, unheated glass bowl provides quick entertainment. When it dies, it's no big deal."

"We did that," I told him, ashamed.

"It's not on purpose. People just don't take the time to educate themselves on caring for aquatic life like they would, say, a bunny. Fur and tails trump scales."

"These are a lot more colorful than those." I pointed out a four by four cluster of sandy bottomed tanks.

"They're reef fish," Vic replied.

"Like, coral reef?"

"Yep. Exactly. Those are all saltwater."

"Aren't those tough to maintain? That's what I've heard, anyway."

"Yes and no. It's easy once you get it established."

"In other words, you don't need a degree in marine biology?"

"Not necessarily, although it couldn't hurt."

"Do you have one?"

"No. I studied botany."

"I see why you and Aunt Jeannine get along so well."

"How is she?" he asked.

"Still in a coma. I think they want to give it a few more days."

"I'll feel a lot better when they wake her up."

"That's the scariest part," I told him.

"Don't even mention it. Remi would be lost without her."

"I thought we weren't going to mention it." I nodded my head in the direction of an interesting item. "Tell me about that."

He followed my inquiry over to a glass enclosure with one strange looking creature moseying about. "What do you want to know?"

"Is it real?"

Vic laughed. "It's an axolotl."

"An axe-uh-what?"

"Mexican salamander."

"He's neat looking."

"She. Her name's Lilith."

"Aww. That's a good name. I always love that part about new pets."

"It's fun, but when you name them, it's tougher when they pass. There's more of a connection."

"You sound like Sadie."

He grinned. "She must be *super cool*, then."

"I'll have to invite her out to Colorado sometime. I think she'd love it here."

"Where does she live, again?"

"New England."

"That's right. Our winters are nothing like they are there."

I thought of the trees in the canyon whose leaves were already showing signs of cold weather. "Either way, I'm glad I won't be here for the snow."

"What do you mean?"

"I'm heading back to Florida in a few weeks."

"I thought you were going to stay for awhile."

"I have stayed a while. Summer's almost over."

"I know. But..." He shrugged. "What's the point of going back if things are going so well here?"

I laughed. "Going well? I don't know if that's true. Look at the shit I've gotten myself into."

"I meant with me and you."

"Are you trying to convince me to stay?"

"Yes. And if you say no, I'll chain you up and keep you as my slave."

"I don't see any chains," I told him.

"C'mon. I'll show you."

"Does the torture chamber have snakes and scorpions?" I asked, following behind.

"Nothing like that. Just a few skunks."

"Eww. Don't they stink?"

Seeing that the joke went straight over my head, he smiled and led me deeper into his basement.

· ◆ ◆ ◆ ◆ ·

On the other side of the tanks, Vic had arranged a guest area complete with a dresser and a bed. To soften the look of the concrete floor and walls, he'd sprawled out a rug and hung matching curtains over the window wells which were drawn to allow light in. It was bright and welcoming – not at all the dreary place I expected a basement to be. From another room I had yet to see, pleasant classical music played.

"Who stays down here?" I asked, spotting a bottle of perfume and a scarf.

"You do," he said, fluffing the pillows and pulling the comforter down a bit.

"Who *was* staying down here?"

"Xandra's ex. They wanted to see if living in separate rooms would improve their chances of getting back together."

"That sounds a lot like our plan."

"Not really. We're just starting out. They were at the end."

"I see the arrangement didn't work."

"That's because they never slept in their own beds. If you're going to draw boundaries, you have to stick to them."

An orchid in full bloom basked in the sun's rays from its home on the end table, purple flecked petals thin and delicate above waxy green stems. Propped against the well-stocked bookcase was an acoustic guitar, the snapped low E string dangling, begging repair.

Vic led me through a series of corridors and into a double entry bathroom complete with a stand up shower, a toilet, and several sinks.

"It's crazy nice down here," I remarked, surprised by the cleanliness. No cobwebs. No insect carcasses. Aside from the drop in temperature, I could have been fooled that we were underground.

"Before I take you into my sanctuary," Vic strangely said, "I want you to know I rarely share this with anyone."

"Your secrets are safe with me," I promised.

"It's not that. I just don't need any trouble."

As I contemplated his meaning, he jangled a set of keys from the depths of his pocket and began the procession of unlocking three deadbolts. Because that didn't provide enough of a safeguard, he dialed in a number for his combination lock and then lifted a latch at the top of the door that was invisible to would be intruders.

The maximum security measures were perplexing, but I refrained from comment. I felt honored to be let in given his predilection for secrecy.

Bright light streamed out and we entered.

"Holy shit," I said, my voice competing over the whir of fan blades.

He disappeared into the underbrush, the only sign of him a teal patch of his shirt poking out from behind the massive plant between us. The skunks he kept in his vegetation room were not of the mammalian variety, rather, genetic clones from a mother plant labeled *Skunk #1* that sat in the corner, her branches bushy with leaves I recognized immediately.

"Come on over," he said, his voice close, his body out of sight.

Heavy duty black cables of electricity linked boxy light fixtures overhead, their bulbs so bright they couldn't be stared at. The top of the crop danced in the fan-forced air, branches flickering as the current swept from one side to the other.

"There's more?" I asked, joining him at the back where there was another door.

"The flower room has a different photoperiod."

"I have no idea what that means."

He cracked the door open and a wave of dank earth spilled out. "They require less light. Well, they don't require it. It happens naturally in nature. But inside, I have to force bud formation."

"It's crazy smelly in here."

"That's the terpenes."

I shrugged. "Apparently pot growing has its own vocabulary."

"Care to learn a bit?"

"Is there a quiz at the end?"

"Not today," he said, stepping ahead to point things out. "These are staggered by a week, that way they don't all mature at once. That one there," he motioned to the farthest point in the room which was all but inaccessible, "should be ready in a couple of days."

"How do you know?"

"This strain is a hybrid, meaning it's a mix of indica and sativa. The flower period is fairly short. About sixty days."

"Wow, that seems like a long time," I said.

"Some strains take double that."

"So, it's an ever revolving cycle, then. Plants moving from one room to the next."

"It's rewarding. And profitable. I don't do it for the money, but it's a nice perk."

"Don't get mad, but Xandra mentioned this to me. I think she was a little stoned."

"Did she take you to bed, too?" he teased.

"She tried."

"That bitch!" He shook his head.

"She didn't mean it, I'm sure."

"I guarantee she did." He crouched down to one plant's level and looked through an eyepiece. "Anyway, the terpenes are made by trichomes. You can see them here."

I recalled Uncle Remi's brief cannabis lesson. "Those are the little mushroom things, right?"

"Very good," he said, a master grower proud of his pupil. "Early on, those turn milky as the plant prepares for harvest. The longer you let it go, the more amber they are, and the higher the CBD and CBN levels. That's what causes the couch-locking effect. Fuzzy – like a peach." He turned every plant a half circle until he made it to the back of the room where he checked on his oldest gal.

"She's ready," he concluded, peering through his thirty-magnification jeweler's loupe. "I don't suppose you feel like trimming today?"

I pouted. "Can we start tomorrow morning when we're fresh? I'd rather spend the night catching up on lost time."

"Okay," Vic said, working his way back to me and slipping his arms around my waist. "But you have to sleep down here tonight. That's the rule. Remember?"

He grinned and kissed me on the lips, his breath spicy from two THC laced mints he'd popped into his mouth at the entrance of the grow room. After locking the bolts from the inside, I followed him up a second set of steep wooden stairs that delivered us to the backyard.

"I have a fire suppression system down there," he told me. "But it's always good to have another escape route. Besides, I need a way to get in when someone is staying in the guest area."

"Did Taz know about it?" I'd seen her name on an envelope tossed in the trash.

"Hell no. I told Xandra if she said anything to that loudmouth she might as well pack both of their bags."

I smiled at the thought of being let in on his secret and wondered how long it would take before I squealed. Sadie was a safe bet.

"Ready to enjoy some of the bounty?" Vic asked, taking a flagstone pathway to the back porch.

I swiped the pipe from his hand and hit it boldly, Xandra's previous warning about its potency resurfacing too late. I blew a huge puff of smoke out and instantly regretted my heroic pull. A heavy body high started to immobilize me, and then I was catapulted hours into the future. When night fell, Vic put on a movie. I faded in and out, my mind floundering to formulate cohesive thoughts.

"I'm going to look for a job this week," I said, having toyed with the idea before mentioning it out loud.

"Shhh, let's not worry about that right now. There's no cost in staying here."

"And I thank you for that. But I'm an adult. And it's not okay to mooch."

"You're not mooching. I am giving freely and without stipulation."

"Take advantage while you can," Xandra interjected, her presence in the kitchen unknown until then.

"Shut the fuck up!" Vic snarled. He paused *Super Troopers* and stood in defense. "Why are you always in my business?"

"I'd answer you, but I think you just told me to shut up."

"Ever since Taz left, you've been a real bitch. What's gotten into you?"

Xandra continued her silence.

"Fine, go ahead. Play the game. No wonder they put you on meds."

"Fuck you!" she belted, lobbing a glass into the sink where it shattered.

"I'm sorry, Xan," Vic called out, realizing he had pushed her too far. She slammed her bedroom door and Vic hurtled down the hall after her.

"Why do you have to be such a dick?" she yelled as he entered her room and shut the door behind him.

Before I could stop myself, I was tiptoeing down the hallway to eavesdrop.

"I know, I know. I've been torn in a lot of directions lately," I heard Vic say, my ears straining through sheets of drywall and multiple layers of paint.

Xandra said something back to him but it was just a grumble from my perch.

"Maybe I can make it up to you," Vic said. Xandra giggled and they were quiet for a few seconds before Vic spoke again. "Get some sleep."

I barreled down the hall to the living room and returned to the couch. My breathing was heavy, so I took deep inhales through my nostrils to bring it back into sedentary range.

Vic swooped down and apologized for his absence.

"Everything okay?" I asked, faking grogginess.

"It's a cyclical thing. One day she's manic and upbeat. The next day, she locks herself in her room."

"Is she depressed?"

"Bipolar. She was diagnosed last year."

"Wow, and it's still not under control?"

"Apparently she stopped taking her lithium this week because it's been making her gain weight."

"Birth control did the same thing to me."

"There are a lot of side effects, but not taking it is even worse. At times, unbearable."

"She totally snapped," I said.

"That's how it is. Unpredictable. Violent."

"Gosh, I'm glad I'm staying downstairs," I whispered, trying to lighten the mood with a little humor.

"Keep the shotgun close," he teased. "She's not all bad. It's mostly self-hate. She'll gain a few pounds, stop taking her medication, work out like a madwoman, and exhaust herself to the point of insomnia."

"She doesn't look fat to me. Maybe the extra pounds are good for her."

"Yeah, well you're not manic depressive."

"Is it contagious?" I joked. My smile faded. "I guess it's not right to talk about her like that."

Vic shrugged a shoulder. "It could be worse."

I imagined Sadie sitting across from desperate patients locked inside their heads. She'd try to convince them their psychosis was a function of traumatic life experiences – that they have a choice. And that the mental disorders plaguing their brains could be eradicated – that they could heal. To them, the only choice was living with their defects; to rationalize with the buzz of voices who, contrary to what the doctor said, swore they were more than just figments of the imagination. Prescriptions would only numb, and the victims of their own minds would simply exist until they could no longer endure the grind of their psychoticism.

"You look tired," Vic said as I continued to ponder the notion of multiple personalities, schizophrenia, and spontaneous senility.

Just as I shook my head to agree, he scooped me up into his arms.

"You make me feel like a princess," I told him, lassoing my arms around his neck.

"You *are* a princess."

Vic laid me on his bed and disrobed me, gently feeling his way up my stomach to my breasts. The hairs all over my body stuck up when he whispered *I can't wait to taste you* in my ear.

48

I examined myself in the mirror of Vic's master bath. With the cut on my forehead scabbing over, it could easily pass for a scratch. Crisis averted.

I leaned in further, and found something new. The summers of unprotected sunbathing had finally compounded to deliver what was promised – an outcropping of wrinkles at the corners of my eyes. I wondered if Camila's plastic surgeon had heard the news; if she would be missed.

After applying eyeliner and mascara, I dusted my cheeks with bronzer. Once the business-flirty look was achieved, I debated a hair style. The darker roots of my henna treated tresses had grown out a few inches, the length a faded burgundy with lighter tips bleached out by the sun.

To mask the growth of my naturally brown hair, I opted for a deliberately messy bun, my side bangs swept into a loose French braid tracking across the front of my head before being scooped up in the back. I knew the service industry look well – if I was going to get a job bartending, I needed to be able to attract clientele.

I slipped into a belted summer dress, an offering of cleavage suggestive enough for a male interviewer, but respectfully flaunted in a way that wouldn't offend a female. Almost all restaurant managers I'd worked for were men, and my image would be the first thing they judged me on – maybe the only thing.

In case he wanted to show me around, it was important to have on sturdy shoes that could defeat bar mats drenched with the previous night's cocktails. I tucked my feet into a pair of flatfooted linen slip-ons that were my go-to for most outfits, their neutral color easy to match to my entire wardrobe, the arch supports worn in comfortably.

"Almost done in there?" Vic called from the other side of the door. I'd taken longer than expected, wanting to get out of the house before he had a chance to dissuade me from my job search. I cracked the door open and let him in.

"What do we have here?" he said, tracing his warm fingers across my bare legs.

"Later," I promised, removing his hand.

"Later's no fun," he pouted. "Got a hot date?"

"Maybe. Are you planning on taking me out to celebrate?"

"What are we celebrating?"

"My new job."

"You got a job?"

I laughed. "Not yet, silly. I'm heading downtown to look."

"I thought you weren't staying past the summer."

"I'm not. But it will be good for me to have something to do until I leave," I said. "Besides, I could use the money."

"I have money."

I turned the bathroom light off and pushed past him. "I'll be back after four."

"Four? It's only ten!"

"There are rules. Gotta hit them up before eleven or between two and four."

"That's the most ridiculous thing I've ever heard."

I chuckled. To service industry whores, it was standard practice. "Customers only get an hour break. That's why it's called a lunch rush. There's no time for interviews."

"If a place wants to hire good people, they should be willing to meet with them whenever."

"You've obviously never worked in a restaurant," I told him, pecking him on the cheek. "Good employees stop by during designated hours. I'll be back later."

·✦✦✦✦·

I'd trolled Craigslist before setting out to see which places were hiring, that way I could avoid them. If a restaurant couldn't keep staff, there were reasons; either it was too slow to make steady money, or the company sucked to work for. I checked my reflection, adjusted some stray hairs, then tucked my folder with a dozen resumes under my arm and rolled out of the cab.

When I'd ditched my last job, the scheduling manager called the following day. He was actually in a good mood and told me he wasn't mad, that he'd been in my shoes before.

"Give yourself some time," he said. "You'll come back. They all do."

I assumed he was talking about Fred's Fish Shack, but as I found myself searching for a new restaurant job, I realized he was talking about the industry in general. The quick money was tough to pull away from, even if it was a soulless occupation.

I ducked into a few spots, glossing over the interior before deciding if I wanted to submit an application. The way a place looked and their signage said a lot about the customers.

Early bird specials meant old people. Old people were notorious for less than adequate tips. The same thing went for college night. You would assume serving cheap cocktails would give you a better opportunity to make money. I knew first hand that assumption was incorrect.

I also planned to avoid multilevel buildings, which meant that in order to deliver drinks to diners upstairs, I'd have to endure the most insane ass workout of my life, every single day. And when I forgot a lemon for some biddy's water, I'd feel that much more aggravated having to fetch her desired fruit knowing that I must literally climb a mountain to appease her. She would have no sympathy – it's my job.

If the restaurant passed preliminary inspection, I'd proceed to the bathroom. If it wasn't spotless, then I'd know they didn't have a professional cleaning crew. That meant I would be the one in charge of wiping down toilets and urinals at the end of the night, scrubbing lipstick off the mirror, and transferring used tampons from their shiny metal boxes into garbage bags. Once I ascertained the level of cleanliness, I was ready to make my decision.

This kind of screening process left few options available. The first two places I walked into, I walked right back out of. The third spot looked promising, until I saw the uniform.

"Can I help you?" a petite blond in a crisply pressed oxford and bowtie asked, her feet crammed into patent leather heels that would be sure to devastate her legs by the shift's end.

"I write for the dining section of a local paper," I said, using my go-to line. "Mind if I look around?"

"Go right ahead." She returned to her bar duties, readying the fruit caddy and filling her sinks with hot water in anticipation of a profitable day.

I knew Chappy's Chophouse wasn't going to fit the bill, so I pretended to browse over the menu until I satisfied my fabricated role as curious foodie and headed for the door.

The bewitching hour was practically up when I checked my phone for the time. I passed a small local publishing house and thought about picking up a writing gig instead. Considering my education, it was ironic that I was searching for a serving job while pretending to be a journalist. But I wouldn't be happy writing stories about local events. It didn't interest me. Besides, I didn't know anything about Ft. Collins.

With fleeting thoughts of rekindling my writing career, I took a deep breath and contemplated what I'd do until after the lunch rush. I turned down a street lined with posh bars featuring pricey menus in their windows, the doors stickered with late hour openings and no listed closings. After jotting down the name of a martini bar, I continued on to the end of the block.

The quaint town seemed to stop there. Across the street, a park full of homeless people gathered, their rickety bikes strapped with stained blankets and tattered tents, their faces unshaven and hair tousled from sleeping on the ground.

On my side, the money flowed plentifully, into robust flower pots and brick walkways that kept the city swanky. Mere yards away, drifters occupied their time by sipping on beverages concealed in brown bags, their next meal unscheduled and often missed. I quickened my pace and circled around the posterior of the building.

Having looped back into the crowded sidewalks of the business district, I set out to burn some daylight. A bookshop built out of an old firehouse sucked me right in. I browsed the shelves until my appetite no longer allowed it. Giving into temptation, I followed the smell of freshly baked bread through an archway which connected the bookstore to the neighboring eatery.

"What can I do you for?" the fedora-topped lad with a handlebar mustache inquired when I approached the counter.

"What's good?"

He didn't hesitate. "You want a breakfast Kolache. With fried caper berries and house-cured pancetta."

"Think it's too early for a beer?" I asked, scanning their expansive draft offerings.

"Not a'tall. Might I make a recommendation?"

"Pour what you like."

"Twelve seventy," he said, handing me the pint.

I paid with a ten and a five. When he returned my change, I dropped it into the tip jar on the counter.

"Thanks! I appreciate that."

"Of course," I told him, and headed off to find a seat.

I took the only table left in the crowded dining area among other Kolache enthusiasts, a few of whom also paired their breakfast with a morning brew. I lifted it for a taste just as some rambunctious person bumped into me from behind. Shocked, I sprung from my chair.

"Gosh, I'm so fucking sorry," the perpetrator said. "These goddamned tables are tighter than a nun's asshole." She sighed, swiping her choppy bobbed hair aside to reveal stormy eyes. "Let me buy you another beer."

Before I could protest, she slung her bag into the chair opposite me and headed up to the counter to place her order. While I was dabbing the front of my dress with napkins, she returned.

"Excellent choice, my friend. I love Breckenridge beers." She set the pint down in front of me, threw her belongings to the ground, and helped herself to my table.

"I don't know where that is."

"Traveling?" she asked, hunting about her bag for something elusive.

"Sorta."

"New to town?"

"Been here a few months."

"Don't you love it?" She grinned, pausing to look at me for a second before continuing her search. She was oblivious to her imposition.

"It's been cool." I attempted sampling the vanilla porter for the second time, taking a generous sip and secretly agreeing with my uninvited guest about its quality. The flavor was bold and impressive but smooth on the finish.

"Here you go." She handed me a wet nap.

I looked down to check my garment. "I think I'm good."

"Wipe your skin with it, doll. You smell like a brewery."

264

Since I'd be returning to my job hunt, I heeded her advice. I didn't want to give the wrong impression to a potential boss who might assume I had a serious drinking problem because I already reeked of booze and it was barely afternoon.

"I've met a lot of people that moved to FoCo in the past year. Where ya from?" She asked this while stabbing out a text on her iPhone, easily running simultaneous conversations.

"Florida," I answered, observing the blackness of her hair in contrast to her pale complexion. "But I'm not moving here. Just visiting."

"I hear great things about Florida."

"It's alright. I needed a change."

"Did you find it?" she asked, tossing her phone back into her bag.

"Find what?"

"Change."

I mulled over her question. I'd given her the same answer I'd given Vic when he asked me what I was doing in Colorado. *Change.*

It had been a change of pace. It had been a change of scenery. But the real change, the change from within – I wasn't sure I'd found that.

"The suspense is killing me."

"I have to get going," I told her. "My job hunt awaits."

"I've got a job for you," she said.

Before she'd even given me her name, she was offering me a position.

"I don't think I'm cut out for the street life," I teased, lightening up a bit.

"Oh, ouch." She shook her hand like she'd just crushed it in a door.

"I kid. Where do you work?"

49

Shauna and I shot pool at Trailhead until hunger sent us into the streets of Ft. Collins to seek out a late lunch.

"Let me give my boyfriend a call," I told her before heading into Scrumpy's, the syllables in *boyfriend* unfamiliar as I formed them with my mouth.

From the sidewalk, I watched her settle in at the bar while I waited for Vic to answer.

"Hey stranger."

"Hey babe. What's up?"

"Just waiting on you," he said. "How's the job search going?"

"I found one!" I shrieked.

"Congrats. Let's celebrate!"

"Well, that's the thing. I start tonight. So I'm going to stay in town until then."

"I can meet up with you if you want."

"That's okay. My boss and I are going to get a bite to eat and head over early so I can start my new hire paperwork."

"What's his name?" he asked with a tinge of jealousy.

"*Her* name is Shauna."

"Okay, well call me later."

"Everything alright?" I asked.

"Yeah. It's all good. I'll see you tonight."

We hung up and I joined Shauna inside, the bartender completely smitten by her as they talked about what they were going to wear for an event called Tour de Fat in September.

"She'll have the same as me," she told him upon my arrival.

"And what if I want something different?" I sassed.

"Oh, well excuse me Miss Thang," she replied, and to the bartender, "Give the lady whatever she wants."

"Miss Thang, what would you like?" he asked.

"It's Tally, and I'll have what she's having."

Shauna flicked me off and whispered. "Bitch."

······

After finishing our third hard cider, Shauna gave the word. "It's about that time."

"If you say so," I told her.

We ducked back onto the street and headed east, my strides sodden with alcohol.

"You never told me what you're doing in Ft. Collins," Shauna said, guiding us through town.

"My uncle owns a funeral home."

"No shit?"

"Yeah. It's kinda strange."

"He must be a weird dude."

268

I took offense to her comment. "No. It's not like that. He's a really sweet guy who cares about people."

"Whatever you say."

I followed her down a set of stairs to a door and she let us in with her key. "Stay here a minute."

Shauna was swallowed up by darkness. Moments later, dim lights came on.

"Voila," she said, emerging from around a corner.

"No flashlight?"

"That's way too smart for me. Sit over there and I'll grab those forms." She pointed to the main bar anchored along the back wall.

I followed her instruction and sat on a stool in the distance. The walls were painted black with dark wood accent panels and brick in all the right places. Brixton's was industrial, yet upscale.

Shauna returned quickly, her left hand clutching several sheets of paper and a pen. "I forgot to grab your ID."

"I'm old enough," I said, peeling my license from my wallet. "This place is pretty nice."

"Yeah. You'd never believe it used to be a whorehouse. I'll be right back."

· ✦ ✦ ✦ ✦ ✦ ·

At seven, employees started to arrive. On a typical night, Shauna and three other barmaids handled drinks while two college jocks brought ice and changed out kegs. A music venue wasn't the kind of place I'd had in mind that morning, but the opportunity practically landed in my lap, along with the beer.

269

Luna, a busty brunette with boyish features, was escaping the service industry for good. She'd graduated in the spring and scored a grown-up job selling pharmaceuticals for Pfizer. I was going to fill in for my remaining weeks in Colorado while they looked for her replacement.

"We'll miss her dearly," Shauna said, tossing a soggy bar towel in Luna's direction and hitting her in the stomach.

"Yeah, yeah. I'll miss you too." Luna swiveled the wet towel into a whip and slapped it across Shauna's ass.

"Oh, baby," Shauna cried, rubbing her butt cheek. "What a tease!"

The other two bartenders chatted about their boyfriends while they stocked liquor bottles.

"He can be such an asshole," I overheard one of them say.

"I know what you mean," the other agreed.

"What are their names?" I asked Shauna discreetly.

Instead of answering me, she spun around. "Molly, Sarah, why don't you introduce yourself to our new staff member. You can continue bitching about your shitty relationships in a minute."

"I'm Molly," the prettier one offered, her smile not concealing her hatred for Shauna.

"And I'm Sarah," her friend said.

"Hi, I'm Natalia." I felt instantly hated.

"At ease, ladies," Shauna barked.

They returned to the other side of the bar and quickly got back to chatting, their voices dwindled down so that only they could hear one another.

"Rich parents," Luna whispered to me. "They only work because they want to. Seriously, who *wants* to work?"

"Sisters?" I asked.

Shauna answered for her. "Sweet, isn't it?"

······

It was quarter of eight when customers started to trickle in. One small group stopped by the bar.

"We're not open yet," Shauna said without apology.

Once they retreated, she told me it was a lie. "You can serve'em early if you want. I just don't like that guy. He never tips."

I nodded and smiled, intrigued by her bad girl attitude. Earlier in the day, I'd seen her softer side, but now she was in work mode, ready to enforce her selective rules and kick out the people she didn't like.

The crowd continued to thicken as a burly, redheaded bassist plucked strings on his instrument, stubby fingers dancing from chord to chord to test their veracity. The only good seats already taken, clusters of people competed for decent spots to stand. Shauna hopped over the bar top and greeted a few guy friends passing a joint, their heads bobbing to trippy music coming from gigantic speakers mounted on either side of the stage.

After a few drags, Shauna slinked off to the bathroom, returning to the bar just as the jam band started its first set.

"Ready to rock and roll?" she yelled to me over the roar of the crowd.

"Let's do it!" I took the shot of Jäger she handed me and downed it without opposition.

50

"You were soaring when you got home," Vic said when I cracked my eyelids open and saw him staring at me.

"What time is it?" I mumbled.

"Going on noon."

Dehydration took my body hostage, every molecule of my being desperate for a sip of water.

Intuitively, Vic handed me a bottle of Eldorado and two ibuprofen.

"Thanks," I sighed, rubbing my forehead as dull pain squeezed at my grey matter.

"Your new friends seem nice."

Tatters of the previous night speckled my memory. "Friends?"

"Shauna and Luna dropped you off," he said.

"I know," I lied, the ride home splotchy in my mind. I remembered shouting last call into a microphone at Brix, but the time between collecting my tips and walking over to Hopheads for a beer after work was blurry. Several rounds later, the three of us hobbled down the sidewalk to Shauna's car while passing a clove cigarillo back and forth.

Vic broke into my thoughts. "When do you want to pick up your truck?"

I sat up and laid right back down, the hangover heavily entrenching my flesh suit. "I don't really need it today. If you don't mind bringing me to work, I'll drive home tonight."

"If you didn't already get towed," he harped.

"I parked a little ways down," I told him.

"How far down? They usually don't allow vehicles to stay overnight."

I shrugged, refusing to be upset about a situation I had no control over.

"Do you have a bike?" I asked.

"Yeah, I have a few in the garage."

"Cool. I was thinking that might be a better mode of transportation for me."

"Why? So you can get sloshed every night?"

"No, so I don't have to worry about trying to find parking. Are you mad at me for something?"

He looked away.

"Listen, I'm just getting settled in at Brix. It was nice to let loose."

"I know," he said. "I don't like you out alone, late at night. Especially when you're drunk."

"I wasn't alone."

"I worry about you. There was something in the paper about a sexual assault that happened just down the road from here. In City Park."

It had to be the same article gun-club-Brad mentioned. To me, it wasn't anything to be concerned over.

And nothing a little pepper spray couldn't handle.

"My job caters to people who work normal jobs. They go out and spend money at night."

"I get it. It's fine."

"You should come visit me some time," I suggested.

"You don't mind being the one with the creepy boyfriend who sits at the bar and watches your every move?"

"Watching the band would probably be *slightly* more interesting." My stomach growled. "What's for breakfast?"

"I think we ought to plan for lunch. I've got work to do downstairs. Mind if we order delivery?"

"Sounds great," I told him, stoked that I could nurse my hangover a bit longer. "What'll it be?"

"Grab a shower. I'll take care of it."

· · ◆ · ·

I let the heavy pelt of water beat down on my back for longer than necessary before realizing how wasteful I was being. Aunt Jeannine had guilted me in her not-so-subtle manner when she once asked me if I was trying to meet my daily quota by letting the faucet run while I chopped veggies in her kitchen.

"The average American uses one hundred gallons a day," she said. "Imagine hauling that much water by foot. You'd quickly learn to treat it as the precious resource it is."

"Sounds inflated to me," I told her, defending my carelessness.

"A toilet uses about two gallons per flush. How many times a day you use the bathroom?"

I grinned. "Five to ten, I guess. It depends on intake."

"That makes ten to twenty percent of the daily average," she replied, unamused by my playfulness. "And you just ran the sink for more than five minutes. That's at least another twenty gallons. Almost half way there."

I missed Aunt Jeannine. Darla was most likely carrying the weight of the mortuary if Uncle Remi was still holding steady by his wife's hospital bed. I hoped Vern had sent him home for some sleep before he exhausted himself to the point of needing his own medical treatment.

Vic was in full conversation with the delivery driver when I strode out of the bathroom in my towel. I dashed into the bedroom before being spotted, the discernible aroma of greasy Chinese food enveloping me as I whooshed the door shut. Nude, I shuffled around in my duffle bag for a change of clothes; all articles were thoroughly wrinkled.

"Shall we do dessert first?"

"Vic!" I shouted, turning my back to him. "Get out of here!"

"No way. I don't want to miss the show." He stayed in the hall with the door cracked open.

I stretched the towel around me and rushed over to him. "I'll be out in a minute!"

I pecked him on the lips and pushed the door shut.

"I'll be waiting," he said, his voice trailing off as he withdrew.

51

The General Tso's chicken was fantastic. I also enjoyed two egg rolls and a portion of fried rice that I picked the shrimp out of.

"Not a fan?" Vic asked as I piled my rejects onto the plastic take-out lid.

I scrunched my nose up and told him why. "They eat poop."

He laughed so hard he started to choke, his face turning beet red as he fought off aspirating his lunch.

"Oh my God, that's hilarious," he said after slugging a whole glass of water. "Good shit. Literally."

"I've eaten them before. I don't think they have much flavor."

"Oh, so you only eat poop on occasion?" he teased. "I didn't know or I would have ordered something else. I figured a Florida girl would be into all kinds of seafood."

"Too expensive for my budget."

"Really? Even right on the coast?"

"It's less abundant than it used to be, especially since the oil spill. They make up for it by charging more. Tourists gladly pay the prices."

"What oil spill?"

I lifted one eyebrow.

"Didn't hear anything about it."

"Three million gallons of oil went into the Gulf of Mexico a few years ago," I prompted, trying to jog his memory. Surely it wasn't news to him.

"That's a lot of money," he said.

"Fuck their money. Eleven people died."

"Whoa. I had no idea."

"It took almost three months to stop the leak after the rig exploded. But that's not the worst of it. Do you know what those assholes did?"

"Blamed it on someone else?"

"No. They dumped dispersants into the water to break up the slicks. Chemicals that are fifty times more toxic to microscopic marine life than the oil itself."

Vic set his fork down.

"And who do you think owns the patent for that?"

"The. Oil. Companies?"

"Bingo."

He looked at the crustaceans loathsomely, their possible contamination impeding desirability. "Well, I think I'm done here."

"I didn't mean to talk you out of them. I still eat seafood *occasionally*. Just not the ocean's filters."

"Point taken," he said, splaying two fortune cookies in his hand. I grabbed the one closest to me and opened it up.

"What's it say?" Vic asked, chomping down on the one defaulted to him.

"It's bad luck to share."

"What? That's absurd. Mine says *Your tongue is your ambassador*. See, I told you we should have done dessert first." He scooped my hand up and licked my finger. "Mmm, salty. Read me yours."

"Nope." I pulled my hand away and pocketed the curled strip of paper.

"It probably says something like *Kick your new boyfriend to the curb*."

I feigned shock. "How'd you know?"

"Hey, that's not nice!" He pinned me down and dug his fingers into my armpits. I squirmed and kicked, but he was too strong. After my ticklish laughter subsided, we started kissing.

In a matter of seconds, Vic was inside me. It was a short session with the sole purpose of reaching orgasm; nothing fancy or frilly – just the means to an end. I'd heard about sex relieving a headache and was pleased to find mine diminishing.

"Alright," he said, jumping to his feet. "We've got work to do."

·· ◆ ◆ ◆ ◆ ··

Vic led me down the stairs to a room the size of a large walk-in closet. Massive branches teeming with mature buds were hanging upside down on twine that was zigzagged from one wall to the other and back again. Upon the table were trays of different colors, a few sets of scissors, and an iPod docking station.

"Have you ever manicured before?" he asked, swiveling one of two chairs around and settling in with a beastly cola he'd selected from the drying rack.

"Nope," I said, taking my place next to him.

"You'll be slow until you get the hang of it. Here in Colorado, we trim wet and tight."

I narrowed my eyes.

"Virtually all crops are grown indoors," he went on. "It's a lot different in California where most of the herb is grown outside. They let it dry first, and then trim it."

"Colorado is too cold?" I deduced.

"That. And hail. But mostly, the restrictions make it almost impossible to grow outdoors. According to the law, it must be in an enclosed and locked space."

"That sounds far reaching."

"It is. The people who passed the amendment have probably never grown a cannabis plant in their life. It also says you can't have more than three mature plants at a given time." He raised his eyebrows to signal his clear violation of the statute.

"What does it matter if you have three or thirty?" I asked him.

"Control."

"What about the dispensaries? They obviously have more than that."

"They do. But it's all registered with the government. So, if they wanted to stop in and take a look around, they could. It's the underground growers they're trying to snuff out."

"That's bullshit," I decided after thinking about being hauled off to jail for growing a plant.

"Yeah. Tell me about it." He spun to face the lamp.

"Alright. The aim here is to cut away all the fan leaves as close to the stem as possible. Those go into the lined trays here." He pointed to two bins with bags stretched over them.

"Trash?"

"No. A client of mine juices them."

"Juices them?"

"Yeah. For lupus. Her doctor had her on more than twenty different meds. With the juice, she only has to take over-the-counter pain relievers here and there."

"Wow. That's amazing."

"She has a hard time getting enough leaves because most growers use fertilizer and pesticides to boost their production output. Jeannine and I met her at an anti-GMO rally last year. When I told her I grew organics, she practically begged me to save the clippings."

"I'll make sure every last one makes it into her box," I vowed.

"Cool. After all of those are gone, move on over to the purple trays. Those are for the frosty sugar leaves like this." He pointed out a few and clipped them off to demonstrate.

"Cut those down to the quick. After they're out of the way, your trimmings are going to go into the green trays."

I watched him sheer away the points on each leaf, tapering the bud at the top to expose tiny tentacle-like hairs.

"I'm kind of shocked at how much gets wasted," I said, a snowy pile growing below his scissors.

"It doesn't get wasted, per se. I use it to make things like hash, tincture, and butter. But I know what you mean. I usually end up with the same amount of trim as I do flower."

I watched him work, regarding the nuisances of his knuckles, his tendons moving beneath a taut sheet of skin. When Vic was done sculpting the nug, he set it on the mesh shelf of a tiered hanging basket that was ready to be loaded up with the newest crop.

"I'll get some tunes in here for you." He stood and offered the scissors my way, sharp point towards him.

I chose a small bud from the rack and settled into my chair. When Vic returned, I was methodically working my way around the crown of my specimen.

"Nice job," he told me, leaning over my shoulder to inspect. "You're a natural."

52

I was high for seven straight days as we whittled away on the crop. An endless monologue carried on inside my head, one thought bouncing me off to another idea that served only to propel me in a different direction. I dissected my entire life three times over and even got into a loop of repeating the word *albatross* until it no longer sounded correct.

The work was tedious and boring, but it kept me occupied. Camila came to mind on a single occasion; it was unlike any other time I'd thought of her. I felt pity for the way her life had gone. She'd chosen the wrong path and paid the ultimate consequence.

By the weekend, our bounty tipped the scales at almost ten pounds. Blisters were left where delicate tissue once was, my hands sore from overuse.

"How much is all of this worth?"

"About twenty grand."

"Seriously?"

"Yeah. But that's not pure profit. On top of other things, the cost of electric is insane."

"You can't just walk into the bank with that kind of money," I said, more of a question than a statement.

"I invest some of it into cryptocurrency."

"Like Bitcoin or whatever?"

"Bitcoin is a dinosaur. XRP will be the new king."

"Never heard of it."

He grinned. "You will soon."

"Digital currency never made sense to me. Why take real money and turn it into something fake?"

"You and Xandra both have a lot to learn. Besides, that's not my only hustle. I have a mining claim up north that does pretty well."

"Any gold?"

"Never looked for it. I'm more interested in crystals and gemstones. Petrified wood. Fossils."

"I want to go."

"Sure. I charge a grand for the whole summer."

"Maybe we can work something out," I teased, nuzzling the crotch of his pants with my elbow, my hands covered in gloves sticky with scissor hash.

Smiling, he weighed out the last of the product that was too small to sell and what he'd smoke until the next go around.

"Who buys all of this stuff?"

"Don't worry about it."

"Sorry. It's none of my business."

"It's not that. If anything was to ever happen, you are better off not knowing."

"Do you think about it a lot?"

"What?"

"Being busted."

"I try not to let it consume me. It's a harmless plant. I'm confident I could convince a jury that this is hardly a destructive way to make money."

"I'm sure Wendy would testify on your behalf." She was the elderly woman Vic donated his fan leaves to.

"Probably. I'd rather just keep it under the radar. Court is an expensive place to be. Speaking of expensive," he went on, "Remi got the bill for Jeannine's hospital stay. Care to take a guess?"

"I didn't even know she was home," I said, appalled that Vic had found out before me.

"Ninety thousand! I only know because I called Darla to see if she needed any help with Josie. She told me Jeannine got out on Wednesday and your uncle was back to work as normal."

I refused to look at him.

"I'm sure if they needed anything, they would have called you."

I continued my silence, upset with myself for not having reached out. With working at Brix and staying busy in Vic's basement, I'd had little time to worry.

"Tally, what's wrong?"

Looking off in the distance, my eyes lingered on some undetectable point of empty space. All physical items drifted out of focus. "I don't appreciate being left out all the time," I finally said.

"No one's leaving you out."

"It's like all these things happen in real life and I have a whole other existence playing out in my head."

"That's how it is for everyone. I've got my own agenda. You do. Your family does. You can only work from your perspective."

"Yeah, but all of you are on the same page. Here I am, floating around in la-la land."

Vic's phone rang and he cleared his throat before he answered, his voice projected in a way I'd never heard it. He relocated himself to the other room, for privacy or to hear better I wasn't sure.

"Do you want to go visit them tomorrow?" I asked when he returned.

"I can Sunday. But tomorrow I have to be in Denver." He shook his phone at me as if that explained why.

"I understand," I told him.

"I wish I could reschedule."

"That's alright. I can go alone."

"I'll give you a few bucks if you want to pick up a card and some flowers."

"Aunt Jeannine would kill me if I bought her flowers."

Vic laughed. "You're right. She would."

"How about some chocolate?" I suggested.

"Great idea. She used to eat these clusters from a place called Kilwin's in Old Town. It's been years, though."

I'd watched an old lady decorating waffle cones in their window when I was roaming around the day I first met Shauna. "It's still there," I told him.

"Perfect. She adores those."

"I'll stop in before my shift tonight."

"Good luck not eating them all," he warned.

53

"You're in the wrong business," Shauna said after nibbling on a square of fudge.

"It's store bought."

"No shit? I really like the tan one."

"Butter pecan," I told her.

"Go figure. Butter tastes great on everything. Where'd it come from?"

"Kilwin's."

"Never heard of it."

"It's right down the street." I pointed in its direction though a wall blocked our view of the outside world.

When I'd gone in, the counter clerk insisted I try their flavor of the day – salted caramel. She knew what she was doing; it sold itself. I bought Aunt Jeannine's cashew turtles as well as several fudge squares to share with my bartending gang.

"Mav, try this," Shauna said.

"What is it?" Mav asked from the other side of the bar where he was nailing down a piece of molding that had pulled away from the corner.

"Pure deliciousness." She dangled her hand over the edge to offer a bite.

Mav, Brix's owner, lifted his head up and took the whole chunk into his mouth.

"Dude! That was like five dollars' worth!"

"Mmm. Did you make it?" he asked her, his mouth chomping away.

"Nope, Tally did."

"I bought it from Kilwin's," I corrected her.

"Never heard of it," Mav said, not taking his attention off his project.

"Thanks for coming in early," Shauna told to me, licking leftovers from her fingers.

"No problem." I grabbed a towel from the sanitizer bucket and joined her on the inner part of the bar.

The private party we were hosting was scheduled for seven, an hour earlier than when we usually opened. I'd arrived at six to help prep and hang decorations, but already the hour was slipping away.

Ciro, one of Mav's closest friends, would be celebrating his fortieth birthday in less than twenty minutes and all our team had managed to do was sweep the dance floor and wipe off the bar top. Shauna and I still needed to trek down to dry storage in the basement, and our bar backs had yet to haul in the two kegs our guests had purchased in advance.

"How much does it cost to rent this place for the night?" I asked as Shauna and I descended steep stairs, our liquor list in hand.

"None of your fucking business."

I let out a nervous laugh, unsure how to take her.

She yanked on the door but it didn't open. "Fuck! If you run upstairs and grab the key, I'll tell you." She grinned, slapping me on the ass as I turned around to begin the summit.

I trotted up the stairs and she called out the figure when I reached the top. "Five grand!"

Ft. Collins' small city vibe contrasted that of its peoples' generous disposable incomes. I'd figured that the luxury bottles displayed behind the bar were for show rather than for sale, but several brands fetching a price of fifty to one hundred dollars a shot were on our restock list. The state sales tax was more than a percent higher than the rest of the country, and staff members were constantly complaining about the city's rental rates which continued to climb.

Luna was moving out over the weekend to her new apartment in Denver where she'd be peddling legal drugs in capsule form. Her entry level job with Pfizer would net her a salary of seventy thousand a year plus commission, more than double what she was making at Brix.

For Luna, it was a step up. For Shauna, it was a step back. Without financial contributions from a roommate, her monthly housing expenses would shoot up to almost twelve hundred dollars, a price she couldn't afford for long.

Shauna was always talking about money. Even on the first day we met, she told me some of the most intimate details about herself, that her student loans and medical bills could have been easily wiped out with the inheritance she was owed. The problem was Shauna's grandparents left it all to her sister – all one and a half million dollars.

There was probably a reason for it, but not one that she cared to share. Instead, she chose to blame her sister.

"Is Ciro rich?" I asked, handing the keys to Shauna who was talking on her phone at the base of the stairs when I returned. His multi-thousand-dollar night of pleasure was enough for me to live on for weeks.

"We'll chat later," she said into the speaker, summarily ending the call.

"He's loaded. I fucked him one night after a party at Mav's place. Took me back to his pad and treated me like royalty. The guy's house is incredible."

Shauna unlocked the door, a wave of musty air immediately assaulting our noses. She coughed but I inhaled, strangely satisfied by the odor.

"Is it going to be awkward seeing him tonight?" I asked.

"Why?"

"Well, you know."

"Because we had sex?" She shuffled over to the light switch and flipped it on, my vision adjusting slowly as my pupils flexed. "It was just for fun. No attachments."

"Oh," I replied, scanning the shelves for the items we needed.

"You've never had a one night stand?" Shauna asked.

I loaded my arms to capacity, clinching the bottles hard against my body to prevent them from falling. "Yeah, but then I do my best to avoid the mistake."

"Ciro wasn't a mistake. I'd been planning my way into his pants for a while," she said. "The only way I'm ever going to dig myself out of debt is to find a sugar daddy."

"I'm guessing it didn't work out?"

"It will if I allow it. I'm the reason he's having his birthday bash here. He knew I'd have to work, so he brought the party to me."

"Sounds like he's really into you," I commented as we toted our distilled spirits up the stairs.

"He is. But I don't know if I'm into him. Well, I am. But he's been married twice and has kids only a few years younger than I am."

"In the positive light," I said, "at least they are out of the diaper and tantrum stage."

54

I was intrigued when Shauna flirtatiously worked her way up the back of an older man who was perched on a barstool facing the opposite direction when we returned from the cellar. His full head of hair was greyed at the sides, his eyes etched deeply into glowing skin surely pampered with lotion. Despite the signs of aging, he was handsome, his upper body fit and strong beneath a trendy tunic in off-white that purposely accentuated his tan.

"Happy birthday, Ciro," Shauna purred, pecking him on the cheek while stroking his clean-shaven face.

"Thanks, gorgeous," he said, his lip creased by a surgically corrected cleft. He winked and turned to me. "You must be Tally."

I looked at Shauna and then back at Ciro.

"Mav told me he hired you last week," he said, tackling my confusion.

Ciro's voice drew Mav out from his office. "What do we have here?"

"I was just telling your new barmaid how much better your attitude has been now that Brix is out of the negative."

"I was never in the negative," Mav argued, greeting Ciro with a handshake.

"That's not what your old lady told me!" Ciro teased.

Mav grabbed him and wrapped him up in a hug.

Shauna leaned over and whispered to me. "This place practically broke up their marriage."

"I'm sure the new business was demanding of his time," I said.

Shauna shrugged. "She's a twat."

"Happy fucking birthday!" Mav kept Ciro pulled tight and wouldn't let him go, both men laughing as they bro'd out. "Let's get you a shot!"

Mav grabbed the bottle of Pappy Van Winkle and two rocks glasses. "I don't sell this. Got it just for you." He poured a double shot of straight bourbon whiskey for each of them and toasted his longtime pal before they downed their drinks.

Ciro motioned to the bottle after Mav poured another round for them to sip on. "Let me see that."

Shauna escorted me over to the ladder which had been erected near a pop-up table. It was covered in psychedelic colored pompoms and a banner with large blocky characters handwritten in permanent marker.

"Hope you're not afraid of heights."

"You'll catch me if I fall, right?"

"I'll try," she said, handing me several crepe paper decorations.

I climbed the rungs one by one until I reached the top. From the ground, it hadn't seemed as high up. I looked down at the table and could no longer clearly make out the hundreds of signatures that tagged the perimeter of Ciro's birthday banner. I could still read the main message, though; *Happy 40th Malaka!*

After taping the entire stack of decorations to the overhead beam, I stuck my hand down for replenishment. Instead, Shauna was absorbed in a heated textersation, her annoyance revealed by her typing cadence.

I cleared my throat and waited. She didn't notice.

"Should we move the ladder over and keep going?" I asked.

Shauna dragged her hand through her hair and sighed. "Give me a minute, would you?"

As I waited, I surveyed my surroundings. In the far back corner there was a tiny window that let in just enough light so I could make out a lofted platform suspended above the dance floor. On the opposite side, I could see the tops of the lights and speakers which hung over the stage. The dust was thick.

"What a cunt," Shauna said to herself before addressing me. "All done?"

"Well, I did what I could. If you want, we can –"

She cut me off. "Fuck it. Looks good to me. It'll be dark soon, anyway."

· ◆ ◆ ◆ ◆ ◆ ·

The band's first set wasn't scheduled until nine; that way, people could mingle and get a few drinks in them. After that, eclectic surf music would drown out conversation.

During the course of Ciro's sales career, he'd forged relationships with people all around the globe. Some had traveled from other states just to be present for his birthday celebration, one he had orchestrated every detail of. And because he'd paid for everything, his guests tipped us fat. Shauna divvied out the tip share at the end of the night as the final stragglers crawled into cabs patiently waiting to escort them home safely.

Ciro hung out at the bar after everyone left. It was obvious he was interested in taking Shauna home for the final hours of his birthday. She'd dressed ultra-sexy for the occasion, having counted on his solicitation. After her shift, she slipped on a pair of heels and invited me to his place for drinks.

"I think I'll take a rain check," I told her. "Vic's probably waiting up for me."

"Bring him with you," she insisted. "It's a perfect night for the hot tub. God, you should see his place!"

It was tempting, but I declined. "I have to get up early tomorrow."

"No you don't."

"My aunt just got out of the hospital."

"Oh, shit. Sorry to hear that."

"It's all good. But I haven't been by to see her yet."

"No worries. I'm sure Ciro won't mind us being alone." Shauna pushed her cleavage together and jiggled her breasts up and down.

"Not at all," I giggled. "He'd probably prefer it."

55

My trip up the canyon took longer than usual because I kept pulling off along the roadside to clip wildflowers. When I finally made it to the turn off, I smiled. To rest of the world, the gravel road led to a destination filled with heartbreak and sorrow. To me, it was starting to feel like home.

A tulip magnolia had dropped all of its blooms onto the ground leaving a blanket of pink petals on the mulch below. Squirrels chased each other up trees where soon-to-be born babies would nap in nests assembled by their expectant parents. As the mortuary came into view, I saw Uncle Remi's truck parked next to a motorcycle and a minivan.

Samantha greeted me from behind the desk. "Well hey there, Miss Tally."

I guessed at which vehicle was hers. "How's the baby?"

"Oh, he's just wonderful. Sleeps right through the night, now. You look great!"

"Thanks. So do you." She'd lost a few pounds, most likely water weight from carrying a seed inside her.

"That means a lot! I've been dying to get into some of my pre-pregnancy clothes." She shook her head. "That ain't happening."

"You'll get there," I said. "Is Uncle Remi around?"

"He sure is. Him and Darla had an especially difficult one this morning." She looked around and, although no one else was present, whispered to me. "A drowning."

"What an awful way to die."

"No kidding. Gives me the willies. I sure hope to go out softly, in my sleep if I can help it."

"That's a miraculous feat these days."

"No kidding. Well, let me grab him for you."

I thanked her, and off she went.

At some point since her return, Sam had rearranged the office. With the furniture better positioned, it was brighter and more spacious. Her workstation was smothered with greeting cards and store bought flower arrangements.

My eyes continued to wander until I spotted the filing cabinet. I wondered if Dabbencove's death certificate was there – an insignificant document lumped in with all the others. Even though the room felt peaceful, I knew the truth. The walls held secrets.

"Sorry for the wait," Samantha said, returning to the office. "We got to talking about this and that."

"No problem."

"Remi said to tell you to go on to the house. Jeannie is up and about. He's glad you're here."

"Do you think he'll be done any time soon?"

She shrugged. "Ten minutes means an hour in his world."

56

"Let me get a good look at you," Aunt Jeannine said when I found her in her garden, a floppy woven hat shielding her face, long sleeves and fabric gloves protecting her skin. She scanned me from head to toe. Spotting the wildflowers in my hand, she asked, "Are those for me?"

I presented them with reluctance, embarrassed by how chintzy they looked against the botanical backdrop that surrounded her. She brought the bouquet to her chest and hugged it. "I love Cleome!"

I didn't know which ones those were, the puffy purple doodads or the white prickly stemmed thingies.

"To what do I owe this surprise?"

"Vic told me they discharged you."

"Isn't it something?"

"I wasn't expecting to see you so active," I told her.

"I haven't felt this good in months. I mean, my head is sore. And my leg." She pointed down to her cast which was all but concealed beneath her pants except for where it came down over the top over her foot, leaving her toes free to wiggle. They were soil stained.

"Where are your crutches?"

"I'm used to the hobble method," she joked. "But I am ready for a break."

Once inside, Aunt Jeannine kicked back on her rocker and elevated her leg. The bottom of her foot was black.

"You probably shouldn't be getting your cast dirty like that."

She laughed. "That's what Ashlynn says."

"Who's Ashley?"

"Ash-LYNN. She's my home health nurse."

"I thought Vern was staying to help you."

"She flew out yesterday. She's got her own life to keep together."

I sat down opposite her.

"That's where Eileen usually sleeps," she said.

"Where is that little furball?"

"Probably somewhere out in the field hunting mice."

"You let her out?"

"Well sure."

"I don't know how I feel about that. She's always been an inside cat. I mean, don't mice carry diseases?"

"It's an animal's instinct, dear. You can't keep her from it."

There was a soft knock on the door and we both turned our heads toward the entryway.

"Who on earth could that be?" Aunt Jeannine asked, struggling to pull herself out of the chair.

"I can get it," I said, easily coming to my feet. I opened the front door and found a woman in scrubs waiting on the stoop.

"Hello. I'm here for Mrs. Forester."

I let her in and she followed me to the living room.

"Oh my. I assumed you weren't coming today," Aunt Jeannine said.

"I called you this morning to let you know I'd be by later than usual."

"Is Patrick still unwell?"

The nurse shook her head.

"Tally, this is Ashlynn. Ashlynn, this is my niece."

"Is this the one you're always talking about?" she asked.

"It sure is."

Ashlynn looked at me and smiled, and then looked back at my aunt. She nodded at Aunt Jeannine's black foot.

"I can see why you didn't answer the phone. Been in the garden, haven't you?"

"I can't stay away," my aunt told her.

"You should be resting."

"Rest is for old people."

Ashlynn laughed and shot me another smile. "She's something else."

"I'm well aware."

Ashlynn turned back to Aunt Jeannine. "I'll go get the tub ready. How's your head feeling?"

"Fine."

"Like you'd tell me the truth," she replied, and took off toward the bathroom.

"I'd like to see you again soon," my aunt said to me, wriggling around in the chair to create forward momentum. "Maybe you could come for dinner sometime?"

"That sounds great," I told her, remembering the chocolates I'd brought. I fished them out of my purse. They were somewhat melted.

"What do you have there?" she asked, spotting the stamped paper bag as she headed toward me.

"Your favorite pecan clusters. They aren't in the best shape at the moment. The heat got'em."

"How'd you know about those?"

"Vic told me."

"Oh, my sweet boy. How is he?"

"He's good."

"Did you two make up, yet?"

"We're working on it."

"Glad to hear it." She pulled me in for a hug and kissed me on the head. "Sorry to break this short, but I can't keep her waiting. Her son's got the flu."

"Ugh. That sucks."

"You can go ahead and put those chocolates in the fridge on your way out. They'll firm up just fine. And take the leftovers. There's enough for the two of you."

"Vic will be happy about that," I said, watching her make her way to the bathroom.

"Love you, dear," she called out before turning the corner.

· · ◆ · ·

I watched the house grow smaller and smaller as I travelled down the driveway to the main road. Meeting my aunt and uncle had given me a sense of family again. They made me feel cared for. Why hadn't my father moved to Colorado after his divorce? We would have benefited from the camaraderie.

Instead of carving out a new life, he'd stayed in Florida and faded away, depressed and alone. To protect me, he'd put up his walls and allowed them to cave in on himself, the outer structure strong, the interior in shambles. Most of his health problems were genetic. The rest I blamed on a broken heart. Maybe he hoped she would come back. Maybe I still did.

I came around the blind curve of the canyon and a deer bounded across the road, into the trees on the other side. When I hit my breaks, the tires skidded across a patch of gravel sending my vehicle toward the drop off which had no protective guardrail. Struggling to maintain control, I yanked on the steering wheel with my entire weight. The truck came to a halt in a patch of grass just off the road on the shoulder.

I shifted into park, thankful to have all four tires on the ground. Aunt Jeannine would consider it a sign. What would she say? *Don't dwell on the past.*

She had become my voice of reason and I was glad to have her as my guide. She wouldn't like me calling her that, though. I smiled and looked out the passenger window. The view was incredible, one I had always missed as I blew by it on my way to town.

I glanced down at the leftovers in the passenger seat and remembered my mission. I picked up my phone and called Vic to let him know I was on my way over. His number went straight to voicemail.

I returned to the road, drove a few miles, and tried him again. The signal beeped three times and hung up. My service bars were nonexistent. Surely he would be back from Denver. The sun had already set behind the mountains and only the light that was trapped in the clouds remained, creating a movie-esque haze that brought out the best in everything.

When cell service returned, I dialed him one last time before I pulled into his neighborhood. It went to voicemail, again. I banked left and right until I reached his street. At the end of the cul-de-sac, I spotted his van. I followed the curve around and parked on the curb behind him. Using the spare key he'd given me, I let myself in.

"Anyone home?" I shouted from the entryway. I carried Aunt Jeannine's leftovers into the kitchen and set them down on the counter. In the distance, drums rumbled. I followed the rhythmic music down the corridor to Vic's room.

At the doorway, I reached out for the knob and froze. Above the instrumentals, there was something more. Vic was not alone.

I tried to swallow the lump that was welling up inside my throat. Millions of scenarios raced through my mind as I inched back down the hallway and out of Vic's house. Once in the street, tears streamed down my face. Before I could regain my composure, anger brought me back inside, quick strides delivering me to his bedroom door. I reached for the handle and turned the knob.

"Who's here?" the female stammered.

As I flung the bedroom door open, Vic's beside lamp switched on. His just-fucked hair was wild, his eyes wide. There, next to him, was Xandra.

57

Without any words exchanged, I retreated. When I got to my truck, I slammed the driver side door shut and sped away.

I was confused. Curious, even. But above everything, I was hurt. Instead of losing myself to my mind, I reached out for company.

"Yo, yo, yo," Shauna answered, fast-paced electronica droning in the background.

"Hey. Sorry to bother you."

"You're not. Now, five minutes ago? We would have had a problem." Ciro's voice came across faintly and they both laughed. "I know you take longer than five minutes," she told him. "It's usually five and a half."

"I'll let you go," I said, regretting the call. "I didn't realize you'd still be there."

"No, no. It's fine."

"Are you sure?"

"Ciro, turn that down!" she yelled without covering the receiver. "What's up?"

It was a loaded question, one that I didn't know how to answer. I'd replaced my job. I'd replaced my best friend. And I'd replaced my lover. But the shit storm continued along its war path.

"You alright?" she asked.

"No. Not really," I told her.

"What's wrong?"

"I don't know. I guess that's the problem."

"Ciro, knock it off," Shauna ordered. Then, to me, "Why don't we get a drink somewhere?"

· · ✦ · · ·

I was two glasses in by the time Shauna got to Café Vino. The bartender had offered me a drink on the house after telling me that I looked like I needed one. I slugged it down in two sips and ordered another. Warmth was seeping into my cheeks, the alcohol numbing my feelings along with my body.

"I'll take what she's having," Shauna said to a random person that looked like she worked there. The pudgy hostess rolled her eyes and a minute later the bartender arrived to fill our glasses.

"I'm Bianca. Let me know if there's anything else I can do for you." She set out a happy hour menu and disappeared again.

Shauna lifted the glass to her mouth and took a swig.

"Vic is fucking his sister," I told her outright.

She nearly spit her wine out. "Whoa!"

I shook my head and stared off into space.

"That's messed up."

"Tell me about it."

"How did you find out?"

"I caught them in bed together."

"Amateurs."

I looked at her and raised my eyebrows. "Shauna!"

"I know, dude. I'm sorry. That was the wrong thing to say."

I sighed and looked away.

"Here," she said, handing me the rest of her wine. I chugged it.

Shauna raised her index finger into the air, tapped the rim of the empty wine glass, and then signaled to Bianca with two fingers. A moment later, she appeared with two more glasses of wine.

I lifted the fresh glass of Grenache to my lips and missed, dribbling it down the front of my blouse. "I think I'm starting to feel a little better," I said, cracking a smile.

Shauna giggled and dabbed my chest with her napkin. "I can see that."

We were quiet for a few moments. I didn't know where to take the conversation and she didn't want to overstep any boundaries.

"So, what do I do?" I finally asked her.

"I literally don't know what to say. I mean..." She paused. "Do they *do it* often?"

Frequency wasn't something I had thought about. Certainly, it hadn't been their first night together. Had it been a handful of times? Once in awhile? A couple times a week? I gulped what remained of my wine, keeping the glass inverted for longer than necessary to secure every last drop into my mouth.

"I have no idea," I replied, raising my finger in the air to signal I needed Bianca's services. I intended to order another glass, but when she arrived, I asked for my bill instead.

"Thanks for the company, Shauna. I appreciate it."

"No problem. I was ready to leave Ciro's anyway."

"He seems like a really nice guy," I said.

"Most definitely."

I pulled cash from my wallet. "I got this."

"Are you sure?"

"Yep. Thanks again for meeting me."

"Duh." She took one last sip of her wine and stood, leaving the glass half full. I stared it down.

Without a word, Shauna picked up the glass and moved it to the other side of the bar, farthest from me. I brought my eyes to hers and she smiled. "You'll be glad for it tomorrow."

"Yeah. You're probably right."

She roped her purse over her shoulder and prepared to leave. "If you need a place to stay for your last few weeks," she said, searching for her keys, "I've got a spare room now that Luna's gone."

"Is there a bed?" I joked, my eyelids heavy.

Shauna smiled. "There sure is."

The timing of her offer couldn't have been more perfect.

"Do you like cats?" I asked.

Her response was unexpected. "Meow."

58

Shauna's apartment faced west, where, just over the foothills, Forester Funeral Home carried out its important task of ushering the dead into everlasting life. I recognized Luna and Mav in a few framed photos, the rest, nameless faces smiling at the lens of a camera capturing but one moment in their lives – a moment when they pretended that everything in their world was picture perfect; a moment worthy of preservation to serve as a reminder to the 3D version of the subjects that happiness is tangible, even if elusive and fleeting.

In the center of the living room a sofa and loveseat in the same geometric pattern faced one another, awaiting sophisticated conversations that never took place. On the coffee table were once white roses approaching the end of their splendor, their petals shriveling, the vase caked with algae. The television was locked away in a colossal rustic armoire, centered between matching shelves that held unburned candles and commercially manufactured figurines.

Although my temporary bedroom's south facing window let lots of light in, a dark cloud of depression loomed over me. *The Fool* in my tarot reading wasn't some obscure element or a warning from the heavens. It was a depiction – a portrait of me. I was the fool.

All those journalism courses on the principles of neutrality and the importance of level-headedness had been thrown out the window. How had I become so out of touch? Camila had played me. Vic had played me. Like a pawn in their schemes, I was set up and sacrificed for their grand agendas.

And then there were the flashbacks from my accident in the canyon. Little by the little, the pieces were coming together. Bright lights. A nudge from behind. I was starting to remember seeing another vehicle. But I was also drunk. So I couldn't be sure. I wasn't sure of anything. Not even my own thoughts.

One morning, when I was lying awake, the sun spilled in over my face. It was warm. It was soothing. In that moment, I felt lucky to be alive.

I got up and headed to the shower to scrub away the blues. I closed my eyes and cleared my mind, trying my best to focus on the moment. I felt my pores open up, desperate for healing.

Shauna called to me through the door.

"Come in!" I shouted, unable to make out what she was saying over the water.

"I'm leaving for a bit," she said once inside our shared bathroom.

I poked my head out from behind the shower curtain. Shauna smoothed dark red lipstick over her pout and smacked her lips together.

"Got a hot date?" I asked.

She leaned into the mirror. "With the bitch from hell."

"Yikes," I said closing the shower curtain.

"She better be ready for me."

"What time do you think you'll be back?"

"I don't know."

"I was thinking about making us dinner," I said, debating where to start taking down the half inch worth of hair that hadn't seen a razor in two weeks. That's how long it had been since I'd walked in on Vic and his sister. We hadn't spoken, either.

I'd sent him one text: "I'm not ready to talk about this yet."

He'd reciprocated with one letter: "K."

"I'll text you when I'm on my way home," Shauna decided.

"Alright. Good luck!"

"There's no such thing as luck. The bitch either wants to get along or she doesn't."

"At least you can say you tried," I said, sticking my head out from behind the curtain once more.

Shauna smiled and exited without reply.

······

Clad in nothing but a towel, I whisked myself over to the pantry and conducted an inspection as I let my creative spirit conjure up a meal idea. The shelves were stocked with the basic staples of rice, flour, sugar, canned sauces, and soup bases. Deep within the cabinet, I found a jar of prepared curry. It would perfectly compliment the frozen pork loins I'd dug out of the freezer and set in the sink to thaw. Behind that, I was profoundly amazed at my next discovery: not one, but two bottles of Chilean Carmenere.

I pictured Shauna and her sister bickering back and forth over a mediocre chef's salad, and wondered if they had been close when they were younger. Shauna had a hard exterior which I imagined Sadie would blame on being the black sheep of the family. Her fickle attitude didn't net her any brownie points either.

It was sad they had let money ruin their sisterhood. But the inheritance couldn't be the only thing dividing them. There had to be something Shauna was hiding.

To slip into the vibe of prepping dinner, I set Pandora to Thievery Corporation and made myself an aperitif with cranberry juice and cheap Cava, three fingers worth of each that remained from the previous night of premeditated intoxication. The inspiration to get started in the kitchen didn't strike me like I thought it would. I tapped into the first bottle of Carmenere and waited.

Two drinks in, my hands began to assemble the items I needed to execute my menu. Rosemary and garlic fragranced the air in culinary collusion as I chopped them into bits. They would be sautéed with the pork which I was serving alongside basmati rice topped with lemongrass curry.

The meat could wait to be cooked until Shauna got home, but the rice needed forethought. I scooped out a cupful and dumped it into the basin of the rice maker. After rinsing it several times, I covered it with fresh water and set it on the counter to soak. Then, I poured myself another glass of wine.

Boredom sent me snooping around as I waited for time to pass. Shauna's schedule was the same as mine. We got up late, ate lunch together, carpooled to work, and partied after our shifts at Brix. Rarely alone, I took advantage of my solitude by checking every closet and drawer that I cared to.

I remembered Sadie telling me about curiosity once before, that it triggers chemical changes in the brain. Human nature imposed its will on me for a half hour until I arrived at Shauna's bedroom.

I'd been in her room before, but never without her. Though it would be dishonest of me to enter, the unrelenting desire to poke around held steadfast. I stared at her closed door.

Just as my hand reached out for the knob, a noise in the front entryway startled me. My heart jumped into my throat as I escaped to the bathroom and waited for Shauna to settle in. Minutes passed by without a word. I flushed the toilet, pretended to wash my hands, and returned to the kitchen to greet her.

"How was hell?" I asked, coming around the corner.

Shauna wasn't there.

I went to the front door and looked through the peephole. Nothing. I poked my head out into the breezeway. Not a soul. I closed the front door, latched it shut, and listened.

Something rustled inside a brown grocery bag atop the credenza. Stumped, I worked my way over to it. Reaching up to inspect, Eileen's head emerged.

"Silly girl!" I squealed. She meowed and revealed herself. "You scared the shit out of me!"

I scooped her up and topped off my wine glass. Armed with two of my favorite things, I headed to my bedroom to assemble an outfit.

59

Several shirts, two pairs of pants, a dress, and two skirts of differing length all looked dreadful on me. With the contents of my wardrobe scattered about the floor, I fell backward onto the mattress. My stomach was churning with hunger. Curious of the time, I rolled over and stretched out for my phone on the nightstand.

Shauna had said she would text me when she was on her way but I didn't have any messages from her. If she wasn't home by eight, I was going to have to eat alone.

"Dinner will be ready in an hour," I typed out with a smiley Emoji. "Don't be late!"

Fifteen minutes later, there was a knock on the front door. On the other side, Vic was waiting for me to answer.

I opened the door and stared.

"Are you going to let me in?" he finally asked.

"What are you doing here?"

He looked at me, perplexed. "You said not to be late."

"Late for what?"

"Dinner."

"Dinner?" I digested his statement, rewinding my actions. He held up his phone with the text message I had meant for Shauna. *How the hell had that happened?*

"I'll go," he said, pointing his thumb over his shoulder.

"No, its fine. Come in."

I showed him to the dining room table and we sat. There, I couldn't help but study him. The nervous electricity that had always accompanied our space was absent. For the first time, Vic seemed human.

"Are you done yet?" he asked.

"There's something different about you."

"Yeah? Maybe the excessive booze? Lack of sleep?"

It felt like he was blaming me. "Put yourself in my shoes," I said, and then gave a guided narrative to help him along. "Imagine yourself walking in on me with another man. Someone you've met and never felt threatened by. A person I introduced to you as my brother!"

"Jesus, Tally, I get it! I'm a piece of shit. I assume full responsibility."

Vic's physical appearance assured me he was miserable. Still, I couldn't find sympathy for him. He had brought this on himself.

Trying to move the conversation in a different direction, I stood and headed for the kitchen. "Dinner's not quite ready."

"That's it? We're not going to talk about us?"

Irritated by his insistence, I returned to the dining area. "Well, certainly there is no *us*."

Vic stared me in the eyes.

"I need time."

"You've had time."

"Well, I need more."

"Xandra moved out." Her name jarred me and he knew it. "Sorry. I shouldn't have brought her up."

"I don't want to know why or how you ended up in bed with your sister."

He continued on despite my wishes. "It's not something I could explain easily, anyway. One day it just sort of happened and then it never stopped. I don't even know –"

"Vic!" I cut in, the alcohol making my temper short. "Enough."

"You don't even care about me anymore, do you?"

"I have to put myself first. My feelings."

"Didn't you hear me? I'm to blame."

"And I agree. But the damage is done."

Vic crossed his arms and looked away.

"I'm not interested in sorting through this right now. When I figure out where I am in my own mind, I'll let you know. And then we can go from there."

"So because you're not ready to deal with this, I have to sit around and wait?" His eyes were still aloof.

I could tell he was sleep deprived. And it was possible he was drunk. I didn't enjoy seeing him distraught. I collected my thoughts before I spoke out of anger.

"Listen, Vic. You hurt me."

"I know." He brought his eyes back to me, tears welling up. "I'm sorry."

I sat down at the table. "I know you're sorry. And I accept your apology."

"I'm so sorry." He wrapped his hand around mine and tears streamed down his cheeks. "I hate myself."

"Everyone fucks up. It's what you do in the aftermath."

"I'm a wreck, Tally."

"You'll be fine. This isn't the end of the world. You've been through so much worse."

He sniffled and wiped at his eyes, returning his tear-stained hand to mine.

I didn't want to give him false hope but I needed to let him down gently. "I've only got a few weeks left in Colorado. Why don't we work on our friendship and see what the future brings."

Vic shook his head ever so slightly.

"I need to use the restroom," I told him, pulling my hand away. When I returned, he was gone.

I sat down at the table and looked at my phone. There was the text message that had started it all – the dinner reminder for Shauna that been sent to Vic instead. She still wasn't home and there was no word from her about her intentions for the evening.

What started as excitement to make a home cooked meal had evanesced and the only thing I wanted to do was lie down. I snuggled up with Eileen and closed my eyes. They wouldn't stay shut. I rolled onto my back and looked up at the ceiling which was slowly darkening.

Had I travelled all the way to Colorado for more of life's lessons? If so, what was I supposed to be learning? I tried to sink into my thoughts but my body wouldn't cooperate. I reached under my head to adjust the pillow and found the source of my discomfort. I'd stowed my notebook there, its metal binding elevating my neck at an awkward angle.

I pulled it out from under my head and opened to where the pencil was. On the page were the words I had written down the day I met Lani.

Fresh.

Fate.

Fail.

Fear.

The utterings of my subconscious.

Despite taking the huge leap into my soul searching journey, I'd fallen back into my old routine. If I was going to return to slaving away in the restaurant industry, I could have spared myself the trouble and stayed in Florida. Serving people was easier than figuring out how to serve myself.

I closed my eyes and pictured Sadie. Everything was working out for her. And Aunt Jeannine – she always seemed to be doing something she loved. Even Camila had an interesting life compared to mine. There were lies and secrecy, but it must have been exciting while it lasted.

The combination of booze and introspection was starting to put me asleep until I heard keys breach the front door. I opened my eyes and the room was completely dark. There was muffled laughter as Shauna made her entrance, her male companion the reason she hadn't come home for dinner.

"Want another drink?" I heard Shauna ask him. The fridge door sucked open.

"Good Lord, woman. What are you trying to do to me?"

"Get you drunk and take advantage of you," she told him.

The fridge shut and they fumbled down the hallway. Moments later, Shauna's bed springs were squeaking.

I listened for several minutes. Maybe I'd overreacted with Vic. Humans were designed to be sexual creatures, otherwise sex wouldn't feel good. If I hadn't been satisfying his sexual appetite, he could have told me. Or maybe there was more to it. Xandra had hit on me before. Was she angling for a threesome all this time? If I had climbed into bed with the two of them, would I have enjoyed it?

Okay, Tally, you're losing it.

I chuckled and stood to close the door. When I returned to my bed, I drew the covers and hooked earbuds up to my phone. Binaural beats put me to sleep quickly, but breifly, because yelling jolted me awake before the track even ended.

Hour unknown, I whisked myself over to the door and opened it slightly. All of the lights in the apartment were turned on.

"I can't do this anymore," the guy snarled. His silhouette bounced off the walls as he paced around the kitchen.

"Mav, you're being dramatic."

Did she just say Mav?

"Dramatic? She's your fucking sister, Shauna."

In their brief silence, I saw a glimpse of reality: Shauna was having an affair with her sister's husband.

"What if she finds out?" Mav asked.

"She's not going to find out." And then, another break in the argument. "Besides, would it be so bad if she did? She acts like you don't even exist."

"I love her."

"That's not what you said an hour ago."

"I'm leaving. I can't take this shit."

"Fine, go. I'll see you tomorrow."

I closed the door slowly, desperate to keep quiet. If Shauna suspected I was awake, she might want to vent. What would I say? *"It's okay, sweetie. You're only sleeping with your boss. Who happens to be your sister's husband."* How would I even look at him the same? What about his wife? What if she came into Brix?

Adrenaline had banished every bit of sleepiness from my being. I packed up my laptop and waited for Shauna to retire to her room. When she finally settled, I snuck into the hallway and exited the apartment.

60

It was three a.m. when I approached the counter at Alley Cat Café. I was wide awake and didn't need caffeine, but not drinking coffee at a coffee shop seemed taboo.

"Pulling an all nighter?" the cashier asked while I searched the menu board for a beverage.

"Not by choice," I told her.

"First time here?"

"Yeah."

"What would you like to try?"

"I'll just take an Americano."

"That's boring."

I looked down from the chalkboard to face her.

She laughed. "Sorry, not sorry."

"Well, shame on me."

"Would you mind letting me tantalize your palate?"

Before I could respond, she drifted over to the fridge and poured half and half into a stainless steel pitcher. While she cranked air into the cream, I looked around to see where I might like to sit. The place was empty except for two people playing some sort of board game and another person sitting alone with his laptop, his headphones drowning out the noise of the frother.

"Try this," the barista said, delivering her caffeinated concoction with inches worth of gravity defying foam, a peace sign stenciled with cocoa powder topping it off.

"How much?" I asked, plotting how I would carry the mug without it overflowing.

"It's on the house. But if you enjoy it, you can pay me with compliments."

I already had five bucks in my hand so I dropped it into a small metal pail on the counter which had a note that said TIPS.

She smiled. "If you need somewhere quiet, around that corner there is the unofficial study zone." Her hands came up to place air quotes around *study zone.*

I thanked her, hoisted my bag onto my shoulder, and lifted the mug with both hands. Heeding her advice, I chose a small table in the far back of the café under a ceiling tile with an abstract painting of a butterfly.

When I was finally seated, I took the first sip of my beverage. It was all foam. Disappointed, I went in for a second sip. It was there that I tasted the magical flavors of caramel and possibly hazelnut. The barista was right. My Americano routine was boring compared to her wizardry.

I set the mug aside and pulled my laptop from my backpack. On the front page of Yahoo! was Max Homestead's picture with a caption proclaiming details straight from the mouth of the killer. Just when I was ready to realign myself, free of Vic's bullshit and Shauna's personal demons, I was drawn back into Camila's drama. I looked into Max's face and clicked on the link.

"It's not every day I get to sit down with a killer," was the statement the interviewer started off with. She had soft features and mousy brown hair pulled back into a ponytail. Her suit was sharp but she seemed tired.

"C'mon Jill. You know me better than that," Max said.

"Do I?" she asked him.

"I'm innocent until proven guilty," he reminded her. "Even if the public has already tried me."

"What do you mean by that?"

"They don't know the facts."

"Please enlighten us."

Max chuckled. "It's not that simple."

"So you have nothing to say?"

"You're the one that insisted on me talking, Jill."

"I wanted to give you an opportunity to share your side of the story, Max."

"What about when Camila came to you?" he asked her.

She stiffened. "I was there to listen and to report."

"Camila told you her story. Now she's gone."

I wondered what he meant, what story was told.

Jill flattened her face. "The public blames you."

Amused, he threw his head back and laughed. "Yeah, well. I'm an easy target."

I paused the video and broke away from the screen to collect my thoughts. I picked up my cappuccino and sipped. Over the far side of the mug, I caught a stranger staring in my direction. He got up and made his way toward me.

"For fuckssake," I grumbled under my breath when he got close enough for me to recognize him.

"Hi," Brad said.

I looked at him and then to my right and left.

He laughed. "I'm talking to you."

"Me?" I said, feigning confusion.

"Haven't we met before?"

I shook my head no.

"Really? You have familiar eyes."

"I don't think so," I told him, returning my attention to the computer screen. I snapped it shut when I saw Max's face on the video.

"Hmph," he replied, and then helped himself to my table.

"I was actually just leaving," I said, loading my laptop into my bag.

He snapped his fingers and pointed at me. "Jackie."

I forgot I'd given him a fake name. There's no way he would connect me with the stolen gun which had been charged under Tally Forester. As far as he knew, we were two different people.

"Isn't that right?" he asked.

"Yeah," I said, loosening up.

"See. We did meet before. You came by the gun club and we chatted for a bit before you went outside to take a phone call and never returned."

Of course I remembered. The chances our paths would ever cross again were slim to nil. And yet, there he was, sitting across from me.

I settled back into my chair. "Brad, was it?"

He smiled. "Can I get you something from the counter?"

"Heavens, no! I haven't even been to sleep."

"Party girl, huh?"

"No, no partying. I was working on some research."

"For school?"

"I took the summer off."

"*Research* doesn't sound like something you would do for fun."

I smiled. "Personal pursuits."

"In law enforcement, we call that Cyberstalking."

I recalled our first interaction – how his charm had pulled me in. He was easy to talk to. I *wanted* to talk to him.

"That's right. You're a cop, aren't you?" I teased.

"And again. I'll correct you. I was a DEA agent. *Was* being the key word."

"Oh my God," I said, pretending to be stunned. "Your buddy. The one from the range."

He nodded his head but said nothing.

"I saw him on the news."

"I'm pretty sure we all have."

"What happened?"

"Hell if I know. I mean, I had my suspicions about him and her."

I didn't let on that I knew his reference. "Her who?"

"Camila," he said.

"I thought she was married."

"On paper." Brad glared at me like I said something I shouldn't have known.

"The news reported that her husband just passed."

"A few weeks ago." He paused. "I hope that motherfucker died in excruciating pain."

I was certain Dabbencove suffered. The Corazole would have thrown his heart rhythm off, causing his breathing to become difficult. He may have clutched at his chest, wondering why his body was failing him. In a moment of clarity, he had known the truth. The poison was already

323

coursing through his body when he realized it was Camila who was responsible for his demise. But why would Brad wish for something so callous?

"That's an awful thing to say," I told him.

"Once she realized what he was doing, she couldn't stand him. More than anything, I think she was embarrassed. We all were."

"I'm not following you," I said. There could never be a reason great enough to justify killing someone. Camila was a murderer. She had poisoned her husband.

"Camila was chasing her tail." Brad looked over his left shoulder and then glanced over his right. The sun was starting to come up and the first wave of caffeine seekers were piling in for their morning fix.

"Look, I don't know if we should be talking casually about all of this. Max is going on trial for murder. I'm a guaranteed subpoena."

"Do you think he did it?"

"Things aren't always what they appear to be. There are layers of truth."

"Anything but the factual truth is…" I searched for the words. "There can only be one truth."

"That's the principle the court system operates on. Regardless of the verdict, the nuances of the trial will shed light on what has really happened here. Max knows that."

"If he didn't do it, who did?"

Brad shrugged. "All I can say is, in my heart, I don't believe it was him."

"The heart can deceive," I said, aware of my own see-sawing speculations. "You have to look at the facts."

"Does that mean you'll accept my offer for a second date?"

"I'm not sure how that even translates."

"Well, the facts are –"

"Wait a minute. Hold that thought. Are you suggesting this was a date?"

Brad cracked a smile.

His connection to Camila and Max was tempting but I needed to keep my distance. If he found out what I was up to, and I was sure he could, it would be a bad situation. Besides, Brad didn't deserve to be played.

"I'll be leaving Colorado soon," I told him.

"We can plan something for when you get back."

"I'm not coming back."

"Oh."

"What I mean is I don't live here. I'm only visiting."

"Ahh, okay. Where are you from, then?"

"Florida."

"See? I knew there was a link."

I waited for him to continue.

"I have family in Florida. St. Pete, Clearwater area."

"The gulf coast is beautiful," I told him.

"What about you?" he asked.

"My college is in Orlando."

"U.C.F.?"

"Yep."

"My cousin works there!"

"Really? What does he teach?"

Brad grinned. "Law."

"An attorney?"

"Not quite. He's a campus cop."

I laughed and shook my head. "It's in your genes."

He grabbed my phone off the table.

"Hey!" I yelled at him defensively. A couple people turned to look at me.

I leaned in and whispered. "What the hell do you think you're doing?"

"I'm putting my number in here in case you want to call me sometime. I go to Florida once a year."

"I doubt it," I said, ripping the phone from his hand when he retuned it to me. "In fact, I'm going to delete it right now."

I scrolled through my numbers and looked up at him. His mouth was curled into a pout.

"Alright, fine. I'll leave it in there. But only because you're cute." It felt good to flirt with Brad. Of course I still cared about Vic, but our chemistry had been forever changed.

"You think I'm cute?" Brad asked.

"Did I say that?" I teased.

He shook his head and smiled.

"Well, maybe just a little."

"I think you're cute, too. Cute enough to meet up with in Florida."

"I get it! You want to meet up. I get it."

"So are we going to?"

I collected my things and stood. Before leaving, I bent down and whispered into Brad's ear. "Maybe."

"I'll settle for maybe," he shouted at my back. "Otherwise, this was the worst goodbye I've ever had!"

He had a point. I turned and walked back over to him. He stared at me, confused. I leaned down, kissed him on the cheek, and whispered in his ear again. "It was nice to meet you."

61

My caffeine fix had finally worn off and I crashed hard. Hours passed. I felt like I could sleep for the rest of the day and all night but my belly wouldn't allow it.

In the same clothes from the night before, I made my way to the kitchen and called out to Shauna. "I'm going to make something to eat."

She didn't answer by the time I'd made it to the fridge. There were several slices of left over pizza in a cardboard box with Krazy Karl's stamped on it. The ease of heating it up was tempting, but I was craving breakfasty stuff. We had all the ingredients to make a veggie frittata with turkey sausage. And if I was really feeling ambitious, I could griddle a few pancakes to have with the blueberry maple syrup I'd been eyeing out for the last week.

I looked over at the sink. Every plate and cup Shauna owned was dirty, the stack higher than the countertop and almost toppling over. Her help would make my cooking event much easier, especially since I'd have to do the dishes first.

"Hungry?" I shouted through her door. She didn't respond.

"Hey lady cat," I tried again, this time with a knock. "How do pancakes sound?"

Shauna still didn't answer. I opened her door and peeked in. She wasn't home.

Producing a large meal seemed pointless for a single beneficiary so I settled for the pizza. After placing two pepperoni topped slices on a plate, I set it in the microwave. Before I could even hit the start button, Aunt Jeannine's voice came in to scold me. *Never irradiate your food, dear!*

I removed the plate from the microwave and looked around for a toaster oven. There wasn't one. The full sized oven would take too long to heat so I decided to eat the pizza cold.

I brought my meal over to the table, took one bite, and regretted it. The dough was dry and hard, and the cheese had coagulated into a flavorless mass.

Just as I was about to take in another disappointing mouthful, there was a knock on the front door. Thankful for the disruption, I dropped the slice and stood.

I scoped out my visitor through the peephole; she wasn't familiar. Before I could decide if I wanted to answer, she knocked again and called out.

"Shauna, its Patrice."

I unlocked the door and opened it.

"Hello," she said with a friendly smile. "Is Shauna around?"

"No," I told her, shaking my head.

"Do you know when she'll be back? We need to talk. It's important."

"I can leave her a message if you'd like."

Eileen came around the corner and stared out the door. She'd been trying to escape ever since Aunt Jeannine had given her a taste of the outside world. Fearful that the apartment complex wasn't a safe place for her adventures, I kept her in.

"You've got to be kidding me," Patrice complained. "When did she get a cat?"

"She's mine," I said.

"Are you living here?"

"No. Just a guest."

"I'm sure you don't know any better, but you have to be on the lease if you're staying more than five days. Even if it's temporary. And I haven't seen Shauna come by the office to make those adjustments."

"I'm sorry. I'll have her add me."

"Also, there's a pet deposit."

"I can take care of that right now. Let me grab my checkbook." I closed the door and shooed Eileen away.

"You've gotten me into trouble, little miss!" She scampered off into my room.

"How much do I owe you?" I asked when I returned.

"It's four hundred."

My jaw dropped open. "Dollars?"

Patrice snickered. "Yeah, dollars."

"Is it refundable?"

"It depends. Is your cat well behaved?"

"She's great," I said with a smile which quickly faded. "I hate to do this, but would you mind if I give you half now and post date the other half for two weeks from now?"

"That's fine," she said.

I thanked her and began filling out the check.

"Florida, huh?" I looked up at Patrice. She was eyeing out my address. "Why the heck are you spending your summer in Colorado?"

"It's a long story."

She laughed. "I've never been to Florida before."

"You should go. I can recommend tons of places." I looked back down and signed my name.

"You can fill in the other details," I said, handing her the first check with a few blank lines. She took it from me and I started on the second one.

"Tally Forester," she read aloud. "Do you have family here?"

"I do."

"Do they happen to own Forester Funeral Home?"

"Yeah. That's my Uncle Remi's place."

She smiled. "Remington is such a kind, gentle soul."

"How do you know him?"

"My grandmother."

"Are they friends?"

"No, no. She died two years ago." I watched as Patrice's thoughts sunk into her past.

"I'm sorry to hear that."

"Look, I'm not here to cause you any trouble," she finally said, tearing the check in half and handing it back to me. "Tell Shauna we got another complaint from the neighbors."

"Oh," I said. After my encounter with Brad, I'd forgotten all about her fight with Mav.

"She and I go way back but it's out of my hands now. This is the third time in six weeks."

"Jeez. I'll definitely let her know."

330

"Please do. They are threatening to get the police involved."

"That's not good."

"No, it's not. And make sure she puts you on the lease."

"Will do."

She thanked me and turned to begin her descent.

"Who was that?" a voice behind me asked once the door was closed.

Startled, I jumped. Shauna was wrapped in one towel and drying her hair with another. "I didn't know you were home," I told her.

"I was in the bath."

"I called your name."

"I had headphones on."

"In the tub? That's dangerous as hell. You could get electrocuted."

"Okay, Mom. Now that my interrogation is over, who was at the door?"

"Patrice."

"From the office?

"Yeah."

"What did she want?"

"The neighbors put in a noise complaint."

Shauna took off to her room and reappeared wearing pajama pants and a shirt that was three sizes too big, her head topped with a towel turban. Quick strides brought her to the door where she slid her feet into sandals.

"Where are you going?"

She said nothing.

"Shauna, wait!" I shouted as she threw the front door open and slammed it upon exit. I ran after her and stood at the balcony to negotiate.

"I don't know if this is a good idea!" I called out.

Shauna didn't respond. She'd already made it down the first flight of stairs to the landing.

"Hey, let's not get crazy over this," I said, trying to persuade her. "I'm sure it's just a misunderstanding."

When she pounded on the neighbor's door below us, I knew there was no stopping her. I returned to her apartment to await the aftermath.

Ten minutes had passed when I realized I'd zoned out. My eyes were fixed on the pizza slice that would have been swimming around in my stomach had Patrice not interrupted my lunch. Disgusted, I promptly threw it out. With hunger pains starting to boil over, I swung the pantry door open and stood in front of it to find a more suitable solution.

It was too warm out for soup. Rice would demand more time that I wanted to invest. And there was no milk for cereal. I spotted a box of graham crackers and a jar of peanut butter. *Score.*

I brought both items over to the counter and laid out a paper towel as my assembly station. I reached down inside the box. My hand went clear to the bottom. Not even the bag remained. I already had the peanut butter on my knife, so I licked it off and called it good.

I couldn't imagine what was taking Shauna so long. She had to have been gone for nearly twenty minutes. I opened the front door to see if I could hear anything. All was quiet. I returned to the kitchen and looked out the window for police cars. There were none. With no signs of an altercation, I decided to move on with my day.

I brought my laptop onto the kitchen table and opened it. Jill's video interview with Max was still on the screen. He was in midsentence, his mouth open as he responded to Jill's question. Though their interaction was strained, it was obvious they had history. And according to Max, Jill and Camila did too.

Then there were Brad's comments. He clearly thought Dabbencove deserved his fate, but did he know Camila was the one who'd issued his death sentence?

"Problem solved," Shauna announced when she made it back to the apartment after what seemed like an hour. "Are you riding with me?"

I broke away from my screen and flexed my eyebrows at her.

"It's almost seven," she said.

I groaned and threw my head back drama queen style. My mental health days had expired and my scheduled return to Brix had arrived.

With a smile, Shauna pulled her phone out, dialed a number, and put the receiver to her ear. "We're not coming in tonight," she said to the person on the other end. "I don't feel like seeing you."

It had to be Mav. He said something and Shauna shot back. "Tally needs one more day." She gave me an over emphasized wink.

He managed to get a few words in before she cut him off. "That's not my problem. Monday's are slow. I'm sure you can handle it." With that, she hung up.

"You didn't have to call out," I told her.

"Fuck it. I don't feel like working, either."

"It wasn't that. I just forgot. All of my days have been jumbled together."

"I know what you mean."

"What are you going to do with your night off?"

"My night off? It's *our* night off! Go get dressed."

I wasn't into partying. "Maybe we should just chill here."

"Ugh. No way. I need to get out."

"What if Mav sees us somewhere?"

She shrugged. "Don't care."

I wouldn't feel right about it even if it didn't matter to her. I was new and he was my boss.

"They don't need us. There's two barbacks. Besides, he pissed me off."

I wasn't sure if she was venting or seeing how much of their feud I had witnessed. I held my tongue and Shauna disappeared into the kitchen. When she returned, she had two shots of something clear.

"Cheers!" she said, offering one up to me.

I took it with reservation. "I don't know. I'm just not feeling it."

"You will be soon," she said, and downed hers in a single gulp.

62

I was sloshed by the time we stumbled out of Elliot's Martini Bar. Fruity vodka infusions were mixing together inside my stomach. There was watermelon followed by key lime pie. Something cranberry based. Then, chocolate raspberry.

Shauna knew the entire staff there. As bartender etiquette goes, your drinks become significantly stronger when you're an ally in the service industry. Determined to drown our woes, they were generous with their pours, and at the expense of our livers, gentle on our bank accounts.

"Any food places open?" I asked when we hit the sidewalk.

"No. But there's a place near us that delivers until three."

I looked at my watch. It was quarter till. "They'll be closed by the time we get home."

Shauna sat on a set of concrete stairs and sifted through her phone. When she found what she was looking for, she placed her call.

"Got any specials going on?" she asked when they picked up.

"That's perfect. Just cheese on one. Tally, what do you want on yours?" I thought of the lifeless slice that had almost become my lunch.

"Make up your mind or I'll do it for you," Shauna told me.

"Pepperoni," I said, deciding there would be nothing to eat once I got home. I couldn't do another heap of peanut butter, especially not on an alcohol filled tummy that would show me no love in the morning.

"Now we need a ride," Shauna said when she hung up. "Give me the address behind you."

I turned to my left and read it to her. "Two-oh-three Linden Street."

Several names were printed on the sign. At Suite #308, there was one I recognized. "You've got to be shitting me."

"Did you get it wrong?" Shauna asked, joining me.

I looked up to the third floor windows. "My fucking mind just got blown."

"Okay weirdo. The Uber driver will be here soon."

"No, listen. I just heard of this chick yesterday and now here I am, randomly standing in front of her office building." I pointed to her name.

"Really?"

"Yeah. She's a part of this crime thing I was researching. I thought I might want to ask her some questions."

"Oh yeah. I always forget you're a journalist."

I laughed. "More like a wannabe."

Shauna went to the front door and pulled on the handle. It opened. She turned around, smiled, and entered. I chased her in to the lobby.

"What are you doing?" I demanded when I found her at the elevator with the up arrow glowing.

"Seeing if Miss Jill Stanley is available." The elevator doors opened and Shauna stepped in. I followed after her.

"It's three in the morning!"

"Maybe she works late."

"Shauna! I can't afford to fuck this up."

"Relax dude. She's a person. You're a person. It's not like you're meeting the president of the United States."

"I'm drunk!" I shouted, catching a glimpse of my reflection in the mirrored elevator doors. "And I look terrible."

"You look great." A bell chimed and the elevator doors opened.

"Please, Shauna. Let it go." I grabbed at her arm to restrain her. She yanked free.

"Why are you being such a pussy?"

I watched as she made her way down the corridor of the third floor, swinging her head side to side as she read the door numbers. The bell chimed and the elevator doors closed me in. Shauna meant well but she never honored my wishes. Jill wouldn't be there anyways. She couldn't possibly be. *Could she?*

I hit the first floor button and the elevator obeyed. Once on the main level, I exited the building to find a car pulled to the curb with its lights on. A voice called out.

"Might you be Shauna?"

I shouted at him and pointed up at the building behind me. "She'll be down in a minute."

"Right on. Are you the second rider?"

"I am."

"Cool. You can get in if you want."

"I'll just wait for her."

"Alright. I'm starting the clock now."

"I don't know what that means," I said.

"It means you have five minutes before I leave."

On cue, Shauna emerged from the building. "You were right. No one home."

I was glad to see her, my irritation transposed to the driver whose comment went right up my ass.

Shauna spotted his idling car. "Is that our Uber?"

"Yeah. He's a dick," I told her. "Let's just walk."

"We can't. Pizza's on the way." She headed for the vehicle, and when she reached the passenger side window, she bent down to its level.

"You're not a dick, are you?" Shauna shouted at the driver, deliberately loud so I could hear her. They both laughed. She opened the door and took her seat next to him.

I was still on the steps of Jill's building when Shauna hit the horn and yelled to me. "This train is leaving!"

I rolled my eyes, annoyed at both of them. I'd had enough of alone time with her for one evening. When we got home, I planned on going straight to bed. Shauna could stay up and binge eat by herself.

63

"Good morning, I'm calling for Miss Tally F."

"Speaking," I replied, my voice barely above a whisper as I was dragged into consciousness.

"This is Diane from Jill Stanley's office."

I shot up out of bed.

She continued. "I found your message this morning and Jill has agreed to meet with you."

My message? What had Shauna done?

"That is, if you are felling well enough."

I forced words into my mouth. "When would it be most convenient?"

"She's available now until ten."

"Today?"

"Well. Given your condition, wouldn't sooner be better?"

Given my condition? I pulled the phone away from my ear to read the time on the screen. It was almost nine thirty.

"Can you make it here by then?" Diane asked.

I didn't have a choice. I had to make it. "I'll be there."

"Okay. We'll be expecting you." And with that, she hung up.

I bolted out of bed. Shauna must have seen me barreling down the hallway to her room because she called out before I got there.

"Yoo-hoo."

I spun on my heel and traced her voice. She was sitting at the kitchen table with my laptop.

"What the hell are you doing?" I shouted at her.

"Catching up."

"You're violating my privacy."

"You left it on the table."

"Shauna! It was closed!"

"So?"

"I can't do this right now. I have an appointment with Jill at ten."

Shauna looked over at me and smiled. "Congratulations." She returned to the screen.

"What kind of message did you leave for her?"

"Your name."

"And?"

"Your number."

"Tell me what you wrote."

"What does it matter? You got what you wanted."

"That's not the point. She made it seem like I was sick or something."

Shauna laughed.

"Why are you laughing? This is serious!"

"Is it as serious as the shit she's being sued for?" She read from a list. "Slander. Defamation. Right of publicity violation. Obstruction of justice."

"What are you talking about?"

340

"Jill Stanley, Ft. Collins resident and author, to file counter suit in charges against her."

I digested Shauna's words as she continued. "Here's a direct quote from yours truly. *This retaliation is a staunch violation, not only against me, but to the community as a whole. We need to unify. We need to fight. And we need to stand in solidarity against –*"

"Tell me what you said."

"This woman sounds like a troublemaker," Shauna went on, avoiding me.

"Please, Shauna. I'm not fucking around."

"Alright already. Don't have a cow." She closed my computer and turned to me. "Everything is fine."

With my arms crossed and my face contorted into a scowl, I waited.

"All I said was that you were..." She paused. "Ill."

"Ill," I repeated.

"Yeah."

"What the fuck does that mean?"

"You know, like you have an illness."

"Okay?"

"So when you get there, make sure you keep that story up."

"Well, I'm not ill so how am I going to act like I am?"

"Oh, c'mon. Anyone can fake that they have cancer."

"You told her I have cancer!" I screamed. "Are you crazy?"

"Some say I am," she replied, relishing the notion.

"That's completely insensitive and outright wrong."

"It worked, didn't it?"

Remembering that my appointment was fast approaching, I looked over at the clock on the stove. Our conversation had already taken up more time than I had. "We'll talk later. I have to go."

I dressed quickly and threw my hair into a bun. Shauna was still at the table when I went to leave. I snatched up my laptop and headed for the door. Before I left, she couldn't help but make another absurd comment.

"I was thinking."

I turned to her, the door half open, part of my body already making the exit.

"What if you really are dying of cancer? I mean, how would you know?"

I slammed the door shut and trotted down the stairs.

64

All in all, Shauna had done me a favor, even if it was under false pretenses. But as the elevator brought me closer to Jill Stanley's office, I felt like puking. I had no idea what I was going to say to her. *I don't have cancer and I had no idea you were an author. I'm here to drill you about your personal life.* I should have never agreed to the meeting on such short notice.

When the elevator doors swung open, I didn't move. Before I could unglue my feet from the floor, the doors started to shut. I let them close and stood motionless. Because it hadn't been told what to do next, it remained stationary on the third floor.

I debated an escape. I could leave the building and call Diane before I was spotted. I'd tell her I wasn't feeling as well as I had hoped and reschedule.

The elevator dinged and the doors opened. A husky man in a suit went to enter, but after seeing me, politely shifted to the side to await my exit.

When I didn't make my move, he inquired. "Getting off here?"

The doors started closing again and he put his porky hand in to halt them. Sweat studded the crown of his head where, over the years, his hair had fallen out. His huge briefcase was overstuffed and I could hear his breathing across the more than five feet of space that separated us. Finding courage, I stepped forward and exited without a word.

"You're welcome!" he shouted at me as I approached Diane's secretarial domain. She looked up and addressed me before I could introduce myself.

"You must be Tally F. Go on ahead through that door. She's expecting you."

There would be no waiting in the lobby – no time to get my thoughts under control. I nodded at Diane and made my way toward Jill's office. I lifted my hand, paused, and then gently knocked on her door.

· · · ♦ · · ·

"Thanks for having me," I said as Jill directed me to sit on a chair opposite her, the workspace between us.

She smiled a rich, warm smile. "Of course, Tally."

Jill probably assumed the meeting was about her book. That I was a fan of her work, and getting her autograph was on the bucket list I wanted to fulfill before I died of whatever type of cancer she thought I had.

But I'd never read her book. Hell, I didn't even know the name of it. I scanned the walls, searching her accolades for something to go on. It was impossible to read anything from the position of my chair.

I looked over at Jill. She was staring at me. In that moment, I decided there was only one way out.

"I'm not here to bullshit you. I'm doing research on the Max Homestead case."

She leaned back in her chair and crossed her arms.

"I have questions about him."

"So why are you sitting in my office?"

"Because I think you know the truth."

The phone on her desk rang and she answered it. "Yes?" A pause. "Okay?" Another pause. "I thought we'd come to an agreement."

I could hear Diane's strained voice on the other side but couldn't make out what she was saying.

"Call Mr. Williams back and tell him he needs to propose an alternative solution."

Jill hung up without waiting for a response. She stood, adjusted her perfectly tailored pencil skirt, and relocated herself in front of the windows that looked down on Old Town Square. There, she gazed out, lost in thought.

Moments later, she brought herself over to the desk and sat on the edge of it, her feet no more than a foot in front of mine. "There is nothing to be gained in fighting for justice."

"If you believe that, then why did you interview Max?"

She answered with one word. "Guilt."

"His?"

"Mine."

Jill returned to the chair opposite me. I watched her as she watched the pendulum on her desk kick back and forth, shaving off time, second by second.

"Do you think he killed her?"

"Absolutely not."

"Are you going to stand up for him?"

"It's not my place."

"What do you mean? You have a voice. And an audience."

"Look, Tally. Don't worry about Max."

I scoffed. "People get convicted on circumstantial evidence all the time."

"You're right. They do."

"It's possible he'll be found guilty without one bit of forensics. Doesn't that bother you?"

"Max will be a free man soon. It was set up this way."

I thought about her word choice. *Set up.*

Jill stood and returned to the window. An eternity of silence passed before she spoke.

"Camila was in a tough place. She was working with Max on a special project involving drug trafficking. When they started uncovering trails that led back to the DEA, she contacted me to write her story. She wanted to blow the thing wide open."

"What happened?"

"We met. She told me everything. And I published *Contriving Justice* a year later."

"What about the lawsuit?"

"Mr. Howes found out he had a lead role in the book. Not by his own name, but still. He told me to pull it from the shelves or he would do it for me."

"Mr. Howes? As in Charlie Howes?"

"Yep. Good ole Charlie. Chief of Police. He's as crooked as they come."

"This is unbelievable."

"When property values and incomes go up, people are willing to turn a blind eye."

"Even as a police chief, he has no legal standing to stop you from whistleblowing. There are laws to protect you."

"His official charge is that I damaged his reputation and it could jeopardize his chances of reelection. More than anything, it's about revenge. He's pissed I ignored his request and now he wants to make an example out of me."

"An example of you? He's the criminal!"

"Yes, but he's the one with protection." She paused. "Is this for a school project or something?"

"No. I'm out for the summer."

"Then why are you so interested?"

"I've been visiting my uncle. He owns a funeral home out in Bellvue."

Jill grinned. "So Martin wasn't making it up."

I shook my head no.

"Tally F." She laughed. "I should have connected the dots."

"I'm sorry. This wasn't my idea."

"I'm not pleased with the circumstances, but I do value your tenacity." She looked off in the distance. "You are motivated by the desire to find the truth. It's the same thing that motivates me. But let me be clear. You have no idea where your research will take you. Often times, it is better to leave things where they lie."

"I need to know."

She shook her head to tell me she understood.

"Why didn't Camila come out publicly?" I asked her.

"She was terrified."

"Of Charlie?"

"No."

"The DEA?"

"No." She paused. "Of her own husband."

"Flynn Dabbencove?"

Jill nodded. "He was the one orchestrating the drug trades. Then he'd turn the dealers out. Higher ups in the DEA knew about it. They used civil asset forfeiture to confiscate whatever they wanted. Money. Guns. In exchange for Flynn's *righteous philanthropy*, they let him buy up all the seized property dirt cheap. Made him a millionaire."

I couldn't believe it. Dabbencove was scum. Camila's undercover work had put her on a trail that ran straight into her own home.

"When Flynn found out Camila was barking up his tree, he warned her. She refused to back off. Then, he threatened to kill her."

"So she killed him instead," I said. Camila wasn't a heartless, greedy murderer. She was a victim. And a hero.

"It doesn't matter that he's dead. His business partners aren't. They've suffered greatly because of her. And they won't stop until they find her."

"Camila's alive?" I gasped.

Jill didn't respond. She didn't have to. The answer was written across her face.

"Do you think they'll track her down?" I asked, suddenly worried for Camila's safety.

She closed her eyes and winced. "I sure as hell hope not."

Epilogue

"Now boarding all rows for flight twelve sixty-two nonstop to Boston," the representative announced from United's welcome desk at the mouth of the terminal. I opened my eyes and gathered my things.

Only a couple of people were ahead of me between the stanchions, ninety percent of passengers having already boarded. I'd chosen the cheapest ticket and thus ranked at the bottom of the priority list, behind the young, the elderly, and the first class. I was pretty certain 34B was going to be a middle seat. Hopefully it would be at least a couple rows away from the bathroom.

I handed my photo ID to the clerk but she was only interested in my boarding pass. She scanned it, looked up, and smiled. "Enjoy your flight."

As I made my way down the jet bridge I wondered if people actually *enjoyed* flying. I didn't. In fact, I was terrified of planes. But Sadie had gotten engaged and I owed it to her to be there.

She had the whole trip planned out: dress shopping, cake tasting, venue exploring. It would to be an eventful four days. And once I got back to Colorado, I'd be packing up my truck to head home, just in time for the fall semester.

I couldn't remember ever being excited to start class, until the previous week, when I declared a new major. The switch from journalism to criminal justice was going to delay me by half a year, only a slight setback compared to the ramifications of giving up on school all together.

Before my paperwork with the registrar's office even finalized, I was searching U.C.F.'s website for the curriculum list, wondering what techniques I'd be learning in a course called *Interviews and Interrogations*. My interest skyrocketing, I had no doubt – I was headed in the right direction.

At the end of the jet bridge, there was a collection of oversized items that needed to be moved to cargo. I took inventory and wondered if I would be able to pick out which passengers owned what. I'd look for twins that would be loaded into the double stroller; a bearded, long haired intellectual who would claim the acoustic guitar; and a little old lady who would need that wheelchair to carry her to the next stage of her travels.

The pilot and a female flight attendant were hanging out at the plane's entrance. He lifted his hand to rub lipstick away from the corner of her mouth. I cleared my throat and stepped into the metal bird. Like a good hostess, the attendant turned to me and said her line. "Welcome aboard!"

I smiled back at her, turned right, and made my way into the cabin. With my carry on tucked tight against my chest, I squeezed through the rows of seats. Instead of playing the match game I'd created, I kept my focus forward and headed to the back of the plane. From my peripheral I could see passengers eyeing me as I walked past, leaning to the inner seats to avoid contact.

The walk down the aisle seemed eternal. When I finally reached row 34, I found another obstacle: a little red-headed girl with tons of freckles.

"I'm sorry, young lady. I believe you're in my seat." I showed her my boarding pass to validate my claim.

"I believe I am," she responded. "But if you're interested, I'd be more than willing to strike a deal." She unzipped the huge backpack on her lap and gave me a peek inside. There were tons of snacks.

"You're sure you want the middle?" I asked her.

She shook her head yes.

"Fine," I said to her. "But I get to pick out whatever I want from your goodie bag."

Her face lit up and she smiled, her front teeth too big for her mouth. "Deal."

I took my place next to her and settled in.

She was anything but shy. "This is my eighteenth plane ride, you know?"

"Wow. You do a lot of traveling."

"Every summer. And Thanksgiving. Christmas. Easter."

"Always to Colorado?"

"Yep. My parents hate each other."

"I'm sure they don't *hate* each other."

"No, they do. My mom tells my dad she hates him all the time. That's why he moved to Colorado."

"Where does your mom live?"

"In Boston, silly. That's where we're going."

A female attendant's voice came over the intercom and asked for everyone's attention. She introduced her

351

assistant who was in the aisle, holding up an oxygen mask and a life jacket for her safety demonstration.

I was only half listening, my mind evaluating the chance of the plane actually crashing. I convinced myself that they only did the safety talk for liability purposes. Planes didn't crash. I'd even read somewhere that I was more likely to be bitten by a shark.

A text from Sadie saved me from speculation. "In the air yet?"

"Soon," I typed back.

"Can't wait to hear about Colorado!"

I cracked a smile. Where would I begin? I was grateful for my season of lessons. About failing, and falling, and getting back up. About honoring the journey. But I was ready for the return of knowns: the familiarity of my apartment, the comfort of my bed, the predictability of a routine.

"Looking forward to some normalcy," I said.

"You mean the exact thing from which you wanted to escape?"

I pictured the look on her face and laughed. When I tuned back in to the voice on the intercom, we were being told to stow our belongings for takeoff. I looked down and pushed my bag under the seat in front of me with my feet. Next to mine were little toes with red polish.

"Do you know why elephants paint their toenails red?" I asked my half pint row mate.

"No," she replied.

"You're supposed to say *why*," I told her.

"Why?"

"So they can hide in cherry trees?"

She looked at me like I was crazy.

"Have you ever seen an elephant in a cherry tree?" I continued.

She thought for a moment, scrunching up her chin and tapping it with her index finger. "No," she finally said.

"They hide pretty good, don't they?"

She rolled her eyes and slipped her headphones on. The sticker on the back of her phone said *Property of* and then a line for your name. *Me* was printed in bright red marker, below it, the name *Kate* in parentheses.

The flight attendant, who was making her way down the aisle to secure the overhead compartments, stopped by to inform me of my disregard to her instructions. "Can you put your seat up all the way, ma'am?"

"Oh," I said, not realizing I was in violation. I leaned forward and depressed the button to bring the back of the chair up to its most uncomfortable position.

"And her carry on isn't properly stowed," she said, spotting another problem. Before I could respond, she bustled off to scold her next rulebreaker.

Kate looked like she'd dozed off, so I unbuckled my seatbelt and reached down to relocate her belongings. Something inside her bag was preventing me from moving it any further. I unzipped the backpack and stuck my hand in to adjust whatever was being stubborn.

"Lemonheads," I said aloud, my mouth saturating with saliva. In that moment, an idea struck me. I tucked the candy box back into her carry on and pushed it once more. This time, it slid under easily.

"How about a day trip to New York?" I texted Sadie.

"Sounds amazing."

"Ever heard of Brookville?"

"Google has." She sent a screenshot of the map. "Call me when you land."

"Will do! See you in a few hours."

I switched my phone to airplane mode and closed my eyes. A smile worked its way across my face as I imagined my final ode to Camila. I couldn't wait to spit on Flynn Dabbencove's grave.

Acknowledgements

Locard's exchange principle is a concept that has stuck with me long after studying forensics in college. For those of you who aren't obsessed with crime documentaries or haven't ever heard of Locard or his exchange principle, it essentially says that every contact leaves a trace; that a perpetrator and a victim create an irreversible connection that forever links them.

This philosophy extends beyond the realm of science. That is to say, every human interaction you have serves to contribute to your identity in some way. *Every contact leaves a trace.* To that end, I am thankful for everyone that I have crossed paths with, whether a brief conversation about cheese at the supermarket, or an in depth discussion about where the wind comes from. For the ones who have laid down a helping hand and for those who have placed obstacles along my path. For those who have conquered and those who have failed. My whole is not greater than the sum of my parts. I am whole *because of* the sum of my parts. Thank you all. This book is for you.

And then there are those who have contributed to my success more intimately. With gratitude to Brian Kaufman, for his guidance and selfless interest in helping me to see my potential as a writer. To my close friends, near and far, for always asking how my novel was coming along and pushing me to complete it. To my father, who believed in my abilities even from a young age and who continues to be a source of inspiration. To my brother, whose humor I will always carry in my heart. To my family, for giving me the space to evolve. To my husband, John Jeffrey, for his unwavering allegiance and encouragement when I needed it the most. And to my creator, whoever that may be, for my opportunity to shine.

Thank you all from the depths of my being.

ALSO AVAILABLE

Messages from the Ether
A collection of poems

Made in the USA
Columbia, SC
16 February 2020